the

REALITY
MELTDOWN

ALSO BY DAN CRAY

Mother Tongue

Piercing Maybe

the
REALITY MELTDOWN

DAN CRAY

THE REALITY MELTDOWN

Edited by Elizabeth Mitchell
Hardcover Design by Carl Graves, Extended Imagery
Paperback/Ebook Design by Damonza

This original work is inspired by a different
Dan Cray work published under the same title in 2011.

Published by Third Quandary Books
An imprint of Delcominy Creations, LLC
8601 Lincoln Blvd., Ste. 180, #301
Los Angeles, CA 90045

Library of Congress Control Number: 2022916332

ISBN 978-1-940317-15-1 (hardcover)
ISBN 978-1-940317-16-8 (paperback)
ISBN 978-1-940317-17-5 (ebook)

Paperback Edition: December, 2025

Like many writers, I decided to experiment with the nascent ebook marketplace back in 2010. My guinea pig was *The Transitory God*, one of several desk-imprisoned fantasy manuscripts. The early interfaces for uploading text and graphics proved highly technical for a mere wordsmith such as myself... but nonetheless, in June of 2011 the deed was done: my ebook appeared online, newly renamed *The Reality Meltdown*.

A softcover edition followed in 2012—again, as an experiment in the process of launching my own publishing imprint and distributing through an online vendor. Once the tests concluded, both editions were pulled from the marketplace.

But one of the book's plot threads continued to fascinate me. That thread became the basis for an entirely new novel that shared only a few remnants from 2010... and the provocative title, which deserved a truly finished product.

So, if you search for *The Reality Meltdown* online, you might come across the unavailable book with the same author and title. Sorry for the confusion, but rest assured that what you're about to read is an original novel that enjoys the benefits of my earlier publishing experiments.

For Jane
"La" always.

And, for Evan
For introducing so much I never knew.

How do you know but ev'ry Bird that cuts the airy way, / Is an immense World of delight, clos'd by your senses five?

William Blake, *The Marriage of Heaven and Hell*

the REALITY MELTDOWN

ONE

My wife's latest painting won't stop talking.

Art speaks to most people, but that's not what I mean. Sofia's simple oil-on-canvas feels like a magnet. My mind reels from my first-ever look at it, as if I'm processing sub-liminal signals. My wife—the focus of my personal, social and emotional world—is standing twenty feet away from me, elegant and coiffed, bedazzling a dark-suited client with lively intellect, yet suddenly the only thing I can think about is that siren of a painting.

I avert my eyes. Sofia's cozy studio, resplendent in brushed steel wainscoting, narrow track lights, and several of her earlier oils, looks unusually tidy. She's straightened the nook housing her cluttered easel and organized her brushes into artistic groupings. A countertop speaker is streaming soft jazz. The blue dress she's wearing only leaves its hanger twice a year, her complexion looks gently burnished, and her mascara-free eyes are more vibrant than ever.

For the buyer, I realize. For Suit Guy.

My phone's vibrating but the only thing I'm paying attention to is the painting, calling me back, an insistent child asking me to look, look, look. So I do, even though there's nothing to see. So-fia's composed an abstract, surrealist landscape: faded, barely visible geometric patterns against a bleached backdrop. *Outset,* she calls it. The entire canvas is pallid, even stifling. Sun, sky, and land are indiscernible from one another, all of them filthy white—a depiction of life, embalmed, to hear her tell it. Drained of pigment, numbed from feeling, a world muted into a bleak, powdered void.

I'd go so far as to say it's her least compelling work. *So why do I feel so drawn to it?*

Maybe it's because I get a sense that I'm somehow *part* of the painting. I study it intently, searching for subtle hints that she's thickened some of the paint lines to form "Matthew Beren" or blended my bushy hair and slender nose into the sallow void, hidden-pictures style—things she's done in the past. But... no. She didn't paint my features or my name into the piece, yet somehow *Outset*'s signaling me that I'm there, so lost in the void I can't even distinguish *myself.*

"A wonderful addition, Ms. Coronado," Suit Guy tells Sofia as he opens his checkbook.

He has a sagging eyebrow that makes his narrow head look as if it's leaning to one side, but more to the point he's about to purchase *Outset.* An easel-shaped wall clock with an especially loud tick catches my attention, counting down the remaining moments before the deal becomes final. I avert my eyes once again, but I swear I can hear the painting calling me with faint whispers, begging me to look, feel, learn.

Maybe I'm simply projecting my own impressions onto the painting since, difficult as it is to admit, Sofia's been aloof lately. She's like that sometimes, ebullient for weeks then sullen for a day, but this is something more, as if there's a leaden tarp over her spirit. Even now, as she glances away from her conversation with Suit-Guy to lock eyes with me, I see pretense and a forced smile. Our wedding anniversary gift guide hasn't even hit cotton but I can already feel a distance that wasn't there before.

The thought makes me sick. Sofia Coronado is the real art in this studio, not the paintings. She has the face of an angel's daughter, a radiant, tender visage that caresses your heart and doesn't let go, not even when she leaves the room. There's something muscular about her dark eyes, not only in the strength they convey but the way they grab you, and hold you, and make certain your glance never shifts. She's about my height, meaning average, and has some meat on her waist, meaning she's never disregarded as mindless, stick-thin camera fodder. When she runs her fingers through her chestnut hair it isn't an absent-minded reflex, it's because there's a tangle. If she paints her nails, it's because the color reflects her mood, or the tone of her latest project, not because some cosmetics company says she should.

That's what fascinates me most: she's as open-minded as I am, yet far more grounded than any other woman I've met. We'll celebrate our two-year anniversary in a few weeks and no, I have no plans to change these rose-colored descriptions anytime soon.

I hear the easel clock again, louder than before. Strange, because I don't usually notice it. Now, though, with Suit Guy scribbling in his checkbook, the message those bracing ticks are sending seems clear.

"It's not for sale," I say, interrupting the transaction.

Sofia, startled, gives me a classic WTF look. Suit Guy recognizes an awkward situation and arches his sagging brow, but says nothing.

"Sorry, but... this one really grabs me, Lily," I say, which I know will get her attention since I usually only call her that in private. "We need to keep it."

I'm expecting a retort, or a finger motioning me to a private time-out. Instead, she nods, as if she understands why I'm trying to keep *Outset* for myself. I must have the only wife in the world who wouldn't be furious in this spot.

"Matt, I know it's special," she says, measuring her words, "but I need to move it along and Doug Halston here is going to put it on display in the lobby over at Three West. It'll have a good home."

The clock answers before I do, not that anyone else seems to notice. *Since when did that crappy plastic easel start ticking so loud?* I introduce myself to Halston, shake his hand, and re-apologize to both of them.

"I didn't realize how personal this particular work would feel," I tell them. "We really can't sell."

Sofia gives Halston an apologetic smile that usually means I've won. Then she puts a hand on my shoulder, and I see the apology was intended for me.

"I'm so sorry, this one was commissioned," she says. "But that's the advantage of an artist-wife. I can just paint you another, right?"

She and Halston share a generic, awkward laugh. I'm too busy removing batteries from the clock, and realizing the only other time one of her paintings grabbed me like this was at Buttercove Pier, on the night I saw *Assembly Required*—a portrait piece of an introspective, raven-haired woman with streaming, mosaic-like skin that was puzzle-pieced together, as if freshly baked. The thing practically held me in place until Sofia wandered over to greet me, and our relationship took off from there.

Assembly Required led to a marriage. What's *Outset* have in mind?

"You're the 'Melds King,' right?" Halston says, interrupting my thought train. "The guy who created those caricature figures that turn into stretchable, shapeable slime when you heat them?"

He twists a hand palm-up, referring to the size of the figures. Nodding, I wait for more. My face is on the Melds packaging; there's always more.

"I know you've made millions of Melds," he says, "but I have Series 17—the bloodied video game characters. Really, truly genius. The way they bleed, pixelate, alter colors to show different game skins, re-form after they cool... I can't even imagine how many ingredients you had to stir together to make that happen."

It's a typical reaction, so why doesn't his feel genuine?

"Drives me nuts, the way the media casts you as Type A," he adds, not waiting for my answer. "As if anyone with a vision isn't, right?"

Normally I'd chat it up with someone like Halston. I know that's what he's waiting for, and it's not like I can't go on for hours about those little products that I so dearly love—hell, there's a prototype for the next line in my pocket right now. But my mind is on *Outset* and I'm just not in the mood. I give him the short spiel instead: how the raw materials come from fourteen countries, with more than seven hundred distinct ingredients, fusing components, capabilities, and cultures.

My big finish is the marketing catchphrase. "Holding a Meld is like holding a piece of the Earth," I tell him. People usually eat it up; Halston's no different.

"Look, it's an honor to buy your wife's painting, and a thrill to talk with you," he says, shaking my hand. "You're welcome to come by Three West any time."

Again, his words are perfect. So why do they seem hollow?

"Only if I can bring Sofia's painting back with me when I come by," I say.

He offers an uneasy laugh as she ushers me toward the studio door. Through the glass, pedestrians scamper through a crosswalk as cars inch up to the painted line.

"I know *Outset* feels personal compared to most of my others," she whispers. "That's because I painted it with us in mind—so I could take some stuff I've kept buried and push it away, strange as that sounds. That's why I can't turn back on this sale."

"Sofia..."

She holds up a hand. "I need this painting out of here. More than any other, this painting needs to go. Not for me. For *us*. Okay?"

It's not the first time she's said something enigmatic. Far from it. That, like superior talent, captivating expressions, and the occasional sullen day, is part of who she is.

I lift my phone, aim it at *Outset*, take a picture. Makes me feel better. Halston looks relieved. After a business-like kiss for Sofia, I leave the studio, phone still in hand. The corners of my eyes see pedestrians, crosswalk paint, and trees in a park across the street. But that's all background, because focusing on the painting splashed across my phone's screen helps ease the pit in my stomach. *Assembly Required* is mounted in our entry hall. *Outset* should be with it. Maybe I can enlarge a digital copy and—

Blaring horn, screeching tires. *Oh god—I've walked into the crosswalk without looking!* Milliseconds loiter; an airborne fire hydrant hurtles straight at my head while images pass before my eyes—of my pier-top wedding, and millions of gooey figures churning along my factory's assembly line. Obscure stuff, too... utensils, desks, clothes, cars, furniture... and yes, easel clocks, phones, paintings.

Why am I seeing this? Unless...

The car skids to a stop, no more than two feet left between the bumper and my leg; the airborne hydrant clears my tilted head by a finger's width, then smashes into the trees across the street. No time to exhale: metallic fencing clatters onto the asphalt near the car, accompanied by a terrified squealing that halts mid-bleat as something hairy plummets, smacks onto the road, then crumples.

What the...?

The air reeks of embalmed machinery. Burned tire rubber, white-hot disc brakes, and whatever the hell just hit the asphalt make my throat, and my heart, seize up. Across the street, the hydrant-bark explosion knocks a singed, wedged tree trunk into a forty-five-degree lean.

Somehow, some way, I'm alive.

So then, why does everything go black?

TWO

I'm only semi-conscious, so the past is the present and the present is me, waking in the night's unraveling hours, hearing the faintest of whispers, noticing subtle curtain movements. So frightening, yet exhilarating too. The warm bedcovers soothed my fears, easing me back to sleep.

A memory, reborn. So much forgotten, now regained. *Triggered by the accident?* My subconscious croaks an instant retort.

No, triggered by Outset.

That first time I noticed the whispers, when I was four, they seemed little more than a bleary-eyed curiosity. When it happened a second time, at age six, I bolted upright in bed, looking for details a three-watt nightlight couldn't possibly reveal, then making up the rest. By age nine, I'd made the connection between the whispers and my belongings, but my dad insisted no one else heard such things. "You're being childish," he insisted. "Time to grow up."

I caved, joining the ninety-nine percent who choose to disregard what lingers right before their eyes. The ensuing, willfully ignorant nights muted the whispers, cementing illusion over truth.

Until *Outset*.

The digital clock says four a.m., my nightlight is long gone. Sofia's bundled next to me in a deaf-to-the-world slumber, some eight hours after my first trip to a hospital since a hernia surgery four years ago. No scars this time; doctors diagnosed a "stress blackout," meaning they think I simply fainted, lost a few seconds, and that was it. All I know is that the car's bumper was still shuddering when I regained consciousness. From the abrupt stop? Yeah, it must have been vibrating from the stop.

Maybe.

The fire hydrant debris was still shuddering too. Same with the metal fencing, all of it just residual motion.

Maybe.

The dead goat—yeah, *goat*, which fell three stories after the bursting hydrant punched a hole through a safety fence around someone's illegal, rooftop animal pen—was motionless. I'm lucky I'm not just as motionless, and that no one else was hurt. The driver, though he smashed into the hydrant while swerving to avoid me, walked away with only a few scratches and a very legitimate auto insurance claim against my inattentive self. Maybe a lawsuit too?

I can already guess the legal advice against apologizing, but that's what I'll do anyway, to both the driver and the goat's owner, along with some sort of compensation. It's the right thing to do, legal exposure be damned; I'm the one who caused the accident, by not looking before I stepped into the street. Plus, I feel terrible about the goat.

But none of that addresses *Outset*'s role in this. It doesn't explain why I suddenly hear a seashell's ocean in my quiet bedroom, whispering memories long wiped clean. I stare into clock-lit darkness, embracing the wonder refilling my soul. The usual night sounds are there, of course: distant crickets, the odd refrigerator clicks that you never notice during the day, the occasional passing car. Those I filter, straining for the rest, for the things I've noticed since coming home.

The things I hadn't heard since childhood.

Tonight, it's the clock. Much like the one at the gallery, it's just sitting there, yet it's not. There's a thickness to the glowing digits, a depth that reaches out, straight to my eyes, the numeral-shaped lights linking with my eyeballs. Conversation, too... some sort of eerie, soundless dialogue that avoids my ears yet still meanders into my head. It's no longer me, darkness, and a timepiece. It's me and the clock as *one*. Each minute-change is a jarring experience, jolting me, shifting the world's permanence... ramming home an understanding that a segment of time is forever lost.

The understanding fascinates me most. The clock is sharing its experiences rather than just telling me the time of day, and I think I might be absorbing some tiny gist of what it's conveying. It's as if we're actually... communicating?

The thought jars me. The bedroom, or at least my awareness of it, reappears. The drapes have a glow around the edges; morning's here. Rise and shine.

I keep what I've sensed to myself, knowing there's a good chance I'm imagining it, that it's a side effect of the accident, whatever. But nothing changes. If anything, the whispers grow more expressive than before, so two weeks later I decide it's time to share.

Sofia, to her credit, is the only woman in the world who doesn't blink an eye when I tell her I have a clock problem.

"What problem?" she says over breakfast. "I've heard it talking to me for years."

I love how she can mock me and still make it sound like she's enjoying, not ridiculing. "And just what exactly is the clock saying when it talks to *you*?" I say, taking her bait.

She looks up from her morning crossword, adjusts her glasses, thinks about it.

"That time will tell whether you're a nutjob," she says.

"Cute."

"Yeah, I kinda thought so too."

I should just let this drop. Discuss possible dinner plans, the weather, anything. But for some reason, if nothing else a test of just how far the love of my life is willing to humor me on something so wild, I feel like risking another share.

"Thing is... what would you say if I told you that it's part of a pattern?" I ask.

No answer. She's deep in the crossword... or maybe in the hope that I'll let this drop.

"It's like our stuff's alive or something," I add, with a nervous laugh.

She lowers the crossword, cocks her head.

"Okay, do I need to call a doctor about this?" she says.

"Probably."

She points to her phone, resting on an end table way on the other side of our living room. "Hey phone, you hear that? The man thinks you're alive! Call him a doctor, will ya? And have the table walk you over to me."

"That's ridiculous. We both know tables only use their legs for dancing."

We giggle at our absurdity. If nothing else, the mood feels good, which is reassuring since I can imagine how crazy the things I'm saying must sound. "Maybe some weird fumes are affecting me, the way some people hallucinate from hot-sauce odors. Did you use chemicals when you painted *Outset*?"

"Yeah, they're called *paint*," she says, grinning. "You're the guy who works in a factory full of Melds, not me."

Good point. But I've been at the same work location for years, so something bothering me now seems unlikely.

"Really, though," I say, refusing to let it go. "Unless it's a hallucination, then I think maybe there's a chance I'm onto something here. What if objects are more than we think they are?"

Her smile shrinks by half, then half again as she weighs what I'm telling her. A few seconds later the levity's gone altogether, she's taking a deep breath, and I'm getting an impression of a vast, unseen set of scales, weighing what I've said.

"I guess anything's possible," she says.

She didn't discount the idea. She didn't endorse it either, but when you bring up the idea that inanimate objects are alive, you're expecting to get roundly slammed. This? It seems like a win.

"So then, you're saying maybe—"

"I'm not saying anything," she insists, as if she doesn't want me to suggest something that might get her thinking about it even more. "Just thinking out loud. I mean, my keys hide from me every day. My slippers, my rings too... or the reverse happens, where my missing, treasured things somehow seem to find *me.* We all notice that stuff sometimes, right? Pretty normal."

"Yeah, but—"

"You're talking about consciousness, not random chance, I get it. I suppose everyone notices *that* too, they just don't talk about it. I sometimes know when a friend's calling without looking at the Caller I.D., don't you? Or when a car's approaching from behind before I see them in the mirror. Some days I know what bills or cards are waiting for me in the mailbox without looking. And, I can tell you for certain that any time I've ever bragged about how good I am at painting, archery, *anything*, my stuff will break, spill, misfire, and so on, as if my things decided to teach me a much-needed lesson. It's all just routine, just a part of our lives we never discuss."

Now don't get me wrong: I'm a pushover for the way Sofia transforms a tedious art symposium into webcam-worthy discourse, and no one livens a Contemporary Surrealism installation like my wife. But hearing what she's just said, knowing she's not joking, realizing how truly open her mind remains... I'm in love all over again.

"You're so easy," she says, with that special half-smile she reserves for me. "Just don't go overboard with this, okay?"

Whatever buried demons she was trying to expel when she sold *Outset*, it did the job. I haven't seen the sullen Sofia in the couple of weeks since we returned from the hospital. She still has her secrets, though. We admire the fragmented woman in *Assembly Required* every day, but never really discuss why, and she continually sidesteps my questions about *Outset* even though it had such a strong effect on me.

"So, what should I do? Rubber room?"

She laughs. "Do like everyone else: ignore it. We can have a very happy life together without ever worrying about what our dishware thinks of us."

I hesitate. "What if I'm more curious? What do I do then?"

One bite of toast is as much time as she needs for an answer.

"Whatever the clock says, within reason?"

Makes sense to me.

THREE

That afternoon, I do what anyone would do: an internet search.

What little information there is on objects demonstrating some sort of... *consciousness*, for lack of a better keyword, focuses on A.I. implications, or philosophies for determining whether extra-terrestrials qualify. But that eventually leads me to something called the Integrated Information Theory... a line of thinking that says even the most basic structures in the universe—protons, electrons, and so forth—add tiny bits of consciousness into their structures when they form.

Meaning there's a little bit of consciousness in every object?

It's a reach, but it's also reassuring, so I copy several links with details.

Lowering my phone, I listen for whispers in the living room. Nothing. Still, the past couple weeks have me thinking there are two ways of describing the place where we live. I can be pragmatic like everyone else, naming our suburban street, the color of our three-bedroom, single-story home, how it's located in the northern California town of Canoga Springs, part of a coastal valley that's about an hour's drive southwest of Palo Alto. I can describe the aging, silver sedan parked in our driveway, and the neighbor's gas guzzler. I can say we keep *Water Lilies* above our bed, a print of *The Kiss* on the far wall, and *Assembly Required* at the entry. I can even mention how I remodeled the garage, and how the property values inflated because of the new shopping center up the road.

Or, ever since I looked at *Outset*, I can tell you what's *really* here.

The sunlight entering our window doesn't shine, it glitters. Our floorboards randomly creak like they're talking with one another, even when no one's walking on them. I smell fresh rosemary all week long, whether we have any in the kitchen or not, and the news headlines on my phone's lock screen refresh even when our cellular service is down. Outside, faces and shapes present themselves in the exterior stucco's cottage-cheese texture. The pool water out back occasionally bubbles like it's coming up for air. We have a forty-foot ash in the front yard; sometimes it's dark green, sometimes light green, other times its mood makes the shade altogether indefinable.

As far as I can tell, our home is not unique in this regard. The Stenders, next door, have flowers with bell-shaped stamens that—I swear this is true, though no one else will vouch for me—jingle in the breeze. The Baxters, across the street, have a dog who can tell time. Since I now remember that I once noticed this kind of stuff as a child before somehow burying those memories, I can only assume the neighbors are truly unaware of such things.

Same with the people I work with at Fustian Industries. We're a young company but thanks to my Melds our facility is chockfull of robotic machinery, cast-iron molds, and all the electronic tech that controls them, so upon returning to work I'm constantly hearing chattering—not from the people working there, from everything else. Our robotic arm assemblies don't simply precision-rotate, they play off of one another's movements like ballet dancers. Heating and cooling units aren't just venting air over the

Melds, they're expelling it with the gusto of a perpetuated rivalry. The liquid polymers gurgling within their canisters? They're announcing their arrival, lion-style.

It's like that everywhere. My doctor insists the stress blackout wouldn't trigger the hyper-awareness I'm experiencing, that medical imaging verifies my brain is healthy. My parents, who live three states away, are nonetheless on board with that diagnosis, assuring me that I'm worrying about nothing. They're off on some sort of backpacking week when I phone, but they insist I never mentioned anything unusual about our surroundings as a child. Then again, Dad doesn't remember telling me to 'grow up,' either. Maybe they attributed my comments to childhood imagination, then forgot all about it?

Another round of internet research leads me to synesthesia, where people experience one sense through another—you hear someone's name and see a color, or see a shape and taste fruit— but that's a lifelong neurological condition produced by an unusually high number of connections between brain segments, not a sudden-onset condition.

Still, a simple drive down the road shows me potholes that yawn and road signs wiggling to rid themselves of birds. People tell me that seventy years ago, Canoga Springs was pure wilderness. I say it never changed.

Apparently, I say it too loud. One month after my blackout, Jerry Darwin calls me into his office for what he terms a "heart-to-heart." Jerry and I started Fustian Industries nine years earlier, well before he grew the bushy mustache that makes him look a decade older than he is, but the company floundered until my Melds rocketed sales to the moon—literally, since our Heritage of Apollo line utilized lunar dust collected by one of the private astro firms. So I know things are serious when he warns me that I'm "not always meeting professional standards" and that the company might have to look at its options if my behavior doesn't change.

It's an empty threat; I'm the face of the company. My Melds lines are the only thing keeping the doors open, and there's a crucial, pending deal with Kelapa Materials International, an Indonesian raw materials supplier, that will never close without me running things. But I like my job too much to cause trouble, so I solve things by shutting my mouth, keeping the crazy observations to myself.

The plan works... for a while.

"Care to explain?" Jerry says, summoning me into his office once again.

After wriggling out from a sport coat that's a size too small, he plays a video that some nameless coworker posted online. The footage shows me with the Melds assembly molds, which the company's 3D printers are using to churn out our lines. I don't see the big deal, until I realize the video was taken yesterday, when I thought no one was in the production room.

When I "heard" the newly manufactured Melds whispering... and responded.

I feel my face redden, watching myself pat the back of the cube-shaped printer then verbally congratulate it as if toasting a brand-new parent. Pretty soon I'm high-fiving the little composite hands on several Melds from my "Blacklisted Filmmakers" line as they exit the 3D printer.

"Proud of you guys," I hear myself say.

Bad as that is, the ensuing segment makes me look worse: me, having a serious, one-sided discussion with the Melds, outlining the business strategies behind their creation and the people and history who inspired their designs.

Cringing, I turn away from the video. "Well at least it's a good online course in how to bring a product to market," I tell Jerry, trying to soften my embarrassment with a joke.

He looks like I just blew my nose in his coffee. "Don't even."

"Viral?"

"Of *course* it went viral, you're the Melds King! People recognize you from the ads, the packaging, everything!"

I hear my video-self tell one of the Melds she's "going to change the world."

"So, I got a little enthusiastic, what does it matter?" I tell Jerry. "People talk to their cars, coddle toy animals, yell at their computers... we personify everything. How is this any different? It's not like I think the things are actually *human*, for god's sake."

He leans back in his desk chair.

"I'm not suggesting you do," he says, "but you're exposing a side of people they want to keep hidden. Like you said, people talk to their shit all the time. Slapping *you* with the 'crazy' label keeps it further away from *them*."

His chair squeaks as he leans forward. "Problem is, it slaps Fustian with the same label."

Which is why the company's Board of Directors places me on indefinite medical leave that afternoon. Walking out of the building, I feel more in the dark than I was during the stress blackout.

Sofia is concerned when I share the news, but she's also irritated.

"I tell you not to go overboard and you shoot the breeze with a bunch of Melds while you're at work?" she says, her voice rising with every word. "Why on Earth would you do something like that?"

"These are people I've known for years. I guess I figured if they saw me, they'd give me the benefit of the doubt, like you did."

Her sharp scoff scratches my eardrums. "And how'd that work out for you?"

My dead silence pretty much answers her question.

"You still carrying one of those figures around with you?" she says.

"Agnes Waterhouse? Yeah. Why?"

Sofia disappears into our hallway without answering. A moment later I hear her fling our bedroom door shut behind her. It strikes me as an odd, overblown reaction. Maybe she's worried about my mental health, and losing my job amplified those concerns? Until now she's seemed very at ease with what I've been seeing. Supportive, even. Watching such an intense reaction from someone who rarely gets upset, I can't help feeling...

That she knows a lot more about this stuff than she's letting on.

FOUR

Snowboarding isn't my strong suit but attending physical therapy isn't either, which is why I've walked with a limp since my early twenties. It's also why my old hernia scar is larger than most; post-surgery guidelines, also not my thing.

Turns out I'm just as stubborn when it comes to believing that Jerry Darwin won't bring me back. Melds are mega-sellers, an international phenomenon, and they're *my* creation. I'm also the public face of that creation. Without me, Fustian Industries goes under—not only because I have a way with composites but because I've managed to turn the little figurines into compelling, anamorphic characters who offer glimpses into topics people consider taboo.

"Inappropriate Icons," our very first Melds line, sold like wildfire. Pretty satisfying line, too: we had Black kitchen servant figures pouring 'syrup' that spelled out "Never Again," extinct animals that reshaped into the mascots of the cereals they peddled, and a Confederate chef that morphed into a vengeful chicken holding a plate of tofu. I won't lie, my first crack at making people think about the products they support felt good.

"Blacklisted Filmmakers" came next, captivating consumers with the way they started in the shape of a person, re-formed into a movie screen, then became a mini motion picture camera capable of projecting controversial old films. From there we expanded into our "Banned" collections: book, cartoon, film and video game characters from media that some people burned because they objected to the content.

Consumer demand skyrocketed; the Melds product lines multiplied exponentially from there. Our all-time revenue leader, "Dishonest Athletes," sold out four times, and "Disgraced Priests" is on pace to sell even better. If the Kelapa deal goes through, we'll be introducing my dream line, "Persecuted Witches"—the line Agnes Waterhouse is part of—this Fall.

Every Meld uses the same principle of combining hundreds of ingredients into a composite product with all sorts of unique properties. Whether it's a heated Meld 1 figure that can be stretched into goo, a Meld 2 that turns translucent, or the Meld 3 shooting spark-filled bubbles, it's all the same challenge from a developmental standpoint: wrangling resources. And no one's better at wrangling resources than I am.

All of which is my way of saying that the company's PR-motivated medical leave doesn't change a thing. Jerry and everyone else at Fustian understands that I'm working my dream job and I'm not going anywhere. To borrow the Melds catchphrase, I hold a piece of the Earth every day. What other job could compare with *that*?

My forced sabbatical has me headed to a local deli on a Thursday afternoon for a late lunch with Jerry and my longtime friend and product manager, Neil Iseli. The deli's one of those hole-in-the-wall eateries shoehorned into a sixty-year-old bungalow, meaning it has a crappy health department grade but tastier food than the chains. You'd think educated, white-collar businessmen would avoid the place. You'd think wrong.

Only Neil is there so far. He's wearing a long, thin necktie over a black T-shirt, and his work shoes have cartoon viruses painted along each side. Everything from his angular face to his threadlike goatee seems scrawny, and he has a thing for lip balm. Neil's always rolling a stick of it across his lips and gets worked up whenever he runs out, which is every few days. Some days he wears a nose ring, but he's left it out today so I know he probably had a meeting with a supplier.

We bump fists, even though no one does that anymore. I ask about Jerry. Neil's eyes dart to the wall menu, and his grainy voice sounds uncertain.

"Yeah... he couldn't make it."

"Couldn't? Or wouldn't?"

He shrugs. We order, a pastrami on rye for him, corned beef for me. Low-cal, all the way. In line, then at the table, Neil gives me the dirt on what's happening at the office: supply snafus, political backstabbing, a rumored affair... the usual stuff, reshuffled with different names from whenever I saw him last.

"You'll be happy to hear 'Persecuted Witches' is lined up for an October release," he says. "You still have the prototype?"

I pull Agnes Waterhouse from my pocket and pass it to him, like a teenager showing off a picture of his girlfriend. Even though it's just monochrome plastic at this stage, her intelligent eyes, narrow lips, and flowing raiment have more extensive etchings than our earlier efforts, and her ornate lantern can actually glow.

"What about the Kelapa deal?" I say, curious about what became of the most important project on my plate.

"Still not done."

"Seriously? I've been on leave for three weeks. No one else can offer the ingredient volumes that the Indonesians have right now. We could double Melds production and they wouldn't even blink."

His eyebrows lift at my use of 'we' but he doesn't mention it.

"I know, and I have a meeting with them at their Jakarta plant next week," Neil says, passing Agnes back to me. "But our competitors aren't making this one easy."

"That's because they're looking for a cheap and easy way to eat into our market share with a knock-off product."

"Damn right. And they might actually pull it off."

I start to sip my drink, then keep it hovering just below my lips. "You need to close that deal, at any cost. Please tell me you're going to make it happen. The future of the entire Melds line depends on it."

Neil hesitates, grimaces, then lobs a missile.

"Would have been easier if you were still in the office," he says.

"Yeah, well you didn't exactly bang the drums for me when Jerry stuck me on this med sabbatical." I'm leaning against the vinyl booth now, half-eaten sandwich in hand. There's a black-and-white celebrity photo on the wall behind me, an actor wearing a highway patrol uniform from a show that hasn't aired in fifty years.

Neil finishes his last bite of sandwich, searches the plate for escaped pastrami slivers, uses a fingernail to spear the ones he finds. "Look man, you were talking to the Melds."

I nod. "I had my reasons."

"You were talking *to the Melds*," he repeats. "Not to yourself, or making absentminded chatter. To *the products*."

"Actually," I say, thinking it over, "more to their components."

He shakes his head. "We can't have potential business partners worrying there's a whack job overseeing our multi-million-dollar Melds production."

Crinkling sandwich wraps and persistent background chatter seems louder now, probably because I'm listening more closely to them than to him. Or maybe because it's really the wraps I hear chattering in the background, rather than the people.

Neil glances at the ceiling but doesn't go so far as an eye roll. "You still think all the crap around us is... alive? Aware? Whatever?"

I give him a single nod. He pulls the little balm tube from his shirt pocket, rolls it across his lips. "I swear, if you tell me your dishware breaks into song..."

My middle finger wants up, but that's not really my style.

"Come on, man, you need help," Neil says. "Professional, right? You're not the first guy to come down with a case of runaway mind after a near-death experience. There's still a chance for you to turn this mess around. Jerry wants you back, and all he needs is a way to show everyone you've turned things around. Get yourself to someone who can straighten out your head—and do it soon."

It's an awkward moment. A one-man intervention, I suppose. I've been friends with Neil since business school. I hate the way this is going down.

"You know I wouldn't make this up," I say, and yeah, there's a hint of pleading in my voice. "I mean, this country spends millions looking for new life... in space, undersea, at the poles. What if it's right here, with us all the time, only no one's seeing it?"

He leans forward. "So, what, an alternate reality like in every crappy movie? Is that what you're telling me?"

"No, not alternate. *This* reality. A whole class of life that we're not aware of, doing stuff we're not aware of. Right in front of us."

Neil sighs.

"I'm serious," I insist. "The tables, the menus, the old photo—there's something to them, something more than you're thinking there is. Just go with me on this, okay?"

But I can see it's not okay.

"I suppose they're as smart as we are?" he says.

"Come on, Neil. They're just *things*. Be real, okay?"

"But you're saying they're alive."

He draws out the 'eye' sound in "alive," to make it sound ghostly, but it's clear he's genuinely upset. At least now I know why he's here. He thought he could drive some sense into his longtime friend.

"Look, I know it's crazy," I say, softly. "If I'm in your place, I'm probably thinking the same thing. But—"

"No buts," he says, standing up. "The table is a table. It doesn't think. It doesn't do anything. It's just a damn table!"

Heads turn. People stop eating mid-bite. All eyes on me. And Neil. Mostly me.

He points a finger at my face.

"You need help," he says. "When you're ready for it, you give me a call."

He turns toward the door.

"You forgot your lip balm," I say, quietly.

His hand darts to his pocket, finds it flat.

"In the groove between the seat cushions," I add.

His face contorts as he pulls the tube from the seat. "You can't even see down there, how could you—?"

"I just know."

He pockets the tube.

"Get yourself some help," he repeats.

And then he walks.

FIVE

My living room's flickering.

The sun set an hour ago, I haven't turned the lights on, and images from some generic television drama are alternating, dark-to-bright. Several hours after my abbreviated lunch with Neil, I'm scrolling through the news on my phone's lock screen the way everyone should: absorbing the nuts-and-bolts information, filtering all the fear-mongering. Problem is, I'm also hearing ambient conversation, and it's not from the TV.

It's from *Assembly Required*. The painting's casting a ton of whispers my way, as if the oils, the canvas, the frame, *everything*, are trying to tell me something. *But even if that were true, what could they be telling me?* Paintings don't *think*. So how could they possibly convey a message? Even if objects are alive, that wouldn't automatically make them sentient. They'd be like plants, or the lowest-level insects. Still an amazing discovery, but—

Other whispers join up with *Assembly Required*, moonshine for my imagination. Opening my laptop, I type "hello... what are you saying?" My next move is even nuttier: drizzling a handful of the sand from Sofia's art supplies onto the kitchen floor—*where are the tea leaves when you need them?*—thinking maybe the grains might arrange themselves into some special pattern.

Neither experiment gives me anything but floor cleanup. *Big surprise.* Still, those whispers are doing *something...* in fact, I'm pretty sure my coffee table isn't thrilled about shouldering my bare feet. The ventilation pipe above the stove is creaking from a light wind, a reminder that it wasn't installed properly, but why does it sound as if it's *literally* reminding me?

Other whispers seem to be repeating things, maybe the same thing, at different times. It's as if a chorus hadn't learned to coalesce their lyrics into a single, distinguishable song, leaving only jumbled chatter.

"Sofia?" I call, hoping she's home from the studio, so someone can corroborate what I'm hearing.

No answer. Nothing spoken aloud, anyway. In my head, I hear... or is it 'sense'... a word whenever my eyes glance into the dining nook. No one's there, but the voices, led by *Assembly Required*, are calling one word that I can't quite make out. Their chorus, though, is finally coalescing. Listening intently, I might be able to understand what...

Amalgam.

Whatever *that* is. But that's the word: 'amalgam.' Nonsense, maybe? My gut, my subconscious, maybe even the china cabinet, are telling me it isn't. In fact, they're telling me I've heard that word before.

Déjà vu hits.

"Even if you wind up marrying Matthew, you'll never shake Amalgam. Ever."

I heard it from a back porch. The voice was faint... emphatic, smothered speech uttered by someone trying to shout at Sofia without anyone outside the room overhearing it, which never really works.

At the time it was gibberish, a brother's odd warning to his sister. His wife seemed to buy into it, reiterating the same warning. Even the couple's dog, a Tibetan spaniel lounging next to my pillow-topped porch chair, gave me the stink eye from that point on.

Sofia, though, she didn't care. Three dates in, she's having to defend her choice in men and doesn't bat an eyelash doing so. Doesn't even raise her voice. Always confident, like she's already played this life game a dozen times and figures it'll all work out, no drama required.

Me, I'm wondering why there's an issue. The meet-the-relatives dinner—intended as a low-stress warm-up to a meet-the-parents dinner set for two weeks later—seemed like it was going great. Her brother Tyler and I, we hit it off pretty well. His dark hair is in the kind of man-bun that hairstylists and movie producers love, but I'm a barbershop guy so I'm clueless about the appeal. Then there's his wife Florence, what a sweet woman, dimpled and ruffly like she stepped out of an old margarine ad. For some reason they both wear clothes that make you think their closet is a time machine, and they live in a wooden, bayou-inspired home that somehow ended up in a downtown cul-de-sac, but you come to like them anyway.

The back door opens. Florence, she's got a prim little "hope-you-didn't hear-that" smile on her face as she beckons me inside. She's in her thirties, short, and thin, but seems like she could play a grandma with the right makeup. Her dark hair's shoulder-length, permed, nondescript.

I give the dog a pat before entering, but the pooch is still giving me the stink eye.

Sofia's clearing the table, moving plates strewn with saucy pot pie crumbs. She gives me the special half-smile, that and a wink, so of course my chest now feels like I've been doused in a warm, scented shampoo. Florence grabs the remaining dishes and disappears into the kitchen, Sofia at her side.

Ty puts an arm on my shoulder, ushers me to a chair. He hasn't hit forty but the living room says otherwise, with hand-made quilts thrown over chair-backs, a dusty organ, and a couple of chiming clocks. Something smells like worn, aging fibers. The vibe has me wondering whether they inherited the place, décor, wardrobe, and all.

"You're different from the others," Ty says, wiping his nose with a handkerchief as he settles into a rocker, making me wonder when I last saw a handkerchief… or a rocker.

I resist the urge to ask about "the others." The man has construction worker shoulders but enough creases at the temples to let you know he made foreman. Wall photos behind the rocker show him in his teen years, drumming up rent money as a rodeo clown. I'm looking at his rugged face, seeing anything but "clown."

"One of those in all of us," he says, seeing me looking at the pictures. "Depends on which face you decide to see, right? But you already know that."

I shift in my seat, uncertain what he's referring to, wishing he'd go back to asking why I left college early, why I ride motorcycles, why things didn't work out with my last girlfriend. You know, the easy stuff.

He's still staring at me, I'm pretty sure he's seeing a silly, painted face. I know he isn't seeing broad shoulders.

"Tell you what, Matthew, that one out there, she'll always be a mystery," he says, leaning the rocker back so far that it rubs against the wall. "Friendly, smart, talented—oh man, can she work a canvas. Close to the vest, though. Real close. Our whole family is, I suppose."

He dwells on what he's just said. Me too.

"Some people, they don't like mysteries," he says, pocketing the handkerchief. "I mean, sure, they like it for a while, but eventually they want it all spelled out for them. They think it's some kind of insult if they're not included in the 'big unknown.' How about you, Matthew? How long can you take a mystery?"

I shrug. "Long as she wants to keep it that way, I guess. It's *her* life, right?"

He cracks a smile, teeth together as if he's trying to clench a pipe. "If you say so. You might get an argument from..."

He mutters another word, but I can't hear it.

Two years, a wonderful wedding and numerous follow-up visits since, I've always wondered about it, especially since I never ended up meeting Sofia's parents—her mother died a few months before the wedding, and she had a falling out with her father in the aftermath. They've been estranged ever since. That left Ty and Florence as my only in-laws. These are people who I see every holiday, and yet I've never asked what he said on that strange, memorable day.

But now, thinking back, approaching his words from a new context, I might have figured it out.

"*... an argument from Amalgam.*"

I'm pretty sure Sofia's brother said "Amalgam."

SIX

The *déjà vu* fades.

My living room television is still flickering, the ventilation pipe's still creaking. Impressions surge toward me, intense, emotional outpourings from *Assembly Required* and the other objects around me. Their wavy impressions rise like heat from asphalt, chugging through my coffee, lounging on my sofa, wrapping around the pen on my table. Doesn't matter whether I stare at a knick-knack or the toaster oven, my entire living environment seems resplendent with curves, knobs, and strokes, each beckoning reinterpretation.

The world swims as I get up, off of the couch. The light patterns on my microwave's lenticular door panel shift as I walk past, like an eye; the bathroom faucet seems relieved when I don't turn the knobs too hard. Even my phone feels pliant, as if the touch screen actually appreciates the finger-to-function contact.

Am I losing it?

I hear Sofia arriving home. I should probably hold off on discussing my imaginary object-friends, but I don't.

"Maybe you *are* crazy," she says, after listening.

She cracks a thin smile. Mostly she acts as if I just told her dirt isn't just dust, but pebbles too.

"I'm not sure it would matter if our stuff's alive," she says, unloading groceries and a wad of tulips from a brown paper bag. "Even if it is, we'll still get dressed, go to work, eat meals. It's a conversation piece."

"Well yeah, but..."

"But what?"

"It's pretty major—an entirely new form of life. How can we keep this bottled up? If this is real, we need to tell everyone."

She looks at me like I've suggested we groom a donkey with our tongues. "Yeah, that'll go well," she says, grinning.

She listens while arranging the tulips into a crystal vase, unsurprised when I mention *Assembly Required* since that's always called to both of us. The china cabinet, though, that's news to her.

"Still doesn't change anything," she says.

"A world chock full of people and *my wife* is the only one who thinks it's normal that our things are alive?"

"Doesn't seem so far-fetched when you consider how we met."

"What do you mean?"

She shrugs. "Most couples come together for reasons they don't even know, right?" she says, snipping a tulip stem with a pair of kitchen scissors.

"Yeah, but this is a lot different from discovering we have the same favorite song."

She trims and places more tulips in the vase, sees me waiting for more.

"Not if someone else, or maybe I should say some*thing* else, discovered it before we did," she says. "I've always kind of assumed mundane objects have a greater say in things than people realize."

An uneasy thought emerges from my subconscious: who *is* this woman?

"Do I need to call a doctor for *you*?" I say.

She laughs.

"Don't forget, Matt, I'm a surrealist painter; I spend a lot of time imagining," she says. "All I'm saying is, maybe objects are the world's thinkers. Maybe they spend all that inactive time contemplating the universe, steering animate beings such as ourselves in the right directions. In our case, toward our careers... and each other."

I'm blown away, hearing her blurt this out. Four years together, two of them as a married couple, she's said nothing of the sort. I stare at her, eager to hear more, but instead she fills the flower vase with water from the kitchen sink, as if she'd just commented on the weather.

"You're suggesting they're not just alive? That they're, what... sentient, too?"

She and I look at each other, knowing we're both thinking the answer is *yes*.

"But an object doesn't have a brain," I say, as a prompt. "How could it think?"

A second shrug serves as her reply.

Objects as matchmakers? What, did the lights near the ocean draw my attention to Buttercove Pier, where we met? Did the creaky pier boards steer my feet to the spot where I could see her painting? Did the paints and the canvas direct my attention to her easel, her brush... her face?

My head spins. I have to admit, things kind of happened that way. I already knew *Assembly Required* seemed to hold me there until she noticed me. And once we saw each other, once we started talking... *oh, no way*. Could Sofia really be right?

My head tells me I'm crazy. My gut says otherwise.

"What's Amalgam?" I say.

She freezes. Several tulips tumble onto the kitchen counter-top, but it's Sofia's face that grabs my attention. She's turned pale.

"Where did you hear that word?" she says.

"Your brother used it a couple years back, then it popped into my head again when our stuff started whispering. I'm guessing it has something to do with your father?"

She sits at our dining table, her face still ashen, then answers with a non-answer. "I don't remember hearing 'Amalgam' from Ty. Did he say what it was?"

"No, but I could sure tell it was a warning. Same way I overheard *Assembly Required* and everything in the dining nook speak it as a warning tonight."

No reply, though after taking a moment she gets up from the table, walks up the hall to our bedroom, sits on the bed.

"Lily, come on... our stuff is *alive*," I say, following her.

Invoking my pet name for her—a reference to her fondness for calla lilies, which she regards as a sweet secret between the two of us—prompts her to glance up.

"Okay... maybe I agree with you," she says. "Not that I'm confirming anything, other than that my family... they're into some stuff that's related to all of this."

"Related to objects? How, through some sort of research program?"

She looks away. "Yeah... you could say that."

"What else could you say?"

Stress lines form across her forehead. "Hopefully nothing. You already know I'm estranged from my dad. Discussing him, or even thinking about him, is the last thing I want to do."

She's never told me much about what went down between them, other than that it was nasty. "I mean, if it was important, then maybe," she adds. "But like I said: even if our stuff *is* alive, nothing changes. It's a conversation piece."

I shrug. "Maybe, but... it'd be pretty incredible."

She smiles.

"You can have incredible," she says. "I just want a normal life. There was a time I wasn't sure I'd get this chance—my family was *that* domineering, their work all-consuming. But now you and I are together, and I don't want to risk that in any way."

"And you think digging into this object stuff is a risk?"

She nods. "It is. I wish I could explain everything but I can't, because... it's sort of like witness protection, without the criminal aspect. I need to keep an ultra-low profile or everything falls apart. So... *please* trust me when I tell you that you should drop it."

That's like discovering fairies are real and being asked to pretend they're just hummingbirds. My job and my marriage suddenly want the same thing: me, pretending I'm not seeing what's really out there, not speaking about it to anyone. Believing in it, that's fine, but mentioning it means they have to address it... to *deal* with it... and no one wants that. *Touché, Copernicus and Galileo... now I get it.* Centuries later, things haven't changed.

I join Sofia on the bed. She's stressed, but not *surprised*, and it occurs to me there might be a reason. *Because she's already thought this through.* None of this 'living object' stuff is the revelation that it is for me. She expected this conversation would eventually come up, dwelled on it, had her answer prepared. And if that's the case...

Then I truly have no idea who my wife is.

7:47 a.m.

Friday, Sep. 4

Notifications

NEWS

* Two embassies close amid dispute, tempers soar.

* "Aerial phenomena" video released; drones suspected.

* Driftwood assists man lost at sea, carries him 300 miles to safety.

* Gun jams inches from diplomat's face in assassination attempt.

Press HOME to unlock Screen Time, Reminders, and Purchases.

SEVEN

The night's sleep feels so good that I don't wake up until well after eight the next morning, more than an hour later than usual. Sofia's already out of bed, puttering elsewhere in the house, so I take a bleary-eyed jaunt to the back patio, swipe past the headlines on my phone's lock screen, then tap one of the 'Frequent Dials' while I have some privacy.

"You ready to get some help?" I hear Neil say, once he's picked up.

I can't mask the sigh before it escapes my mouth. This isn't going to be easy.

"Yeah... kind of," I tell him, pulling my phone close to my mouth, hoping my voice doesn't carry inside the house. "I ran things past Sofia, to get a sense of whether she's on the same page you are."

"Finally," Neil says. "And?"

I hear him chewing something crunchy on his end. Time was, people didn't eat and talk on the phone. One of those lost courtesies.

"And," I say, "things got even weirder. She, uh... I think she's seen the same stuff that I have."

The chewing stops. "Say again?"

"She thinks there's a chance objects are alive too, Neil. And from the sounds of it, she's thought that for a long time."

"Get the hell out."

"I'm serious."

The crunching starts up again.

"Maybe she just thought you were messing with her," Neil says. "Or maybe she was messing with you by agreeing."

"No, she was serious. Kind of bothers me, to be honest. I thought I was the only one keeping a secret."

"She probably wants to shut you up so people don't think she's married to the local loony," he says. "Anyway, it's nice to hear that your wife's supporting you but it doesn't change a thing. Jerry won't bring you back until he can tell everyone a shrink says you're ship-shape, so I did some digging, got a couple names for you. Good people, they can get you right again."

Meaning he's convinced I'm flat-crazy. Maybe I am?

I hear a drawer close from somewhere inside the house. Sofia, working in her home office, I think, until some pan-rattling tells me she's actually in the kitchen.

"I've got to go, but I want you to have a look at something," I say, using my phone to forward him links to the Integrated Information Theory. "And I want you to make sure Jerry understands: without me, there's no Kelapa deal."

The sound of a liquid-filled swallow follows the crunching. Soda, judging from the distinctive carbon dioxide fizz.

"Fine, I'll see what I can do," he says, though I can tell his heart isn't into it.

We end the call. Sofia's in the kitchen window on the far end of the patio, packing a heaping chicken Caesar salad into one of those lunch bags with an ice block inside. The fact she's dressed in a dark pant suit tells me today's gallery business doesn't involve any actual painting.

She hasn't noticed me looking, and we're more or less newly-weds, so I tell myself it's not creepy to spend a few moments watching her even though it probably is. The thing is, she moves so gracefully it's hard not to stare. All she's doing is basic life tasks: munching the excess salad, sorting the mail between bites, tidying the counter... yet I'm watching like it's the final moments of a televised thriller. There's something poetic about the way her footfalls seem to glide rather than thud. Her hair rises and falls as if she's choreographed the movements, and when she handles simple things like envelopes or napkins it's as if she's caressing rather than carrying. Sometimes she sings while tidying, just a verse or two from a favorite song. Her voice isn't Grammy-worthy, but it isn't bad.

Then, the unexpected: Sofia leans over the kitchen counter and says something to the bread box.

My chest tightens. *Did I really just see what I thought I saw?* I couldn't hear what she said, but her lips moved and this time it wasn't for song lyrics. No, she spoke to the bread box.

Easy now, I tell myself. She might have been thinking aloud about her plans for the day, giving herself a vocal reminder, or talking to herself. There's no reason to make a big deal out of nothing.

But her lips are moving again, and her lively facial expression isn't suggesting memories, it's indicating an active conversation. I move closer, beneath the window so she can't see me, then slowly raise myself up until I can angle my right ear against the window's bottom edge.

No sounds, other than Sofia's gliding footsteps and a drawer closing. I linger, listening as she goes through her tidying motions, but that's it.

See, I tell myself. Stress and imagination, nothing more. Until...

"Just make sure they leave him out of it, like we agreed," Sofia says.

My chest tightens again. I lift myself a bit higher, enough for one eye to see inside. Sofia's still tidying, and cleaning... and talking, though it doesn't seem directed at the rack. Her hands are in motion, waving and dancing about like they do whenever she holds a conversation.

"All of you," she says. "There's no need for this, none whatsoever."

She says it to the room, while returning food containers to the refrigerator. Maybe she's talking to herself, or recalling some prior conversation? But no, that's not the sense I get. She looks as if she thinks someone's listening to her words, understanding them, readying a response. *Wait... is she on a speakerphone call?*

She isn't. I can see her phone on the dining room table, the screen's dark. Since we don't have any digital devices listening for verbal instructions to find a recipe, switch the lights on, and so forth, she can't be talking to one of those things either. I tell myself to stay calm, that I'm probably misjudging this in some way. There has to be a logical explanation, one that I'm missing.

"Yeah, yeah, they're probably using the network on me, I get it," she says, again to the empty room. "Gotta' love the irony. But that doesn't mean Amalg—"

She stops mid-room, whirls, looks at the window... right where my eye is. *How did she know?* I stifle a gasp, but don't move a muscle. More importantly, I don't blink. There are potted calla lilies on our windowsill, and a lot of glare. This isn't a guaranteed crash-and-burn, plus if I have something witty at the ready...

Sofia turns, leaves the dining room. I exhale; maybe she didn't see me. More importantly, how did she suddenly suspect I was there? And did she really start to say "Amalgam," or was my mind playing tricks on me?

Later that morning, after she's left for the studio, I phone Tyler Coronado.

Yeah, it's a bad idea, approaching her brother without asking, especially since it's Friday and most people just want to wrap up and get to their weekend. But Ty's the only person I can talk with who has known Sofia since childhood, and he probably knows the details about Amalgam. So, I go for it.

He invites me to meet at his office, which just happens to be situated at a toxic waste cleanup site at the north end of the valley. Aerospace was king out here until budget cuts and consolidations hit, then the companies moved away, leaving their wartime construction detritus behind. Now neighborhoods ring the site and cancer clusters still pop up every few years. This location is the thirty-fourth worst on the continent, or something like that... it might have improved once the cleanup effort began.

Driving in, I pass covered vats, rusted cranes, and towering debris piles lumped atop sprawling pallets, as if someone raked up leaves from the biggest, deadest tree ever. The place smells like rancid fish pudding, if there were such a thing. Entering the bungalow provides aromatic relief. It's nearly five o'clock, so I'm figuring everyone but Ty has gone home for the weekend. I find him near the reception desk, signing off on disposal permits. The place looks modular because it is, no doubt hauled to the site for the five-year cleanup period. Seams are visible along the walls and the window frames pop out for easy removal. Throw in some composite countertops, speckled-tile flooring, and harsh fluorescent lighting, and it's pretty much what you'd expect from a government-funded operation.

"Here for your spa appointment?" Ty says, then chuckles even though it wasn't funny. He's wearing more time-machine apparel: wide-collared flannel with dated jeans. His boots hint of his job, singed and stained. I always knew he was an environmental engineer, but never really considered the daily health risks it entailed.

"Your tanning equipment might scare me," I say, and he chuckles at that too, even though it wasn't funny either. "Actually, I'm hoping we could crack open up some of those Sofia mysteries you warned me about."

He nods. "Can't say I didn't red-flag it for you. She's close to the vest, right? But like I said, the whole family is, myself included.

"Yeah, why is that?"

"You run an operation like I'm running here, you have to be," he says. "The people sending their kids to school up the block, all they want to know is that the cleanup's being handled. They don't want to hear that this waste's being hauled away in trucks that have to travel the same roads they do. So, I just do the job without talking about the job, know what I mean?"

"Is that how Sofia approaches things too?"

Ty sets the permits on the reception desk. "What makes you say that?"

I notice he's answered a question with a question. *Close to the vest, indeed.* I suddenly see how hard this is going to be, getting answers without mentioning anything about living objects. *Even though Sofia gave the impression her family knows about them, I don't want Ty to know that I do too.*

"Important things come up, she acts as if everything's still normal," I say. "It's not denial, because she's aware... she just doesn't attach the same importance to certain things that I might."

That earns me another chuckle. "Seems like you're not too bad at this close-to-the-vest stuff either," he says. "Look, my sister learned a lot of weird stuff, mostly from our parents, and she got to a point where she decided the only way she could move forward was to ignore it. So yeah, she compartmentalizes it. Same thing I do with all the stuff here at the site, in a way. Because if we don't, it'll all come racing back at us."

This isn't getting me anywhere, so I go for broke.

"Where does Amalgam fit into all of this?"

That sure gets his attention. His eyes pop like the window frames, soon as I say the word.

"Where'd you hear that?" he says.

"From you. You mentioned it before Sofia and I married."

Ty chews on that forgotten memory for a moment before answering.

"I'm going to be honest with you," he says, fiddling with his man-bun. "All I can tell you about Amalgam is that it is not something any of us likes messing with. And that's from a man who dips his hands in toxic waste every day, right?"

"Fine, but is it a person? An organization? A thing?"

"Yes," Ty says.

"Yes? What does that mean?"

Ty takes a breath, walks to the closest window, slides it open. A fresh blast of rancid fish pudding blows inside, curling my nostrils.

"You smell that?" he asks, though all the bathroom spray in the world couldn't change my answer. "There's a lot of angry out there. This site has items that shouldn't be in the condition they're in... stuff that was mangled, tossed, trashed, and chemically altered in every conceivable way. The ramifications of that affect everyone. My job here isn't cleanup, it's making amends and meeting obligations. Bills come due, Matthew, and when they do someone has to go out there and collect."

Takes me a moment to digest what he's saying, and even then, I'm confused. "Are you saying Amalgam is collecting a debt? From Sofia?" I ask.

"I'm saying, repeating really, that it's not something any of us wants to mess with," Ty says. "That's why my sister's happy she's with *you*, just the way you are. Yes, she's crazy in love with you, I happen to know that for a fact, but I also know that without you, things change for her. Honestly, they'll probably change anyway, but she's done a nice job of creating something different for herself, against a huge pile of odds."

A metallic crash sounds from elsewhere on the cleanup site, but Ty keeps talking, as if the sound is routine.

"So, if you're thinking of using that word you heard, or going public with anything you might come across during your marriage, that'd be the worst thing you could do for Sofia," he says. "Because Amalgam, well that's something she and I have known about since we were playing hide-and-seek in our backyard. It's something for us, not for general knowledge, same as any other... unusual... knowledge you might come across during your marriage."

He pats me on the shoulder. "I mean, sorry to be a jerk, but the reality is you're now part of a very private family that engages in private matters, and that's how things need to stay."

He slides the window closed, then locks up as we exit the bungalow. "So, there it is: mystery, close-to-the-vest... can't say I didn't warn you."

I shake his hand and wish him a good weekend as we head to our cars, but it's all performed in absentminded fashion because the only thing that's really on my mind is how much everything stinks.

And I'm not referring to the fish pudding.

EIGHT

Y ou spoke with my brother."

Sofia's waving an aluminum arrow in front of my nose like it's a pointer. She doesn't seem angry, which is good because we're spending our Friday evening at the local archery range and I don't want any of her arrows piercing my nethers. I try shifting the subject to salad recipes and rain gutters, but given what I've done she understandably has a different agenda.

"I needed to talk about our… situation," I say, "and he's known you the longest."

She utters a dainty scoff while nocking an arrow. "Ty is the last person you should have gone to. He's aligned with my dad. They do dangerous work."

"You mean handling the toxic waste?"

She lowers her bow, giving me an unimpeded view of some newly formed stress lines. "I mean handling the things we can't discuss in public. But you're not wrong about it being toxic."

Okay, so she's upset after all.

"Well to be fair, Ty seems a decent enough guy. Not that he said much."

"He's an expert at not saying much."

She raises her left arm, extends her bow, then straightens her back while broadening her shoulders. People think archery is about aim, but posture's the key.

"I saw you talking to the towel rack," I say.

She lowers the bow, looks askance.

"Five minutes earlier you'd have seen me chatting up the silverware," she says. "I think aloud sometimes. Don't you?"

I love her, but she's a crappy liar.

"Come on, Sofia... give me some credit here."

I glance around, suddenly conscious that there are other people here at the range. They're some distance away but possibly within earshot.

Sofia smiles, the placating variety in case someone overheard.

"Okay, Matt... you caught me," she says, lowering her voice. "Yes, I talk with our belongings, and not because I'm an imaginative person."

At first, I can't tell if she's being serious, or messing with me. Then she gives her bow an earnest, wistful look, as if wishing it could offer some advice on what to say.

"And look," she adds, "I get it: you've discovered something mind-blowing, and you want to learn everything about it. I remember when I experienced the same thrill."

She pulls her arrow until the drawstring reaches full tension, keeping her elbow level, then releases. Her arrow pierces the target's secondary ring.

"But then I found out the only way to have a normal life... to have *us*," she says, continuing, "is to think of your things the way you always have: as objects."

I watch as she fires her four remaining arrows; three hit center-target, three edge into the secondary rings, but with her you pay more attention to the poetic way she works a bow. Her movements are smooth and methodical, like she's having a dance with her equipment—very similar to her style with a brush and canvas.

Before meeting Sofia, the women I dated were... *interchangeable*, much as I hate phrasing it that way. Sure, we had common interests, and the sex was nice, but it always seemed like two puzzle pieces where the shapes weren't quite right. Plus—and I'm not proud of this—I basically gave relationships very little priority, as if each woman was just another item in my pile of *stuff*. One late arrival or mismanaged social situation and I would end things, with few second thoughts. And if *they* dumped *me*? Big whoop. Inventing Melds taught me that anytime the fit isn't right, there's always another component out there that'll work just as well.

All of that changed with Sofia. Suddenly, the puzzle pieces felt perfect. Best of all, we made each other *better*, something I'd never experienced. Those secrets Ty referred to? Who cares, we all have secrets. She and I are those rare components that fit perfectly.

Now, though, I'm learning there are things that can put a strain on even the most fitted of puzzle pieces.

"Maybe for now we ignore the objects and talk about Amalgam instead," I say. "I understand it's a secret you need to keep, but..."

She steps back, away from the firing line. "I already told you: it's not about keeping secrets. It's about keeping the most precious thing in the world to me: *us*."

She tugs an arrow from her quiver, steps back to the firing line, notches it. After straightening, she fires; another center-target hit.

"Now I'll let the arrow decide," she says, notching another.

She aims fifteen degrees off-target, maybe more, and releases. The arrow sails off, destined for a plunge inside the protective hay bales piled along the target's right side... except that's not what happens. Somehow, some way, its aerial course inches toward true, as if a heavy wind is pushing its trajectory... only there's no breeze.

The arrow hits the target's outer ring. Not dead-center, but still...

"You can put backspin on an arrow?" I say, startled.

She moves to the bow rack, behind us.

"Sure," she says, setting her bow atop the horizontal rack. "That's what happened. Backspin."

She walks out of the range. I flash back to the question Ty asked when we met, about where I stand with mysteries. He knew this moment would come, tried to warn me.

I rack my bow and toss my remaining arrows into a return bin, exiting the range a few paces behind Sofia. I'm so intent on keeping up with her that I scrape my elbow against a ragged bow rack on my way out, nothing a bandage won't cover but enough to draw blood.

"Sofia, wait!"

But she's not waiting. She waves me off, shaking her head, making clear she wants space. *Not because of the question*, I'm thinking. *Because she's realizing my questions might never stop, going forward.*

I'm such an idiot.

She's already disappearing around a grassy hillside, which is in an urban recreation park spanning several acres. Except for the dirt lot where our car is parked, and some overhead power lines running from the range facility to who-knows-where, there's nothing else nearby.

Some twenty minutes later, right around sunset, I find her crouched atop an arched bridge, looking at tadpoles darting in the stream underneath.

"No, come over here," she says, seeing me hesitate.

"Even though I'm a thick-headed clod?" I say, crouching beside her.

Her reaction smile is more alive than any object could ever be. "*Especially* because you're a thick-headed clod."

The reed-lined stream bisects a flood control basin just outside of the city. During winter storms the area is a news chopper's dream, what with firefighters battling Natural Selection every hour, hoisting obtuse hikers from flash-flood waters. Today it looks like an English waterway, herons and terns frolicking, minnows nipping the surface, puffy pampas grasses shrouding the inlets, sunshine crisping the shore.

"Don't hold back," Sofia says, when I comment on the beauty. "Tell me the rest."

She's right, I was holding back. "The pampas grasses are whispering among themselves, and the bridge timbers seem to have some sort of... persona," I say, observing. "All's quiet and yet everything is chirping like frogs, only it's from the twigs and mosses, and the "sounds" are coming from within my chest rather than my ears."

I hesitate, hearing how crazy I sound. "Maybe I really am losing it."

"More like 'regaining it.' When we're children we see the life in everything, and why wouldn't we? We're immersed in living things, and it's glorious. You've only scratched the surface."

She notices my scraped elbow, digs around her lunch bag, finds a small bandage.

"Look, I want an honest marriage so I'll fill you in on what I know," she says, applying the bandage. "But I'm telling you right now: if we go too far down this road, we'll lose the life we share together."

She lowers my bandaged elbow, looks me in the eyes. "Promise me that you won't let this divide us. That you and I will always be the priority."

"That's the easiest promise ever."

We share a kiss, then an even more passionate one, our feelings so intense that it's almost as if can hear electrical sparks flying.

Then I realize it's because I do. I pull Sofia toward me as one of the overhead power lines snaps from its pole, producing spark-filled explosions the size of fireworks. The explosions, though menacing, aren't really the problem. It's their trajectory, because if I'm seeing it right, then...

The sparking cable is whipping straight at us.

NINE

Everyone imagines they have the skill to dodge danger with ease.

In reality, things happen too fast. Not only is the loose, electrified cable repeatedly whipping sky-to-ground at cobra-speed, it's "spitting" enough sparks to obscure our surroundings. Worse, aside from the waterway Canoga Springs' terrain is desert-dry, so the sparks are igniting drought-stricken bushes along either side of the trail.

Instinct drives us backward... a strategy that's not working since the loose power line is long enough to periodically strike the ground behind us as well as in front, jumping like an animal jabbed by a prod as it lashes the shrubs near our bridge.

We freeze, uncertain. Avoiding the electrified line means trying to find a pattern in how it curls and strikes... but there's no pattern whatsoever, as the current sends it in every direction, at variable speeds. Ducking narrowly saves us from the sparking tip, but then the entire cable dips and returns in a horizontal slash pattern that sends it sweeping into our legs, upending us. My legs throb. *Oh god... are they broken?*

But no... I'm okay, and Sofia's already pushing herself to her knees.

Standing hurts, but there's no choice. We hobble off the tiny bridge, reaching the pathway on the other side just as the dancing power line springs skyward then dives... straight into the stream. A sizzling explosion rips through the park, showering us in mud, shrubs and murky water.

Sofia staggers to the nearest power pole, places her right hand against it, then drags it downward, pushing hard against the weathered wood. Grimacing as splinters slide into her palm, she casts the pole an empathetic look.

"Thank you," she whispers, as if concluding an unspoken conversation.

Her hand looks speckled as she backs away; it's full of slivers. Another mud-and-shrub-filled explosion sounds as the power line again hits the stream. The line is dancing like a strand from Medusa's hair, and the air is hazy with smoke from random, spark-ignited brushfires.

"Get down," she says, pulling the two of us into a protective crouch.

Before I can ask why, something cracks.

At first, I can't tell what it was. Then I hear more cracks and understand: it's the power pole, splintering as if a *kaiju* just leaned into it. The pole wobbles, then topples away from us, dragging the dancing power cable as it crashes onto the grassy terrain, grounding the electrified tip.

"You okay?" I say, breathing hard.

Sofia nods.

I have so many questions, but approaching sirens convince me to wait. Minutes later, firefighters are snuffing brushfires and the power company has the line shut down. As paramedics pluck splinters from Sofia's palm, I tell authorities what we saw.

Except, of course, there's no real explanation for what I just saw.

Back at the parking lot, we unlock our car doors and collapse inside.

"Do I even need to ask?" I say, after several exhausted, silent moments.

Her sigh steams the passenger window. She closes her eyes, contemplating, then reaches for my elbow and rips off the bandage she'd placed over my scrape.

"What was that for?" I say, rubbing it.

"Your tutorial," she says. "The Band-Aid... it's an element."

"Element?"

"Yeah. Try not to use the word 'object.'"

She looks like she might be sick to her stomach. *Whatever's going on here, it's tearing her up.*

She holds up the Band-Aid. "How many other elements do you have on you?"

I add up the things I carry with me, like my keys, phone, and wallet. Pocket change, too, and Agnes Waterhouse, my de facto good luck charm. I also wear a watch, plus my wedding band. No glasses or contact lenses, but I do keep a pair of sunglasses with me.

"You're forgetting the biggest items," Sofia says, as I give her my rundown.

Takes me a moment to figure it out. "Duh—my clothes. I never think of them that way."

So that's a shirt, pants, underwear, two socks, and a pair of shoes, every day.

"Meaning a minimum of seven clothing items, plus the wallet, watch, ring, and phone," she summarizes. "Add to that the sunglasses and—how many coins?"

"Eight."

"And how many keys?"

"Can't we count them as one key ring?"

"No."

"Seven keys," I say, looking them over. "Plus a Bram Stoker keychain and a push-button LED light. Wait, I have two dental fillings—do those count?"

She nods. "So, if the keychain alone is nine elements, that brings you up to thirty, then thirty-one if we count the Band-Aid, more when we count the fillings."

I have to admit, it's a much higher number than I would have thought. Still...

"I carry a lot of stuff. Most people do. What are you getting at?"

She forces a smile, but it's not my smile and it's not even her smile, at least not her usual one.

"You sure you want to know?" she says.

Her expression tells me she's truly worried.

"Yes," I say, remembering her earlier concerns, "but I promise... I absolutely promise... that I won't let this divide us. You and I will always be the priority."

She takes a breath, lets it out slowly.

"Every object you're carrying—each and every one—is alive, as you've already figured out," she says. "But the significance goes much deeper than that."

Her face tightens. "They're also sentient."

"As in...conscious? Like us?"

She nods. "As is every object... every item in the world. I'm not saying they all have the same intellect that we do, but they do have consciousness."

Sure, I'd suspected it, but still, to hear her blurt it out...

"So, they're... aware."

"Very much so."

"Even though the very meaning of 'inanimate' is 'lifeless?'"

She blows a puff of amusement out her nose. "A definition written by *people.*"

For a moment, I'm not sure how to react. Then I break into a suspicious grin.

"How could you possibly know for sure that objects are conscious?"

She shuffles in her seat, uneasy.

"It's like I told you at the house," she says. "My family... they're into some stuff that you and I never want to be part of, ever. Their work... well, let's just say they uncovered things no one ever knew about elements."

"Like sentience."

"Yeah... and more."

"More than being sentient? What else could there be?"

Her long, loud exhale ruffles the hair on my arms. "The short version? Human, object, there's no difference. They're just stages of an overall life experience."

What?

"I know," she says, extending her fingers above her head in a 'mind-blown' gesture. "It sounds crazy, but it's true. Our lives have biological stages and inanimate stages, but they're all part of one long lifespan with varying degrees of sentience."

My thoughts fluctuate between genuine fascination and a deep-seated conviction that's it's all a bunch of bunk. Sofia grips my hand, then lifts it.

"When people are buried or cremated, their bodies return to the earth," she says.

I nod. "Yeah, we end up in the ground. So?"

"You don't *end up* in the ground. You return to being *part* of the ground. You rejoin your base, organic elements."

"Well duh, but..."

A light flicks on inside my head.

"My base elements," I say, repeating her words. "They're... inanimate."

Human, object, no difference.

"So, you're telling me that... people are objects too?" I say, incredulous.

Another deep breath. "Basically, yes. What's more important right now is that you come to grips with two things: first, that every element is sentient, as we've discussed."

"Okaaay... and the other thing?"

She swallows, hard.

"The other thing," she says, "is that some of them are trying to kill me."

TEN

Hearing Sofia say yet another thing that's not only bizarre but smacks of paranoia, I suddenly understand how Neil must have felt when he saw the video of me at work.

"Lily, the power line was just a freak occurrence. Why would an object—okay, *element*, whatever you want to call them—why would it want to kill you?"

She fumbles with the sedan's seat controls, adjusting until her seat reclines.

"Because of my family, and a whole history that I'll tell you about when we get home, okay?" she says. "This is so hard, and the more I say, the more I feel *us* beginning to crumble. So, please... give me the time I need to adjust, both here"—she taps her temple, then taps her heart—"and *here*."

She holds the hand to her heart long after she finishes her sentence. "Those elements you sensed were alive... have any of them tried to hurt you?"

"What? No. Even if they're alive, they're *objects*. They're not out to hurt anyone."

"Normally, you're right," she says. "Elements help people every day; all the stuff people credit God for, without thinking maybe God delegates. But in this case... I'm not sure."

I flash to the car that nearly rammed me... the airborne hydrant, the plummeting fence. Is she suggesting it wasn't driver error, that the car itself might have had something to do with starting that crazy event chain? Did that bumper shudder because it was distraught over how close it had come to killing someone?

Could a power line detach and fall of its own accord?

"Hold on—we discussed this before, inanimate objects don't have a brain," I say, thinking aloud. "Even if they did, they have no eyes, no ears, no mouths, no nervous systems to convey emotions. How could they hurt us?"

She shrugs. "Just because a table doesn't have the same physical structure that we do doesn't mean it can't have the same *function* we do. It just means we haven't noticed, or even looked for, the way such a function works in a table."

"So, you're saying an object can think, even without a brain?"

"I'm saying elements have structures that function, for them, in similar fashion to the way a brain does for us. They may not have eyes and ears, but they interact with the world using electrical, olfactory, and visual signals... physical and chemical techniques that give them an understanding of what's happening around them."

I'm not sure what to say to that. Part of me is concerned for my wife's mental health, another is trying to give what she's saying actual consideration.

"Sofia, really..."

"Listen to me: elements may have other means, but they *do* think. And believe me, they *do* understand."

In a world where most of our electronics are listening and talking to us, what she's saying doesn't seem like such a leap. Still, there's a big difference between a phone and a paper clip.

"You're done with Fustian Industries now that they put you on leave, right?" she blurts. "No more Melds?"

The comment seems out of left field.

"Done? No, not at all, they'll need me to finalize the Kelapa deal. Why?"

She curls her knees to her chest, looking concerned. "You should consider the ramifications."

"Ramifications of what? The deal? The price-point?"

"Think bigger," she says, without elaborating.

I have no idea what she's getting at.

Her phone rings: an incoming call from Ty, which she puts on speaker.

"You two have a problem, he says. "Meet me at Espousa. I'll be on the second-floor balcony."

He ends the call without waiting for a reply. Sofia and I exchange glances, then she returns her seat to an upright position as I start the engine. Some forty minutes later we're at Espousa, a mom & pop Mexican restaurant a few blocks from the waste dump. It's dark when we arrive, so garden lights are glistening from a patio out front. When we give the hostess Ty's name, she points us to a staircase leading to the balcony.

After a short climb we see him seated opposite the stairs, beneath a light strand hanging from the adobe roof. "Sit—this won't take long," he says. "I've arranged for us to have the balcony to ourselves."

He studies us, then just me, his finger circling around a loose hair that's fallen from the bun. "So... you've met your belongings."

Guess he definitely knows about sentient objects.

"I imagine the world seems different now that you recognize there's so... *much*... life," he says. "It's magical, finding out—like a secret your company's witch-shaped doorstops might keep. Sofia tells me you're still planning on making those."

He's circling. Why, and what, is he circling?

"They're not doorstops... but yeah, 'Persecuted Witches' is our next line if we can close a deal with the materials supplier. People like Bridget Bishop and Petronilla de Meath might actually become household names."

The deck vibrates as a waiter rolls a guacamole cart past us. I use the opportunity to lift Agnes Waterhouse from my pocket. "First woman executed for witchcraft in England."

He nods. "What about Viola Cantini?"

I'm surprised he's heard of a woman burned to death in the seventeenth century.

"Yeah, we have her too. How do you know about Viola?"

"How would I not?" he says, as I repocket Agnes. "Little piece of those women in all of us."

Sofia's patience thins. "Okay, enough," she says, to Ty. "If you have something to say about Melds, say it."

He smiles. "I don't have anything to say that you wouldn't say yourself."

"Maybe so, maybe not," she says. "Either way, I made it very clear to you long before I married Matt that my involvement with 'family business' is over. That hasn't changed, and won't. So, if this little meeting is Dad's idea—"

She pauses as the deck vibrates from another guacamole cart.

"It's *not* his doing," Ty says, after the cart passes. "It's mine. No one else knows."

"Good. Then we're done here."

Ty wags a finger at her. "We're not, because now there's someone else involved."

They both glance at me.

"That's my business, not yours," Sofia says, to her brother.

He shrugs. "I realize he barely knows anything, but it's still enough that he's no longer just your business—not if you expect to hang on to this 'normal life' you cherish."

"Maybe, but dealing with Matt's knowledge is up to me, not you."

Normally I'd interject that I'm actually *here*, but the two of them are staring daggers and it's clear there's a long history in play, so I keep quiet.

The deck vibrates as a waiter rolls another guacamole cart, this one to our table. He removes several avocados, two tomatoes, and a dish of chopped cilantro, then proceeds to mix and serve the fresh guacamole—which tastes delicious.

"Fine, go your own way as always," Ty tells Sofia, after the server leaves. "But this man needs to know that his newfound awareness means he now has responsibilities."

I'm tired of them talking about me like I'm not there, so I address him directly. "What responsibilities?"

"As you know, these beings aren't just alive, they're sentient," he says. "That means you're surrounded by opinions and dispositions."

"You're telling me the objects have opinions?"

He cringes. "Not a polite word, 'objects.' The term is 'elements,' if you please."

"So I hear. Why should I care that they have opinions?"

His stare feels physical, like it can sift and probe.

"Because it's vital that you understand there is an entire civilization of opinions, right under our noses, outnumbering us exponentially. And, like people... a tiny fraction of them are fed up."

I can't help myself; I laugh. "*Fed up*? With what?"

He acts as if it's obvious. "With people abusing them."

He says it as if I should already know. *Wait—is he referring to me?*

"Now, my sister doesn't want to associate with our family, doesn't want you involved, doesn't want my help—fine," Ty says, looking at her as he speaks to me. "But you need to know that Sofia is in extreme danger from that fraction of objects."

I look at Sofia. "They're upset with *you*, specifically? Why?"

"Like I said, I'll fill you in when we get home," she says. "But he's not wrong. It's like I already told you: there are elements out there that are trying to kill me."

Ty nods. "And by extension, Matthew, that places *you* in danger as well... especially given your line of work."

My line of work? Melds are beloved, harmless tchotchkes, winners of educational and marketing awards worldwide, so I have no idea what he's talking about.

"So many resources, so little need," he says. "Deadly combination."

He lifts his sister's hand off the table, like it's a court exhibit. "Sometimes it's the hammer that smacks your fingers rather than the nail," he says. "Today it was a power line that unclenched from its pole. Occasionally it might be a car that jumps a curb."

I feel chills. *Is he referencing the accident?*

"That's enough," Sofia says, pulling me as she gets up from the table. "Leave us alone, Ty—I mean it. And you can tell the rest of them that if they even *think* about—"

I hear faint words, so at first, I think she's lowered her voice. Her motionless lips tell me otherwise. *Something else is whispering.* The table? No, it's coming from underneath the table. *It's in my head, yet under the table... maybe even beneath my feet.*

Suddenly my mind's filling with dozens of jumbled, unintelligible whispers, floating up from the restaurant's patio as if every object, from floorboard to guacamole cart, is conversing. Judging from Sofia and Ty's shocked expressions, they're hearing it too—and that they, unlike me, can understand the words they're hearing.

"Get out of here!" Ty says, leaping to his feet. "Now!"

"Wait, I can—" Sofia starts.

"Too late! Both of you, go!"

Ty shoves us forward as we race toward the steps, feeling the restaurant's deck rumble from yet another guacamole cart... only this time, there's no cart. As I register that odd disconnect, screams sound, a deafening crash slams our ears...

And the restaurant's second floor patio—the one we're racing across—plummets.

8:49 p.m.

Saturday, Sep. 5

Notifications

NEWS

* Intelligence officials raise spy ring accusations; no clear evidence.

* Witness says shooting suspect didn't kill students, "the gun did."

*Fabric awning saves plummeting child after fall from high-rise.

Press HOME to unlock Screen Time, Reminders, and Purchases.

ELEVEN

Screams fill the air—mine, Sofia's, and Ty's, but also the screams of however many people are dining on the restaurant's first floor. For a split second, my stomach feels as if I've leapt from an airplane. Food, glassware, place settings, tables, *everything*, is sliding, spilling, and crashing as it falls alongside of us.

Meaning in this moment, human or object, we're all just falling *stuff*.

We smash onto the first floor. I roll my body upon impact, even as pain races up my ankles, knees, and hips. Dust rises like smoke; everything goes hazy. I don't lose consciousness, but it still takes me a moment to shake off the shock, and the horror. *There are people under this rubble.*

It was only a ten-foot drop, but the impact was so hard I feel like I fell off a high-rise—and that's after rolling, which I did because martial arts film stars always tell you that's how they survive a fall. I'm not convinced it made any difference, but since I'm not feeling any broken bones as I shuffle out from under loose debris, maybe it did.

"Sofia?" I mutter, searching the rubble.

"Behind you," I hear.

Like me, she's covered in a mashup of food, dust, and broken floor tile, but claims she's okay. We can't find Ty, but we do manage to dig a couple of the first-floor diners out from under the patio wreckage during our search. Groans and pleas from buried victims tell us there are still more people below us, but by now firemen and paramedics are arriving, guiding us away from the site.

Their checkups confirm what we already know: we're both bruised, sore, and generally banged up, but intact. Thirty minutes later the firefighters find Ty, and to our relief he looks like he's in better shape than we are.

"Somehow found a pocket," he says, brushing himself off.

It turns out nine diners and two waiters were below us at the time of the collapse, and though a few are being taken away in ambulances, all are expected to survive. The restaurant itself might not, at least not without several months of rebuilding.

"Deck collapse," a craggy faced fireman tells me. "Looks like a couple of the supports gave way."

"Gave way? The patio only had three people on it."

"Yeah, definitely suspicious," he says, rubbing debris from his chin stubble. "Usually happens at overcrowded condo balconies. We're looking into it."

Sofia, Ty and I exchange glances. *Fed up*, Ty mouths, then follows the fireman out of the restaurant.

Exhausted, Sofia and I head home. After showering, we're quiet, preoccupying ourselves with anything that helps us destress. For me, that's a narrative video game that's heavy on tombs, light on guns—a relaxing hour, until *Assembly Required* starts whispering from the living room entry. It's in my head, yet from the painting, like the voices I heard at the restaurant, and there are voices from our ottoman and the coffee table too. None of the chatter seems directed at me, it's just floating through our home, as if every object, from door jamb to floor lamp, is conversing. *Are my things talking with one another telepathically? Or how?*

I set the video game aside to watch Sofia paint. Up close, her brush dapples aren't much more than a gumball thicket, yet she somehow knows just how they'll converge to form her impression of reality from afar. She adds a final dapple, then exchanges the brush for a glass of Riesling and plops herself onto our couch.

It seems like a good idea so I perch myself on the dimpled cushion next to her, stroking the dark, microfiber surface, then switch to stroking her cheek. The room's still full of whispers; I can't imagine she isn't hearing them too.

"Still no idea who the disintegrating woman represents?" I say, taking a long look at *Assembly Required*.

She shrugs. "Just an image from my imagination. Same as *Outset*. I'd get warm feelings about the two of us and lift up the brush. Though I suppose..."

I give her a moment to process whatever idea she's formulating.

"I suppose the brush picks up on those feelings," she finishes, still thinking. "So does the paint, the canvas, the easel... everything. Every painting is a community of sentient objects, and this community was built on our feelings of love."

I nudge myself closer. "But one's showing a woman breaking into bits, the other is a blank void. Why would warm feelings inspire *that*?"

She shrugs. "Feelings can inspire *anything* because they reflect existence, and existence is itself an art. All we do is emulate it from our own perspective—a fancy way of saying there's probably a deeper layer to this. We just haven't found it yet."

Neither of us have any insight on the settings, or why the raven-haired woman's skin looks like a streaming, puzzle-pieced mosaic. And yet, whenever I look, I feel like I'm somehow a part of the painting. "Is every object aware? Or just certain things?"

"All of them, to varying degrees," she says. "Woods, metals, plastics... man-made, or natural. Plants, for sure."

"But animals would have more sentience than all of them, right?"

She shrugs. "Usually. Not always."

I keep waiting for her to burst out laughing and tell me the whole thing is a joke, but she remains serious. "People like to think we're the world's centerpiece, way above 'lowly' objects. But no... we're all just different varieties of one giant, diverse species."

I walk to the kitchen and pour myself a matching glass of Riesling, suddenly wishing we stocked something harder.

"This is crazy," escapes my lips, though I hadn't meant to say it aloud.

She cocks her head. "Is it, though? When the elements are identical? When the only difference is shape, the need for food and water, the degrees of sentience and motion?"

"But—"

"Yes, when we're in human stage we're highly animate and conscious, but that's only a very brief time in our lifespan. For nearly all of our existence, we're inanimate."

My Riesling is already gone. Surprised, I pour another, then think better of it and set the glass on the counter. "So, Ty was right about them outnumbering us exponentially. *We're* the exception. Not them."

She joins me at the counter. "Look around; it's not even close."

I top off her glass, but given the conversation it's hard to do without feeling callous for not considering whether the glass is okay with that. "I guess it's a good thing they only have limited sentience."

"*Some* of them. There are times in our lives when we're highly sentient—like now, during our human phase—and other times when we're the simplest of beings—the dust particle phase comes to mind. Most of the time it falls somewhere in-between."

The wine glass is back in my hand, because I need *something.* "And how long ago did this sentience begin?"

"Not sure. When did it begin for humans? The Big Bang, maybe?"

"You're saying cave men had sentient spears?"

She smiles. "Probably helped them drive off the saber-tooths. Not that they knew; people never caught on to the sentience. Or at least, they never admitted it. Not until my parents documented it as part of a think tank study that they were involved in."

"Let me guess: they got laughed right out of the study."

"Oh, yeah. The very next morning."

It's mind-blowing: humankind, surrounded by sentient life throughout history, never noticing. *Or did we?* I suddenly remember how the leather recliner in my living room appealed to me amid dozens just like it at the furniture store... how my favorite omelet pan is the off-brand version of our other pan, but the only one I'll use when I cook. Our dining room chairs are identical too, and yet we never shift where we sit, as if our specific seats are familiar friends.

How many of us have a bond with the objects in their lives? Is there some unseen reason that certain pens, books, glassware, and other items, become our favorites?

"I'm sorry for not discussing this stuff with you before," she says, between wine sips. "It's just... I walked away from it for a reason, and you're one of the..."

She cuts herself off, but continues staring at the woman with the streaming, mosaic skin in *Assembly Required*.

"Why are you so convinced that objects are coming after you?"

"Elements," she corrects. "And it's not all of them. Ninety-nine percent are either ambivalent or enjoy our company. The Leopards are only a tiny fraction."

"Leopards?"

"That's what we call the sentient elements who hate people. They're like the big cats: able to hide in plain sight, aggressive when they feel they're being attacked."

"Why do they think they're under attack?"

She takes another sip before answering. "People abusing natural resources. Using elements without thought or respect, as if they're unimportant. Basically, our total ambivalence about how we create stuff, and how we treat the things we create."

She says it the way Ty did: as if I should already know. *Maybe if objects told us they're alive, rather than keeping their sentience secret, it would solve the problem.*

"So, if the Leopards are only a tiny fraction of objects, why is this an issue?"

"Because one percent of a billion elements is still ten million, and there are billions upon billions of them out there."

She's right; even objects we think of as a singular item, like phones, jewelry, or a baseball cap, are actually *collections*—as I know very well from my work with Melds. Something as ordinary as a car has about thirty thousand components. "Think about how many elements team up to create our home," she says. "Drywall, receptacles, conduit, wiring, plumbing, tile... the list is immense."

"That still doesn't explain why the Leopard objects would have it in for you."

She clasps her hands, raises them to her chin. "Because I made a big mistake a few years ago, one that only I can correct... but they don't want me to correct it, because the mistake benefits them. That's why they consider me a threat."

"That's it? They want you gone because you *might* correct a mistake?"

She nods. "The mistake ties into me having certain... communication skills. Basically, I can interact with elements better than anyone—or at least, I could, until I found a way to curb my skills. That was the mistake."

"Seems pretty innocent to me."

She nods. "But not to the Leopards. Remember, ninety-nine percent of elements are opposed to their beliefs. When I used to share my opinions with that majority, it usually swayed them into snuffing the Leopards' plans. That's why the Leopards are convinced I'll correct the mistake. They think I want to give myself that kind of influence again."

She thinks objects... plan things? This just gets better and better. "You make it sound like our stuff manipulates our lives."

She looks at me like I should know better. "Sure, haven't you seen it yourself? They're the key that goes missing; the paper cut you never saw coming. On a larger scale, the misshapen stone that triggers an avalanche or the tiny metal scrap that takes out an airplane engine. There's an endless list of elements operating under the guise of random chance before an oblivious public."

I'm speechless.

"Like Ty said, the Leopards are fed-up with the way people treat objects... especially the people"—she gives me a look—"who act as if elements are an unlimited, unthinking resource."

"Seriously?"

"Oh, they're very serious," she says, "especially the elements who are bitter about their current form. I used to be able to stop their plans, but... no longer."

"Because you found a way to limit your own skills. I take it something bad happened, serious enough to make you do that?"

Her face grows rigid, like a jack-o-lantern; perfect exterior, but completely hollowed.

"There were several reasons," she says, her voice cracking. "Among them, the horrific impressions you get, communicating with elements... things you can never un-see. I had to stop, I just *had* to. But my family... they disagreed."

A methodical nod is all I can muster.

"My Dad, and Ty... they have the same communication skills, just not as developed," she says. "Mom too, when she was alive. Maybe it's genetic, I'm not sure. A few years before I left, they swung some private funding and started training people, to give them similar skills. Hoping to create a dialogue with the Leopards, to save lives. Even gave their project an obscure name."

That much I can guess. "Amalgam."

She nods. "If I were to help their efforts, like I used to... I mean, objects influence everything. I can literally stop wars."

A tear streams down her left cheek.

"But I can't do it, Matt. I just *can't*. I need a normal life, with the chance to do the art I choose, and now, with us... I never want to lose *us*."

She shakes her head, frustrated. "The Leopards are convinced I'll go back to Amalgam... back to influencing objects. That's why they want me dead, but they're wrong. After everything I've seen, everything I've learned about this world, this existence... I won't go back. Ever."

She looks at me, squinting through her grief. "And people will die because of it."

I'm not liking the direction this is headed. "This is why you're estranged from your dad. Because you left his life's work."

Her eyebrows lift as she dips her head. "It was maybe the most wondrous, virtuous project ever, but I was done. I turned my back on Amalgam."

I feel my emotional world collapsing.

"And you left because...?" I begin, my gut already feeling the answer.

"Because of you," she says. "I left them to marry you."

TWELVE

If I could tether myself to the house, I would, for no other reason than it looks stable. Right now, hearing everything Sofia just said, not much else does.

Her information alters everything. Or at least, that's the way it feels as I get off the couch, attempting to digest this new reality and how it affects our relationship, my career, my entire world view.

"How come you never said anything about this before now?" I say, running a hand through my hair. "We've been married for two years."

She raises her eyebrows. "This isn't something I could just bring up one night over dinner."

She has a point. My eyes travel the hundreds of objects in this, just a single room of our home. If I was any good at painting, I'd create a completely empty scene, like Sofia did with *Outset*, to find calm but also to jettison this overwhelming baggage.

I rub my hand across our living room window, clearing the dust film. Sofia's saying something but her voice is trailing off, too muted for me to hear. Then she's back, more forceful than before, telling me to leave if the Leopards come after her again, to stay as far away from her as I can.

She knows I'd never leave her. Besides, what would it matter? Ty seemed to think they want *me* gone too.

"He's probably right," Sofia says, when I tell her.

I throw my hands in the air. "Why? What have I ever done to a bunch of rogue objects?"

"Are you serious? Think about it."

I don't want to concede what she and Ty have already hinted at multiple times.

"Matt, you manufacture things that require more than a thousand ingredients, for a product that's not the least bit essential," she says.

I honestly don't understand the objection. Are Melds essential? Maybe not, but they're also not the cheap, crappy junk people use once, then toss. They're collected, and beloved. *Am I really supposed to believe there's something wrong with that?*

"Sofia, the car that nearly hit me... was it intentional?"

She hesitates, then seems to choose her words carefully. "Let me put it this way: if you're not around, Melds probably go away, and a lot of resources are saved. That's the logic the Leopards might use."

"And you're saying this is something that happens all the time? That right now, random Leopard objects around the world are trying to hurt people they consider problematic?"

She takes a deep breath. "Absolutely—but only rarely is it through noticeable events like deck collapses. The influence of a certain pen in the hand of a lawmaker, a certain gavel in the hand of a judge, or a certain smartphone in the hand of a social media-loving government official... those affect the outcome of events on a daily basis."

I try telling myself what I'm hearing isn't all bad. So what if equipment helps guide us to new medical and scientific breakthroughs? Do the Old Masters' paintbrushes deserve as much glory as the artists themselves? If so, great.

But then a personal, disturbing thought hits: *does this mean there's a reason sentient objects brought Sofia and I together at the pier?*

I ask Sofia; she isn't sure. "But imagine," she says, "what happens when it's the *Leopards* making those kinds of decisions, leading an orchestrated effort."

The enormity of what she's suggesting staggers me. Could political coups and assassinations be as much the responsibility of the weapons as the people? I'm suddenly wondering whether my dinner fork might be conspiring with my cheese grater, or if doornails aren't so dead after all.

Ridiculous. They're just objects.

No, *not* objects, I correct myself. They're faceless, unseen, sentient life forms... millions of them, living with us. How do we defend against *that*? If Sofia's right, she's been attacked twice today alone.

"Maybe the answer is to take this public," I say. "Share this with everyone, to warn them but also to inform them. People deserve to know this world is filled with much more life than they think."

She smiles. "Imagine what would happen when people realize there's no such thing as privacy... that for their entire lives they are never, *ever* alone. You already saw the way people at Fustian reacted when you treated the Melds as equals. It probably cost you your job."

"The job's not gone yet, not with the Kelapa deal on hold."

"Well maybe it should be. Either way, going public about sentient objects is a terrible idea. People never believe in things they can't see."

I walk the length of the room, thinking. "Maybe we'd post a few videos online."

"Videos of what?"

She's right. Sentient or not, real objects aren't the cartoon variety that talk and walk. If Neil were here, he'd double over with laughter.

"Lily, come on... our stuff is *alive.* There must be a way we can get people to understand that."

The carbon monoxide alarm blares before she can answer. Standing where we are, only a few feet below the ceiling-mounted alarm, it's deafening. But something else grabs our attention, a smashing noise loud enough to pierce the din.

"From the bathroom," Sofia shouts, as we run up the hallway.

We push the bathroom door open, peer inside, see glass shards all over the toilet lid. They're opaque, which means...

"The window," I shout, pointing.

It looks like someone hit a baseball through it, but there's no ball on the floor, just the broken glass. It's hard to focus with the alarm blasting, but there's no apparent reason behind the busted window.

Another crazy noise erupts, this time sounding like Yosemite just loaned us one of its waterfalls. We glance at the shower, and the faucet. Both are dry.

"It's from one of the other rooms," Sofia calls, running from the bathroom.

The geyser spraying near our kitchen faucet makes finding the problem easy. Sofia reaches underneath to shut the water valve off, while I grab our wooden stepladder from the closet and climb up to the blaring alarm. The readout says carbon monoxide levels are normal, and the backup batteries are fully charged. *Meaning there's no reason the alarm should have gone off.* Determined to snuff the cacophony, I pull the wires. The house shifts into total silence.

Exhaling, I make my way down the ladder... until the third step from the top splits. My right foot plummets, banging the rung below and jamming my ankle, which was already sore from the deck collapse. I'll live, but the ankle's going to hurt for a bit.

Rejoining Sofia, I find her with a pipe wrench in hand, leaning against the kitchen counter. The geyser's gone, and though the kitchen floor's now a giant puddle it still feels like a win.

"Pipe split," she says. "Near the faucet handle."

Gee, what a 'coincidence.'

"The bathroom window was propped up, remember?" she adds.

She's right; the slider mechanisms are so old that we usually prop it with a wooden stick to keep the window from dropping to the sill. Sure enough, we find the stick on the bathroom floor, amid the broken glass.

First time it's ever come loose.

"The alarm goes off, the window crashes down, a kitchen pipe splits, and the ladder busts, all at the same time," I say. "There's no way."

Sofia sets the wrench on the counter.

"No, there isn't," she says. "It's a warning. Unless..."

I move toward her, my tender right ankle feeling halfway decent now that a couple minutes have passed.

"Unless what?"

She looks at her toes, thinking.

"Unless it's a threat."

THIRTEEN

Later that night, emotionally wrecked and torn over what I should do, I decide not to believe.

A little late in the game, maybe, but who cares. My mind needs the rest. It's inundated with sentient objects, Leopards, and the eerie sense that everything, everywhere, is alive and keeping track of me.

I have to let go. I *need* to let go.

So, with Sofia's blessing, I leave the house. Leave my phone too, a monumental event. I walk block after block, all of them empty because it's a Saturday night and people either have plans or don't want anyone to see they don't have plans. My shadow stretches, shrivels, and re-stretches as I move between streetlights. I dwell on baseball, chicken piccata recipes, forthcoming Meld lines—things I enjoy.

Eventually I find myself near a headless, armless figure crouched in a fetal position. The community sculpture garden is normally a paradise of imported cycads framing the bronzed imaginations of a few dozen artists. Now, though, its appearance stops me in my tracks. Nightfall turned the verdant garden into a shadow realm, encroached only by sodium spotlights. Metallic ribbons and rotating spires spring from darkness on the slope just ahead; off to my right, beyond a blackened hollow, a floodlit, ovular knob beckons.

I walk, and look, but mostly I contemplate the pros and cons of what I'll gain versus what I'll lose if I continue delving deeper into sentient objects. Permutations abound, but they boil down to the usual dilemma tough choices present: do I remain in my comfort zone, or not?

Remaining definitely sounds good. It's much easier, too: ignore what I've learned, live life as always. Sofia won't mind, that's for sure. She's pushed for it from the moment I mentioned sensing that our objects might be alive.

Tomorrow I'll touch base with Neil, reassure him that I'll get some help. Then I'll call Jerry, to make sure he knows I want to get back to work as soon as possible. Just the thought of those calls, of placing my life on a normal track, is a load off my mind.

The sculpture garden's stone pathway winds toward an installation that's either a giant triangle, an origami bird, or neither. I barely register it since I'm still focused on what I'll say when I get home... how I'll tell Sofia she was right: ignoring objects, embracing normal, that's the only reasonable path. I'm smiling, just imagining how happy that's going to make her. I should've listened to what she said in the first place: to do whatever the clock asks, 'within reason.' Chatting with paintings is *not* within reason.

There's a driftwood horse up ahead, about the same size as a real horse but with lots of interesting twists in its framing. I head toward it, my stress easing. Next time I feel like befriending inanimate life, I'll compliment my overactive imagination then move on, same as I did when I was nine.

But what if there really are malicious objects, and they really are after Sofia? What if me producing Melds genuinely offends them, triggering even more hatred?

Water's flowing, nearby. I look through an orange sodium beam that's splaying from some unseen pathway light, past the driftwood horse. Another installation is tucked between ferns, this one shaped similar to a piston and embedded inside a concrete basin, enabling water to spill from sculpture to pond. I admire the craftmanship, though all that trickling water makes it difficult to hear.

Wait—to hear what, exactly?

Listening, there's nothing. No speech, no breeze, no footsteps. So, what is it I'm so worried the water will stifle? The sculpture garden's empty. Not another soul, just me.

Right?

Then why am I "hearing" something?

My pant leg is pushing Agnes Waterhouse against my upper thigh, so I remove her from my pocket and glance at the expressive eyes. They're directed at the horse—because that's the way I have her angled in my hand, not because they're actually *directed.* Right?

The horse's skeletal, driftwood structure is unsurfaced, as if its open framework is an attempt to expose an inner self, revealing there's more to it than skin, muscle, or frame. Maybe without speaking a word or physically communicating, it's actually telling me something?

That's what good sculpture does, right?

My mind's already insisting: *not like this, it doesn't.*

Jogging back to the origami bird that isn't really a bird, I sense something new: unbridled freedom. Not my freedom, the sculpture's. I so very much want to rationalize it, but I can't. All I know is the installation exudes freedom. It's grown beyond a bird, beyond art. There's *meaning* to it.

The ribbon, the ovular knob, the headless-armless figure, they're 'speaking' to me too. Grief, experimentation, excitement, fear... I'm feeling all of it. Energy, too—from them, from the artists who created them, from the evolutionary eons it took to form their components... maybe a mix of all three. Years of visiting this garden, of seeing only greenery and rigid structures, and only now am I understanding what's here.

There's nothing rigid about these sculptures at all. This artwork is like *Outlook,* and *Assembly Required*: *alive.*

I glance at Agnes, wondering whether she—*it*—somehow steered me into noticing all of this, the way Sofia suggested objects guide people toward certain information, careers, even each other. The concept seems so unlikely, and yet...

I run from one installation to the next. Vibes are coming at me from everywhere. Some I like and some I don't, but who cares, because if these inanimate structures are alive, then...

Am I really doing this? Am I actually going to stand here and let my imagination talk me into believing this anthropomorphizing craziness?

Then it hits me: applying human traits to objects is the *opposite* of what's happening here. This isn't about objects being human, it's about whether they're more than simply inanimate. Suggesting objects have eyes, ears, or noses would be like defining alien life by whether the aliens have the same functions we do. But that doesn't mean they can't be "aware" in other, unknown ways. If so, the clues might be subtle... like, in this case, the emotions that the sculptures impart.

I slow my jog through the sculpture garden, then stop altogether.

I think I can do this. I can move outside my comfort zone.

It'll be a struggle, but I think I can accept a world where everything, and I mean *everything*, is alive. A world where objects influence our decisions, where some of them might even cause troubles.

I'm still nervous. But I'm not overwhelmed.

Or at least, not as overwhelmed as I was.

FOURTEEN

The walk home is everything the earlier walk wasn't. The burden I'd felt seems easier to bear. Yeah, I'm still worn down, but I feel as if I can wrap my head around the concept of objects as sentient entities. Maybe that's why I arrive at the house with a light heart and an enlightened mind.

Sofia humors me when I tell her what happened at the sculpture garden, but her heart isn't in it. Her red-streaked eyes resemble a rush hour traffic app, and stress is wiring her face into an uncharacteristic pucker.

"Not another word," she tells me, heading kitchen-to-hallway as I follow. "I already know the art is alive, Matt. I'm trying to forget it. What I need now is *normal*, don't you see? I need *us*."

She pulls me close. We kiss, a forced, preoccupied kiss, but we go through the mechanics anyway, to see if there's any spark. Two, maybe three more of them, and everything else drops away. We're together again; the rest doesn't matter. She's right, normal is best. It's comfortable. Reassuring. Consuming, even.

Seems she feels the same way. She kisses me harder, and suddenly it's one of those moments where the sun could turn green and we wouldn't notice. Before long we're writhing and rolling, our tongues wrestling playfully. Joining, sharing, gasping. I lose track of time. I lose track of everything. All I know is that the only woman I've ever truly desired is gasping and lurching with my every movement, but it feels like so much more, like joining her means something far more wondrous than a simple, physical action. Sometimes I hear what she's thinking, or at least that's how it seems. Other relationships offered rote pleasure; being with Sofia is an all-consuming, soul-massaging experience, driving me on in a haze of lust and passion. Our utterances coalesce into one body-wrenching, guttural cry.

She's up by the time I recover—for quite some time, judging by her hazy eyelids, her quarter-full wine glass, and the untied robe draped around her shoulders. I check the clock: eleven-thirty, so it's still, barely, Saturday. Kicking my clothes from the bed, I hear Agnes roll from the pocket.

"Thank you for normal," Sofia says.

The experience is too fresh for me to let that slide.

"That," I tell her, "was anything but normal."

She smiles, my special one, admiring me while I admire her. Thinking, though. So many thought layers behind those beautiful eyes.

Since my hands are already curled around her shoulders, I use the opportunity to pull her closer. "What you gave up, to marry me... it had to be an impossible decision for—"

She stops me. "No, Matt. It was the easiest decision I've ever made."

Her heartfelt sentiment washes clear through me, knocking my emotional barriers away. "You understand that this... us... no, *you*... you're everything to me... right?"

She laughs at my sappiness. "I need to force-kiss you more often."

"No argument here. But I mean it, Lily, and I want you to know that's how I feel. Sure, I could go through the motions with someone else, maybe even be happy at times, but it wouldn't be the same. Somehow, you and I are a perfect match."

She seems surprised, hearing me vocalize my feelings.

"It's why I could always turn a blind eye to your mysteries," I add, rolling with my momentum. "Something I'd never do with anyone else. But with you... there's something about *us* that's more important than any of that. Or at least, that's what it feels like to me."

Her eyes moisten. "It feels that way to me, too."

She says it so easily. For me, expressing feelings comes about as naturally as asking for directions.

"There must be something we can do about the Leopard objects that are after you."

"We're in love," she whispers. "Can't that be enough? Can't we just forget about objects and go back to normal for a while?"

It's one of the million questions I've been asking myself.

My phone vibrates; the screen tells me it's Neil.

I offer Sofia an apologetic look. "I'll ignore it."

"Ignore a late-night call from the company that suspended you? You better take it."

I glance at the phone, then her, before reluctantly taking the call.

"The Kelapa deal's about to fall through," Neil says, his voice laced with urgency, and something more. *Fear, maybe?*

"So just bite the bullet and give them whatever they want."

"I did. The terms are set, but you've been their point person so they won't sign without your assurances. They're saying I either put you on the phone, or they're moving on. Can I conference you in? They're on my other line, Jerry is too."

I get out of bed, pulling my gecko-patterned lounge pants on while answering. "Oh, so suddenly the guy who talks with objects is okay?"

"Hey man, I never wanted you out, I just wanted to get you some help—I still do. I told Jerry the board was making a big mistake, and now that it's all about to fall apart they're finally realizing it. Far as I'm concerned, you're our guy on Melds, period."

"Convenient."

"I'm serious. Screw management, if Kelapa says you're the only one who matters, then I don't care if you're talking to your john every time you pee, I need you to be a part of what we're doing."

Sofia seems to get the gist of Neil's call even though she can't hear what he's saying. She's shaking her head at me, signaling I should decline.

"Look Neil, this is a really bad time..."

"I wouldn't do this if I had any other choice. This deal will set us for the next five years. Millions of Melds, Matt. *Millions*."

I feel my adrenaline surge. Even now, there's nothing like the charge of knowing products you designed from scratch are *this close* to making it into the marketplace. *But what about the Leopards? Should I really worry about what a few objects think about me manufacturing products that people enjoy? Do I even have proof that Leopard objects are a real thing?*

"I'll get Jerry to take you off medical leave, first thing tomorrow," Neil says. "For real—no doc's signature, no shoving you out the door a day later. Hell, we can throw a line into that contract that says Kelapa can back out at any time if you're no longer with Fustian, that's how serious I am about this. Just help me out here."

Sofia waves a hand across her throat in a slicing motion, then gestures in a sweeping motion, toward everything inside our home.

"Matt, did you hear me?" Neil says. "I need your help, man. Everyone working at this company needs you. You need it too—

this is for Persecuted Witches. You've been wanting to do that line for years. Don't even pretend you don't want in on this."

I take a breath, uncertain. Sofia's shaking her head, her eyes imploring me to decline. *Of all times, it had to be now?*

"Yeah, I hear you. Patch the Kelapa reps in."

"Perfect! One sec..."

Sofia throws her hands in the air, disappears into another room.

A ten-minute conversation, me talking business with Kelapa and offering personal assurances, seals the deal. After the conference call ends, Neil phones back to tell me I've saved the company, saved peoples' jobs, kept a fun, popular product line going strong, and am generally the world's best person.

Truth is, I'm feeling pretty good about it myself. *Millions of Melds headed into production, thanks to me!* I grab Agnes Waterhouse from where she'd rolled onto the floor, holding her up high in celebration. She feels ice-cold.

"Wait!" Neil says, just as I'm saying goodbye. "I, uh... well, I did some checking into those links you sent."

"So?"

He sounds sheepish. "So, I still think you should go see a shrink, but that research gives you something solid to pin your hat to, with the board and... well, with me, I guess. I'm willing to hear more sometime."

Was that an olive branch from Neil? Or is something else going on, something he's dancing around?

We end the call. I'm still pumped from securing the Kelapa deal, but it's tempered by Sofia's irritated reaction. She just doesn't get it—they're Melds, the most fun, beloved product ever, and they were created by, well... *me!* What's so bad about growing a popular, successful business?

And why is my subconscious so bothered right now?

Sofia emerges from the bedroom, her face tight.

"You did it, then?" she says.

"They're signing tentative papers right now. Neil heads to Jakarta in a couple days to finalize everything in person."

"How many?"

I'm leaning against the hallway entry, trying to stifle my basking. "Over the five-year lifetime? Tons of Melds. Kids, collectors, they're going to be thrilled. Fustian too."

She curses, under her breath but still loud enough for me to hear. "I meant, how many ingredients to make the new lines?"

I'm not sure how to tell her in a way that won't upset her. "That's the best part: we have just enough materials guaranteed for my palm-sized composites to do everything those poor women were accused of—to mock how *insane* the accusations were, right? They'll convey exactly how unjust the witch trials were, and the anti-feminist motivations behind them. It's long overdue."

I use Agnes Waterhouse to demonstrate how, on command, her lantern re-forms into 'Sathan,' a spotted cat that could change into a toad and supposedly taught her witchcraft.

"But how *many* ingredients, Matt? Give me numbers."

"Well then listen to this: we managed to get a superstitious thirteen for the marketing department."

The tension in her face eases. "Thirteen ingredients? Okay, that's not too excessive. The Leopards might let things slide on thirteen."

I grimace. "Actually... it's thirteen hundred."

"*What*?"

"I know, it sounds bad, but all the enhanced capabilities means that each Persecuted Witch needs a composite of thirteen hundred materials."

She looks sickened. "My god... you've just signed your death warrant."

I want to plead my case... re-emphasize that this is my chance to finally give name recognition to a group of people who were horribly, tragically mistreated. Who wouldn't want to get behind that? But that would just tug an open wound. We make our way back to the flooded kitchen, mop and towel the worst of the puddles in silence, then collapse. By now it's just after 1 a.m., and though we've taken care of the worst of it, our place still looks a mess. *Or maybe we're the mess*, I think.

"The real problem here isn't your Melds," she says. "It's that they aren't an isolated occurrence."

She sees my tired, baffled expression. "Did you ever consider that the Leopards raise a good point? People are always abusing resources without thinking twice. I mean, look at *this* place."

Our living areas are a disheveled, product-cluttered mess, and not just because of the evening's chaos. Contemplating the number of materials that went into the sofa, the TV, the wall hangings, and all the smaller stuff seems impossible... so many objects. *But who cares?* It's not wrong to want a nice sofa or a good living space. If that's what it takes to make the things we need, so be it— *and dammit, we need Melds, too!*

Still, the longer we look, the more Sofia seems deeply bothered.

"We'll get it straightened up tomorrow," I say.

She grasps my arm, apprehension tightening her face. "Will we? What if the only way to straighten up is to stop people from creating all of this in the first place?"

Come morning, I might have an answer to that. Right now, my brain is too fried.

"I'm serious, Matt. I need you to reconsider why you feel free to plunder the natural world... why you shouldn't be using your talent to invent systems that benefit all sentient beings instead. Because in my heart, even though I know how much we love each other... how much we're *part* of each other... I also know that putting a stop to this sort of element abuse is really the only way we'll ever have any future together."

Is she suggesting I discontinue Melds? She must know that's not an option. I nudge her toward the bedroom, thinking we might finally get some sleep and leave the discussions for morning.

Instead, the house shudders from what sounds like something smashing against the front wall. The deafening, terrifying bash sends us running for cover, just as a second thunderous shudder hits. Our lights flicker, then extinguish.

Scrambling though the pitch-black, wondering what the hell is happening, we tuck ourselves into the cavity between our bed and our dresser just as a third crash pounds the house. I'm envisioning a battering ram trying to bust through, again and again, impressed that the front wall is holding firm.

Then I hear the support joists splinter above our ceiling. Even in the dark, I can see the ceiling sag. That's when I understand: no one's trying to burst *through* the wall. They're beating *on* it, probably in multiple spots, with a very clear purpose.

They're trying to knock our home down.

1:09 a.m.

Sunday, Sep. 6

Notifications

NEWS

* Isolationism surges as 3 nations seal borders, 16 others threaten same.

* Soaring temps blamed on pollutants from increased manufacturing.

* Demand for raw materials reaches all-time high.

* Micro-drone "swarms" sighted over Canada, Guam and Iceland.

* Collectors rejoice! Discussions underway for multimillion Melds deal.

Press HOME to unlock Screen Time, Reminders, and Purchases.

FIFTEEN

The house shudders again. Our battery lights kick in, the ones designed to get you through a brief power outage. They're equivalent to the faint glow of a dropped flashlight, but bright enough to see plaster dust sprinkling down from our sagging ceiling, which looks like it might crumble.

"Do what you want!" Sofia shouts, at whoever is out front. "I am *not* going back!"

So much to ask, but there's no time. I pocket Agnes and grab my clothes, which are still lying on the floor next to the bed. Sofia does the same. Then we race across our buckling living room to our shuddering entry foyer, lugging our clothes under one arm as we burst through the front door, onto what's left of the porch, ready to confront whoever's doing this, or run, or both.

There's no one outside.

Next to me, the driveway concrete is curled against the house, like a giant roll of sod. *Did it roll itself into our home? I mean, of course it didn't, but that's sure what it looks like.*

"Sofia, what the hell's going on?" I yell. "What's happening to our house?"

"Leopards," she says. "Probably a few of them, bringing the place down. We need to get out of here."

My life is suddenly a slide show: running, fishing spare keys from under the calla lily planter in our front yard, realizing I don't have my phone, wishing for the first time ever that I owned a big SUV rather than the aging silver sedan out front.

By now, neighbors are looking out their front doors, pointing at our collapsing house and my gecko pants. We're near the front curb when my senses *zing*.

"The car," I say, pointing to where I keep it parked, out on the street.

"Yeah, I heard it," she says.

Hopping inside, I fire it up and open the passenger door, only to see Sofia is still standing by the curb.

"I'm not sure we can trust it," she says, clipping a small belt bag around her waist. "So many components. Too many to be sure whether the car is really with us."

I use her indecision as a chance to wriggle into the clothes I'd grabbed, somehow tugging the jeans over my gecko pants. "This car got us across the desert last year, clanking and smoking the whole way. I'm going to call that trustworthy."

She doesn't look convinced, but eases into the passenger seat. I'm ready to gun us out of there, until a sudden thought hits.

"Our phones," I say, opening my door.

Sofia gestures toward the belt bag. "Grabbed them from the table."

"But wait, there's still the painting."

"What painting?" she says, exasperated.

"*Assembly Required*. There's no way I'm leaving it behind."

"We'll come back for it tomorrow."

"But—"

"It'll be fine! Trust me, of anything in there, that painting will survive. Now go!"

The engine's on, the shifter's already in drive—though I have no memory of moving it out of park—and somehow, I can *feel* the car urging me to step on the gas.

I take another mystified glance at the sod-like roll of concrete indented into our crumbling house, then pull away from the curb, whipping us around the corner and onto the closest major road. Sofia points to the northbound freeway ramp so I steer us on, slowpoke-to-seventy in half the time I thought our little car could manage. The nearby drivers review my lane-weaving technique with some well-deserved horns.

"You're going way too slow," Sofia says, though we're well beyond the speed limit. "We're not going to make it if you don't bump it up."

"Make it where? Is someone following us?"

No answer—I think she's still trying to figure out whether the car's really with us or not. Our dashboard vibrates as we accelerate up a steep grade, into the mountain range bordering the valley. Mini-mansions and tree-costumed cellular towers loom, as does the transition lane toward the neighboring metropolis, but Sofia keeps us headed north, up the mountain, toward the coastal cities that lie on the other side. Traffic slows along the steep climb; commuters don't seem to notice their cruise control systems are just as affected by psychology as we are.

I hear a pop: the familiar, jarring sound of a pebble hitting the windshield. Sofia doesn't seem to notice. She's on her phone, texting, her frantic fingers hitting the device's screen so hard I can hear them pounding.

Another pebble smacks against the windshield. I'm ready to shrug it off as coincidence when a third one hits. Leaning over the steering wheel, I study the roadway, looking for fresh asphalt or indications of road work.

Nothing. No construction trucks trickling asphalt pebbles either, but there is a wide-bed pickup several car-lengths ahead, with... *that's it*. It has a dark, sand-like mound piled up in the back. I slow the car but Sofia insists we pass, so I change lanes and floor the gas pedal. Soon we're close enough to the pickup that I can see asphalt stones scooting out through the gap between the tailgate and the sidewall. Several of them smack against our bumper and, for the umpteenth time, our windshield. I horn the driver, but it's too dark to separate his silhouette from the cab's interior, so eye contact isn't an option. No brake lights either, even though smoke wisps are beginning to stream up from under the pickup's hood.

"Jerk's got no clue."

"No, but the pickup and the pebbles do," Sofia says. "They're working against us."

I glance at her, incredulous.

"*Against* us? What are you talking about?"

She glares at the dashboard as if our car, rather than me, is the one doubting her. "I'm telling you they're all Leopards. The pickup's willing to burn itself out, blow itself up, or do whatever it takes to stop us. The asphalt pebbles, too."

"The *asphalt*?"

Our car shudders from attempting to pass on a steep grade. The pickup guns its engine, maintaining its lead on us, but I'm more jostled by Sofia's claim that a pile of pebbles is intentionally trying to inflict harm.

"I'm not even sold on the truck part," I say, "but it *can't* be the asphalt."

Sofia looks away, as if she's trying to avoid confirming anything—*meaning, what*? That she thinks damage from road debris isn't always happenstance? That loose highway pebbles aren't simple, inert blacktop? *That the whole damn road is made from sentient, asphalt pebbles?*

"No... there's no way. It's *not* the pebbles."

"Yeah, well... it is," she says. "In tandem with the truck. Maybe the driver too, I can't tell."

My logical mind thinks she's crazy, but even *I'm* feeling something up ahead of us, projecting disgruntled emotions. Smoke wisps from the pickup are intensifying and its bed is shuddering, worse than my car. *From engine strain? Or is it trying to shake the asphalt pebbles in our direction?* Some fall over the sidewalls, scattering just far enough for the pickup's tires to launch them straight into our windshield. Others smack against our headlights, bumper, and wheels.

As the roadway curves, the truck's tailgate pops open and a huge section of the pebble pile slides down, over the tailgate and off, spilling onto the road, headed straight for us. I manage to swerve around the thickest portion, but the asphalt pebbles aren't acting normally. Instead, it's as if they can defy physics, spraying up at us from the tailgate, the lane, and the median.

"Go straight through them!" Sofia says. "Don't slow up!"

Her advice defies logic; the asphalt pebbles are going to crack our windshield to bits. Sure enough, one of them smacks the upper right corner, splintering the glass.

Tires screech behind us, a gut-wrenching sound. The rearview mirror is an action film realized, all swerving cars, cracked windshields, and fender benders. Gravel's splashing against our wheel wells and the lanes ahead of us are now covered in asphalt pebbles, so many that it's hard to steer.

I look for an off-ramp—never, ever have I wanted to exit a freeway so badly—but there's nothing in these hills but an old, city-owned reservoir, and the road signs say there's no exit until we get over the mountains, another four miles down. Worse, this is one of those remote areas without streetlights, so everything's dark except for my headlights and the reflective road dots.

The rest of the traffic falls away, stymied by pebbles and accidents. Ignoring Sofia's objections, I ease off the gas and weave across lanes, trying to make us a more difficult target. The pickup reduces speed to match. There's so much smoke billowing from its hood that it's like driving through fog.

Then, at the rim of the valley, the right guardrail shimmers.

"That's it—that's our exit," Sofia says.

She points to a gap in the oleanders bordering the freeway about a quarter-mile ahead, where the shimmering rail ends. It's windy on this side of the ridge, so the roadside bushes are leaning far enough over for a Batmobile to come racing out, but likewise clearing a makeshift off-ramp for us.

"You want to take *that*?" I say.

"Yeah, but not until the last minute. Once we're right up on it, swerve us in."

Our headlights are just bright enough to make out an asphalt margin breaking up into an unpaved, dirt slope with a fairly steep grade. A couple of startled deer are standing to one side, frozen from fear. Sofia's leaning toward the windshield again, eyes as wide as before. Then I see why: just ahead of us, the exit lane is bordered by orange construction pylons.

The good news is that the asphalt within those pylons looks freshly paved. The bad? Construction crews haven't yet cleaned the surface. Even from our distance, we can make out hundreds of asphalt pebbles... and after everything I've seen tonight, I have no doubt that those things will somehow fire straight at us if we try exiting the highway.

"We'll take the next off-ramp instead."

"*Four miles away*?" she says. "We'd get pebbled to death long before we got there! No, this is our best shot."

She's nuts. But she's also right: even if I put us in the lane farthest from the construction lane, there's no chance we drive all that way without getting slammed by pebbles. Here, if we somehow make it up the dirt incline...

Now I'm as nuts as she is. Assuming we can get past the pebble onslaught, taking the unpaved incline means jumping our car off the fresh asphalt, onto the dirt incline, then driving over the dirt without losing control before miraculously jumping back up, onto whatever asphalt road lay beyond.

"No chance," I mutter.

Another pebble volley nails us; the windshield's midsection cracks, then splinters into a foot-wide spider-web. Our car's bouncing over pebbles like we're in a cross-country race, but I can sense this old silver sedan of mine has no intention of letting a rinky-dink pickup and some lowly asphalt pebbles beat it. Or at least, I *think* it's telling me that, which is probably about as real as thinking a pickup truck and a bunch of pebbles are out to get us. Still, feeling that the car is on our side, whether true or imagined, helps.

We hear a loud bang, just ahead; I'm hoping the pickup's engine finally blew out. Instead, one of its tailgate hinges has broken loose. A huge wedge of the remaining asphalt stones pours over the bobbing, angled tailgate, coating the lanes. My car feels like it's careening across ice, but I manage to keep from wiping out.

With so many of the piled stones now on the roadway, we're able to glance inside the pickup's back window. It's too dark to see details, but bright enough to understand something's missing.

"No driver," Sofia says. "The pickup's a self-driving vehicle."

Just beyond the initial construction pylons, asphalt pebbles are wiggling, skittering, and now popping from the roadway's surface like grease on a hot pan. Suddenly the stones fling skyward, as if a thousand tiny catapults released their loads at the same time. The pieces don't look like pebbles anymore, just a massive black swarm that's filling what's left of our windshield view as they hurtle straight for us.

"Get down!" Sofia says, leaning herself below dashboard level.

That's hard to do when you're trying to steer. Swerving, I plow us through the pylons, over the fresh asphalt, toward the unpaved, sloped, makeshift offramp. My fingers clamp the steering wheel as fresh pebbles slam into us. Careening forth, the car fishtails, straightens, accelerates... then soars straight off the road.

SIXTEEN

We're airborne, giving us a weightless microsecond. Then a hailstorm of asphalt pebbles slams into the front end of our sedan, obliterating the windshield. Pebbles and glass shards pelt my head, neck, and chest. Sofia screams out a curse, matching my own. My subconscious registers the sound of smashed headlights, our front grill cracking to bits, debris grinding its way into our engine casing.

The airbag's deploying and my body lurches forward as the barrage, probably several hundred asphalt pebbles, nearly stops our forward momentum. Somehow the car shoves through, then belly-flops onto the dirt roadbed, the tremendous force of the drop pounding my bones.

I've still got the gas pedal floored, so the wheels are already peeling out. The sloped, uphill off-ramp feeds to a paved, empty road, but as I guessed earlier that road is a few inches higher than the dirt we're driving on.

"We're going to hit the lip!" I warn, as if Sofia hasn't already seen it herself.

Our front tires ram the edge of the pavement, flipping us forward and over, nose-first. My body buckles from another jarring impact as the car slams down on its roof, flips upright again, rocks side-to-side, then goes still.

It takes me a moment to absorb that we're no longer in motion. I'm not sure how long I sit there, dazed. I'm so out of it that everything in sight—debris, steering wheel, air vent, empty soda cup—feels alive with sentiment, and thought.

"Matt."

The word sounds familiar.

"Matt, we made it."

The angelic voice dilutes my confusion, enough to know that I'm hearing Sofia, and that I'm Matt, and maybe, just maybe, I'm actually alive. My wife's next to me, more of a filthy silhouette than a person. Blood's dribbling down her face and arms, dusty saliva's trailing off her chin, and she's pockmarked with pebbles and glass, yet she seems more alert than I am.

There's not a single scrap of windshield left and the hood's covered in pebbles, pouring off to either side. The dust cloud in my dangling, rearview mirror looks like someone launched a nuke. Something feels heavy, painful even, in my lap; a downward glance reveals I'm chest-deep in asphalt pebbles, some of them sparkling because they're mixed with windshield shards.

I shove enough of the pebble mounds aside to place a supportive hand on Sofia's shoulder, then pull out my phone, thinking I should call 911, wondering what to tell them.

"No," Sofia mutters, spitting debris. "Absolutely no calls."

I hesitate, not really ready to process conversation.

"Our home's squashed and the highway's a gravel pit," I finally say, in a babbling tone, "but you're dreaming we can keep this quiet?"

She nods, wiping the blood from one cheek. "People will make up their own explanations for what they find. That's good enough."

"Seriously?"

"Yeah. Seriously."

I'm too dazed to have this discussion right now. Truth is, whether I call for help doesn't matter since someone will report the destroyed roadway, and the car's electronic emergency beacon—assuming it wasn't smashed to bits—is probably alerting emergency crews that we've been in an accident. I slide the phone back inside my pants pocket.

Some mild shifting and stretching exposes more cuts and a ton of bruises, several of them a dark, nasty crimson color, but I'm not feeling like anything's broken... though, in looking around, it seems more like *everything's* broken—everything having to do with the car, at least. Streetlight beams prism through glass shards stuck in the dashboard, all that's left of our missing windshield. The car's hood is missing a few chunks too, and maybe part of the front end. If we still have an engine, it sure doesn't look like any engine I've ever seen, bashed with pulverized asphalt.

Sofia and I open our doors to let some of the asphalt pebbles roll out, then stumble out from the car. Damned if we're not in the middle of a road, just beyond the incline we used as our off-ramp. The road seems as welcoming as the pebbles were conniving. It has a concrete surface—no asphalt!—and a stone border rather than a guardrail. Every vibe I get projects hospitality, relief, safety. *Maybe I'm delirious?*

The highway is way below us, down the incline. I don't know the area very well, but if the city reservoir is somewhere up in the hills then we're probably on an old surface road that closed after the highway was built.

Our sedan's looking like roadkill, crumpled and steaming. The tires are blown, the wheels and axles look just as shot. The whole front end looks as if a machine gun hit it, and the right fender's missing altogether.

Of course, I'm keeping the car anyway, even if it stays on blocks. Sentient or not, there's no way I'm getting rid of a car that helped get us through *this*.

Wait—Agnes!

She's not in my pocket—*how did I know that without checking?*—so I lean inside the car and dig through asphalt pebbles until I spot those familiar, expressive eyes. Relieved, I shove the discolored Meld straight into a pocket.

"He'll be here in a minute," Sofia says, apparently finishing some unspoken thought train.

I don't pursue it because right now, there's something more important on my mind.

"How is it possible for asphalt pebbles to physically *move*," I say, kicking the debris closest to my toe, exacting unsatisfactory revenge. "Or our driveway? Sentience is a big enough hurdle, but I'm sorry, objects do not fling themselves at things."

She takes a breath, holds it for a moment, then releases it slowly.

"Legs and arms aren't the only way to move," she says, mumbling the words. "Stuff builds and stores kinetic energy over time. Things suddenly fall off shelves for no reason, computer cables pop out... happens all the time."

"Yeah, but pebbles?"

"All sorts of objects move. Polymers lengthen or shorten like muscles, gels raise and lower objects, tubes extend, retract, and roll. And then there are the bigger systems: drones, cars, the automated stuff."

"Those are mechanical," I manage, my voice hoarse. "This was *asphalt*."

She acts as if there's no difference. "Our driveway was concrete, and it rolled itself right into our house. You ever think maybe stuff gets embedded into highways for more than just tallying the number of cars?"

I don't answer because another voice does.

"Sorry I couldn't get here sooner," someone says. "Things are breaking apart faster than anyone imagined. You two okay?"

I look behind us and see a tall, dark-suited man with a sagging eyebrow, leaning against our trashed car. *Wait—is that Suit Guy, the one who bought* Outset? *Why would one of Sofia's art clients— Doug Halston, was it?—why would he be here... at nearly two in the morning... and how could he possibly know where to find us?*

He sees my confusion. "She texted me while you were driving," he says, and I do vaguely remember Sofia tapping away on her phone. "I'm parked on the side of the highway, a few yards past the unpaved incline. Oh... and she was right. *Outset* really does look good inside Three West."

I'm looking at him, and Sofia, speechless. She's glaring at Halston. Marching up to him, she slams her hands against his chest, shoving him backward.

"*You*, and my own family, sending *Leopards* after us?" Sofia says, her eyes narrowed. "In our home? And then on a *highway*? What, because they couldn't handle that they lost me to Matt? Because *you* couldn't handle it?"

I move to intervene, startled since I've never seen Sofia strike anyone, but Halston's already backing away, hands raised in surrender fashion.

"No, no, no—it wasn't your family!" he pleads. "Or me, or anyone in *our* group either. This is all on the Leopards!"

He hesitates, looking at me, apparently uncertain whether he's said too much.

"He knows," Sofia says.

"Oh, wonderful," he says, loosening his tie. "Well, the Leopards still want you *gone*. They probably want the 'Melds King' here gone, too. Moreover, they're stoking conflict everywhere, carrying out deadly attacks. War in Asia is a week away, and it's certain to domino into the superpower nations... but hell if that isn't our secondary problem."

He puts a hand on her shoulder. "Amalgam's leaders are telling everyone the 'extremists' are trying to ignite a *null*, and they're scary close to pulling it off."

Ignite a what? Much as I want to butt in, I figure I'll learn more by listening.

She whisks the hand away. "Let me guess: 'extremists' is their placeholder word for the Advocates."

"Some things never change," he says, tossing the tie onto our wrecked car. "Thing is, they're not wrong about someone prepping up a null. Our Flies are telling us the extremists specifically engineered it so three people can survive inside, instead of the usual two."

"They still wouldn't last long enough to re-tool all the *scratch* before the null breaks down."

He shrugs. "Probably not, but they think it'll give them a shot."

"That's not a strategy, it's just their usual *crazy*. You really think someone would try it? A null?"

He shrugs. "That's what the elements are telling us. Every interface I have, 'reset' comes up. But you know how esoteric it is, communicating with objects."

"Uh-huh. I also know that even extremists wouldn't make a null. It's way too risky. We all learned that the hard way."

They stare at each other for enough of an extended time that I know 'the hard way' refers to something from their past... something that they're not inclined to share.

"That's why a few of us are hoping we can talk you into lending a hand, even if it's temporary," Halston says. "You're our best liaison, our only real chance for figuring out what's real—and for regaining control if there really is a problem."

Sofia mock-laughs. "Right. Like the rest of you can't handle it yourselves."

"We've tried. We just don't have the same rapport with the elements."

He looks at me, does a doubletake, then points to my head. Turns out I have a nasty split in the skin above my forehead, so I grab a towel from the car's smashed trunk.

Walking back, I see his hand on Sofia's shoulder again.

"Think about it," he tells her. "I'm here, exposing my connection to—" he glances my way— "someone who definitely *shouldn't* know who I am. That should tell you we're worried this is a *real* crisis. That we really do need you."

I notice Sofia hasn't backed away or broken eye contact with him. I also notice she's not wearing her wedding ring—because we left the house so fast? Or is there another reason?

"The only crisis here," she says, to Halston, "is my family—and *you*—interfering with my life, against my wishes."

"You know I wouldn't do that... and in your heart, you know your family wouldn't either."

She scoffs. "Do I? After they turned on me for wanting to lead my own life?"

He sighs. "And that was messed up. But they didn't send the Leopards after you, and they didn't use the Flies on you either—not now, not ever."

She wriggles free of him, seeing me approach.

"Just get us out of here," she tells him. "I messaged you for one reason: to tell you firsthand that if any of you ever mess with me again, I'll get back to interfacing alright... but you won't like what I tell those elements to do."

That shuts him up. He hesitates, then gestures for us to follow.

"Something I need to know?" I say to Sofia, as he walks away.

"No."

Well okay, then.

Sofia watches Halston for a moment, then calls out to him.

"You can also bring *Outset* back from Three West," she tells him. "Consider the sale revoked."

My heart warms.

Halston stops, stands there, then turns around and marches back. "Seriously? For *him*?" he says, speaking to her but looking at me.

He folds his arms, irritated, but our attention shifts to a strange sound erupting from the hills above us, similar to the rush of pouring gravel, but muffled. The sound grows in intensity but softens in tone, sounding fluid, like something spilling.

"The reservoir," Sofia says.

Halston's tightening face tells us he agrees with Sofia's guess.

"The spillway doors on that reservoir might be against us," he says. "If they've opened..."

"Then there's a huge flood headed downhill," Sofia says. "Straight toward us."

1:58 a.m.

Sunday, Sep. 6

Notifications

NEWS

* Suspected drone strike kills vacationing security commander.

* The brazen attack sparks retaliation vows from multiple nations.

* Govts., extremist groups deny responsibility, but suspicions rampant.

* 22-year High Court justice William Donne chokes on peanut.

Press HOME to unlock Screen Time, Reminders, and Purchases.

SEVENTEEN

Never has distant, rushing water sounded so terrifying.

"We need higher ground," Halston says, urging us up a hillside.

Sofia and I break into a run behind him, heading above the scrub-lined mountain pass. My nose and hip are aching, and my cuts burn, souvenirs from crashing, but adrenaline sweeps away the pain. It's pitch-black and there's no trail, so navigating up and across the darkened hillsides is a stumbling, chuckhole-strewn challenge. Unseen creatures rustle the bushes and faint sirens reverberate in the distance, but mostly we hear rushing water, loud enough—and close enough—that it sounds as if we're standing on a beach.

Then I hear someone nearby, calling to us... no, wait, not calling, there's no voice, it's just... there's someone in the darkness nearby, trying to get our attention.

"I feel it too," Sofia says.

Halston shrugs out of his suit coat, tosses it onto a boulder, then hurries us toward a deep gully with a rickety-looking bridge running across. Even in the dark, I can tell the hand-holds are just rope and probably frayed. The footboards extend forward in a line, each a step or so beyond the previous board, but several of them are missing. Halston doesn't hesitate, he just steps onto the shaky thing.

"The bridge will help us," he says. "Hurry!"

Hurrying seems a mismatch with what we're seeing.

"This thing won't hold three of us," I say.

"It will if the bridge is truly with us," Sofia says, following Halston.

I'm no longer sure who Sofia is to me, but I still trust her so I step onto the footboards, bringing up the rear. The sound of rushing water intensifies to frightening levels, and suddenly I see a starlit, tsunami-like wall surging straight at us. Terrified, the three of us break into a run across the unstable footboards, certain we're about to be swept away in a colossal flood.

Movement fills the dark hills above and around us, rippled and reflecting starlight. It's the reservoir water, but it's also the array of strange shapes jammed within. I'm too scared to sense whether or not they're sentient, but my gut already knows the answer: tree limbs, rock shards, and other debris are using the water as their taxi, roaring and pouring toward us.

The sound is deafening, the speed terrifying. I'm expecting a tsunami but we're hit with wind first, frenzied gusts driven by the approaching water wall, knocking us against the bridge's weathered ropes. Grabbing a rope, I hold my breath just as the torrents gush into us. The liquid's pounding like an avalanche, smacking us with debris, shoving us closer to the bridge's edge... closer to the gully, and a fall we can't survive.

The bridge swivels. Maybe the deluge is pushing it, but no, it's somehow swiveling *against* the current, meaning the footboards are blocking some of the water. The deluge continues but we're partially shielded and holding firm.

Then it ends. The bridge re-swivels as the flood eases, then subsides. Behind us, the water drains down the gully, headed toward the freeway and an unsuspecting city below... a terrifying thought I hadn't considered until now. We're drenched, cold and covered in debris, and my dripping phone seems incapable of displaying anything but lock-screen headlines, but here we are... still alive, somehow. My asphalt-stained skin feels a little less filthy. Halston and Sofia have their hands flat against the footboards, as if sharing their appreciation. After thinking it over, I do the same. Maybe the thing helped us, maybe it didn't, but I'm so grateful to be alive that I'd caress my toilet if I thought it played a part.

After catching our breath and squeezing water from our soaked clothes, Halston takes a long look downhill, studying what's left of the terrain we climbed. Even under dim starlight, it's easy to see ripped-out shrubs and hillsides stripped clean from flood damage.

"Both my car and the highway probably washed away, so driving you two out of here is no longer an option," he says, then glances at Sofia. "I know this isn't what you want but if we hike the cutover, I can get you to The Tiny in an hour or so."

I have no idea what that means, but the prospect of a soggy, nighttime hike when we're already shivering makes me happy to hear her scoff at his suggestion.

Halston nods. "Yeah, that's what I figured you'd say.

Sofia shakes her head. "Can you blame me?"

"I guess not, it's just... we're really in a bind."

Even left unspoken, it's clear he's alluding to their earlier discussion. Sofia glances at her waterlogged, bloodied, disheveled clothes, then takes a deep breath and closes her eyes. For a moment I think she's going to throw up again.

"Look, I'm sorry," Halston says, "but what if your Dad's right? If extremists really *are* building a null, you're our best shot at stopping them."

She shakes her head, but I can see it's from frustration, not disagreement.

"Fine," she says, to my chagrin. "We'll go with you. But I'm agreeing to nothing. Understand? *Nothing.* Someone can drive us out in the morning."

They start walking, but I can't keep quiet any longer. "Hold up—you two need to tell me what this 'null' is that you're worried about."

They pause, looking at each other.

"You're right, we do," Sofia says, though Halston doesn't look as if he agrees. "A null is a zone where people, elements, *everything*, dissolve to the point where all that's left is a gooey stew of base components. Think mush, over an area the size of a small neighborhood."

Halston nods. "Yeah, except this mush is like clay. You can reconfigure it into pretty much anything."

"But wouldn't anyone close enough to reconfigure it be mush too?" I say.

If only, his expression says.

"Not if it's engineered to allow them to be inside," Sofia answers. "It's like your Melds: a specific blend of materials gives them special capabilities."

She picks up a fallen pine cone and squeezes it, like a makeshift stress ball. "With a null, that blend is the product of gathering up millions of custom-selected elements, then igniting them into a fiery stew at a chosen site. Combine it with someone's DNA, they can usually enter and survive—for a short time, anyway."

She gestures for me to follow Halston. "We can discuss the details at The Tiny."

I hesitate. "You don't think we should call for help?"

"Believe me, if I thought anyone besides Doug could help us, I would."

I follow the two of them up the darkened hill, but only because our drenched phones aren't working, everything between us and the highway is washed out, and I don't have a better plan. To my relief, we hear distant sirens below—first responders headed to the scene of the flood, meaning they'll eventually reach the dam as well. *Maybe the rescuers will find our wrecked car and search for us.* Then again, it probably got hit by the flood, meaning it'll be a while before *anyone* finds it.

Chilled, soggy, and tired, we head along a trail that Halston seems to know well. The plants muffle our footsteps—I can't explain it but they're actually doing something that's quieting our passage. Aside from a couple of distant streetlights, we're in the dark. Overhead, a night bird's shrill call stops us in our tracks; everything's a menace when shrouded in darkness. Oaks assume their creepy, tendril-topped alter-egos. The southwestern hilltops swallow their diet of stars, fed by Earth's rotation. The evening smells of jasmine, dampened grass... and Amalgam.

"The 'Flies' you two mentioned before the flood... are they the objects that the people in Amalgam communicate with?" I ask Halston.

He nods, but waits for Sofia's approval glance before elaborating.

"Harnessing objects to gather information is how we keep the peace," he says. "We have them in strategic locations worldwide."

He says it with the same pride I convey when discussing Melds.

"You use objects as... *spies*?" I say.

"And to stem conflicts. It's genius, right? Like having a fly on every wall. No one ever suspects their own stuff."

My mouth drops open. The thought of everyday objects tracking people, influencing their decisions, reporting everything they do or say... it's both brilliant and terrifying.

"Like I told you," Sofia says, nudging me forward, "my family is involved in some things that you and I want no part of."

I'm not sure what I had imagined when she said that, but it wasn't *this*.

"How?" I mutter, my throat dry. "How do people 'work' with these objects?"

She places an arm around my shoulder. "They 'interface' with them. It's a touchy-feely communication method, like a medium reaching out to objects rather than spirits. Chock-full of misses, but it generally works. You'll see it at The Tiny."

I'm still trying to wrap my head around the idea of objects as spies.

"The information we gather de-escalates a lot of political situations," Halston says. "Hopefully it's about to help us with what's going on in Asia right now."

It's the second time he's mentioned the situation there. "I check the headlines on my phone all the time. Haven't seen any problems in Asia, or anything suggesting a problem that's about to domino into other nations."

"And hopefully you never will. That's where we're fortunate that the objects keep us a few moves ahead of everyone else. It's a huge advantage given the aggressive politics in play these days."

That strikes me as problematic. "What if the issue isn't political? What if it's a cultural philosophy that portions of the world disagree with?"

Halston shrugs. "Sometimes a peanut gets lodged in a throat."

My stomach twists. "Yeah... that's what I figured."

He stops, turning to face me. "Am I hearing an ethical judgement from the man who grinds thousands of innocent elements to bits every year, just to make idiotic figurines?"

I continue walking, right past him.

"Melds have won 'Product of the Year' twice, and prizes for education and scientific innovation," I say, without looking back. "So sure... I'll share ethical judgements any time you want."

He still hasn't moved, not that I'm bothering to look back at him anyway.

"It's true, then," he says. "You actually think bludgeoning intelligent beings into knick-knacks is something to be proud of. Do you have any idea how much hate you've propagated within the sentient object community?"

This time, I stop. My resentment for Halston just ballooned, but everything else has shriveled into a single, disturbing thought: *Is there any chance he's right?*

"You're as much at fault for the breakdown in human-object relations as anyone," Halston says. "Abusing resources because you can, never stopping to ask whether you should. This world is graced with entire races of sentient beings that could be respectfully, cooperatively fashioned into genuine needs. Instead, you forcibly crush them into toys that'll litter the landfills. And you want to question *my* ethics?"

"Okay, Doug, you've made your point," Sofia says.

Halston looks at me like I'm one of the trail rocks. "The woman next to you once persuaded the triggers on a battlefield full of assault rifles to malfunction. She literally stopped a war in its tracks. *That's* ethics."

He looks at Sofia. "'Product of the Year,' my ass. I don't know how you put up with him."

"Very happily," she says, but I notice a tinge of regret in her voice.

We continue up the trail, skirting property lines as we approach the uppermost ridges. Expensive homes dot the mountaintops, jeweled by the distant city lights reflecting off their windows. Three brief dog-barks steer us away from one of the homes, but there's no other indication we've been spotted. Even faint siren wails seem a world away.

So does a night's sleep. Between the darkness, the terrain, our slow pace, and frequent breaks, we're well more than an hour in before Halston points toward the silhouette of a Seussian blufftop that's shouldering the smallest, narrowest home I've ever seen. The house's exterior lighting shows spade-shaped sidings and a dark, thatched roof, but the entire home is no wider than a camp trailer and less than double the height. If Goldilocks wanted a new cottage, this is probably what it would look like.

"The Tiny," Sofia says, as the porch light flicks on.

The home is built so close to the blufftop's edge that half the structure is on stilts. You want to question the crazy architecture until you see the payoff: a panoramic city view.

A screen door bangs. I'm startled to see Sofia's sister-in-law coming out of The Tiny. Her outdated, bayou-inspired appearance hasn't changed, the curler-laden hair and plaid, hillbilly clothes looking out of place next to the upscale city view. On the other hand, the stilted house is on a dirt road, up in the hills with very few neighbors, so maybe it's a good fit after all. Her Tibetan spaniel's here too, must have followed her out of the house just to give me another stink eye.

Someone else opens the screen door then stands in front of the porchlight, eclipsing everyone's facial features. It's not Ty, but if posture and movements are any indication it's probably a man, probably middle-aged, and definitely impatient.

"Criminy... all banged up and drenched, and look at those clothes," Florence says, giving us the once-over. "But thank goodness y'all made it."

"'Bout goddamn time," the guy next to her says.

Sofia puts her hands on her hips and looks skyward. Florence hesitates, clearly bothered, then glances directly at me.

"I don't believe you've met," she says. "Matthew Beren, this is Anthony Alfaro... Sofia's father."

EIGHTEEN

I don't quite stifle a gasp. Sofia's *father*? This is how, and where, I'm meeting my father-in-law for the first time?

He steps forward, allowing a bit more of the porchlight onto his face. The guy looks old... Moses old. His scarred facial creases are similar to Ty's but sprinkled with white sprouts, as if his ear hair spread like mushroom patches. He's wearing an Einstein T-shirt tucked into saggy pants that seem hand-woven, maybe hand-dyed.

"We'll talk in the morning," he says—to Sofia, as if I'm not even there. "That is, if you can bother yourself to stick around that long."

He points a bullhead cane at his daughter while speaking. The skin of his arms sags like a quilt kicked to the edge of a bed. I've only seen him in pictures, but I don't remember him looking this old.

"Maybe," she says. "Maybe not. We're only here because the reservoir failed."

He nods. "And the reservoir only failed because you weren't here. Poetic."

Sofia curses under her breath as her father goes back inside The Tiny.

"Okaaay then... welcome home?" Florence says, exchanging an awkward glance with Sofia.

Home? Of course—Anthony is here, so this is Sofia's home. But I never knew their last names were different. Sofia sees my questioning look. "Ty and I use my mother's name," she says. "Lesser of evils."

Florence gestures toward the house. "You three must be ready to fall over. Let's get you set up, so you can grab some sleep."

We follow her inside. To my relief, there's no sign of Anthony—and he'd be easy to spot because the place is a dollhouse come to life: pink walls, dainty window treatments, and parlor furniture with ruffled, fabric edges. Everything from the maple end tables to the leafy davenport seem miniaturized; the parlor fireplace is as small as a waste basket.

It's all so charming that you almost miss the captivating things taking place right before your eyes, like billowing tissues riding air currents across the room, jellyfish-style, and steaming coffee stretching a full inch above the edge of its cup, as if peeking out.

Subtle things are happening, too. Atop an entry desk, sheets of paper arch themselves around a pen tip, then drop back down, exposing a freshly written "welcome." Below the TV, a trash can for recyclables is ever-so-slowly growing in height, even as the paper within is ever-so-slowly lowering. Then there's my instant favorite: smoke rising from a tray of pillar candles has formed a wispy image of Sofia's face.

Three people are seated on the floor, Sukhasana-style, and apparently have something to do with the unusual happenings in the room. One, a fortyish man with mutton chops, has his hands clasped around a sealed soda can, eyes focused on it as if he's in a trance. *Maybe in the midst of interfacing, as Sofia mentioned earlier?* Two others, both women, are concentrating on a silver tape measure as it extends and retracts.

"More of an obsession than a home," Sofia says, seeing my mouth agape. "People with Amalgam come here at all hours to practice interfacing. They'll coax expressions, or capabilities, trying to learn the best ways to work with each type of object."

The longer I look, the more I see, and it's wondrous. How can any place where smartphones lounge on tabletops, exchanging affectionate tones, not be great?

"We've documented sentience in millions of elements," Florence says. "Not just here—there are about three hundred of us, in locations all over the world. We'll try interfacing with anything, emphasis on 'try.' Your wife, though... she's the princess of paranormal. The rest of us, we're more like commoners."

Her reference to 'we' redirects my attention. With so much happening in the room, I hadn't noticed there were several people coming up a staircase from some sort of basement. Nearly every one of them is riddled with acupuncture needles, concentrated in patches; knees that look like pincushions, backs that could double as a bed of nails. One, a twentyish male, has so many in his eyebrows that they *are* his eyebrows. Even the people who don't have needles stuck in them bear the scars of having repeatedly done so, their limbs and faces covered in so many tiny dots they look like motion-capture film actors.

Sofia turns to Halston. "It's nearly three-thirty in the morning—you should get back into the city before people notice you're gone."

His eyes shift my direction. "What about him?"

She shrugs, like she's that parent who brought a toddler to an adult party.

His sigh hemorrhages frustration. "Okay, then what about *us?*"

Florence does a doubletake.

"There is no *us,*" Sofia says, shooting Halston a venomous look.

"I meant everyone here at The Tiny. We can't have this guy exposing things."

"Matt's my husband. Your cover's safe."

He scoffs. "Don't think I don't read you," he tells me.

The screen door slams as he leaves. Through the window, we see him climb into a small pickup and drive off. I'm not at all convinced he's actually leaving.

Florence hands us clothes to change into—basic jeans and tees, but they're the perfect size, and dry, and I'm grateful. "Glad you two got here in one piece," she says, as she leads us to a guest bedroom. "Me and Ty had a good bit of sass from our picket fence yesterday. Doesn't compare to asphalt and a reservoir, but it seems no one in this family's safe right now."

"You're both okay?" Sofia says.

Florence nods. "Ty's already met with the folks here."

"Good, he can be the one to fill us in, instead of... Option B."

Florence frowns, deepening her dimples. "Sorry, sugar. 'Option B' already sent Ty off on some sort of assignment at the Whitmore Art Center. You're stuck with Anthony. I'll stay with you, though. Might help him swallow the bitter pill."

She glances at me while saying "bitter pill."

The guest bedroom is the size of a horse stall but decorated for unicorns. We collapse onto our rainbow-colored bedsheets the moment Florence leaves the room. When I wake, I'm feeling like a few hours have passed, which is why it's annoying to discover the "few" isn't much more than "two." Sofia is already up, sitting at the foot of the bed. Her legs are tucked up to her chest, arms wrapped around them, head perched atop her knees.

"What if Doug and Dad are right?" she says. "What if the only reason we're facing a null is because I left?"

I sit up, rub the sleep from my eyes. "How could that possibly fall on just you?"

"Because no one else had the same rapport with objects. I could've convinced the null-triggering elements to reject the plan long before they ever gathered together."

"And you would have, if your family hadn't driven you away. Seems to me that puts this mess on them."

She offers a half-hearted version of her special smile. "Maybe. But even that would never have happened if not for my big mistake a few years ago."

"You mean the modest change you mentioned after the restaurant collapsed? Dampening your own communication skills?"

She looks like she's sorry she brought it up. "What a pleasant word: 'modest.' But no, this was part of a serious enough decision that it set something terrible in motion... something that never should have happened."

"But you said you can still correct the problem, right?"

Her hand squeezes mine. "I'm honestly not sure. Maybe, but... look, I'd tell you everything, but I gave my word to the others involved that I wouldn't, and..."

I give her hand a squeeze in return. "We're married, not fused. You're allowed to keep things to yourself."

She seems to appreciate the support, but I can tell it's still bothering her.

After a morning shower, I transfer Agnes Waterhouse from the waterlogged pants to today's dry pair then head to an early breakfast—Florence's southern biscuits and gravy, because *of course*. The first hint of daybreak glistens as we finish. It's a relaxing setting, but Sofia and Florence look anxious as the three of us walk to the staircase I saw when we arrived.

Anthony is already there, waiting. The man offers no greeting, no welcome, nothing more than a neutral expression, as if he's spent so much time with the objects in this remote, diminutive home that he's forgotten how to interact with people. Behind him, the stairs wind downward into darkness, headed somewhere beneath The Tiny.

"You've got five minutes," Sofia tells him.

He grunts. "Unless you've changed, that's four minutes more than we'll need."

"Unless *I've* changed?"

He turns and heads down the staircase without a reply. Florence is already following. Sofia looks conflicted but gestures for me to come along. The spaniel starts to follow too, then seems to think better of it. Pathway lights activate as Anthony plants his feet on the stairs, but it's still a dim journey. Some fifty steps down, the steps feed us onto a concrete slab, the pathway lights deactivate, and everything turns pitch-black.

Something snicks shut.

"Light it," Anthony says. His voice is smooth for a man who looks so old.

A match flares, igniting the wick of a single pillar candle. That's when I see that we're surrounded by the needle-people I saw last night, except more of them. Standing in silence, their expressions solemn as candlelight flickers reflect off their cheeks, I feel like I've unwittingly walked into a sorcery ritual.

Unlike The Tiny's entry parlor, this room—or possibly *cave*, it's too dark to tell—has no visible furnishings, no electronics, no décor, nothing. So far as I can tell, it's completely empty, except for the candle and the twenty or so people gathered.

Mutton Chops is one of them, sporting so many needles in his dark-skinned chest that he looks like a porcupine. Somehow, he and Sofia manage a hug. Pin-cushioned chest notwithstanding, he's a lean, scarecrow of a man.

Sofia glows as the others rush forward to greet her. They shake my hand as well, so many of them that names are flying faster than I can attach them to faces and features. What's clear is their genuine admiration for Sofia, as if Babe Ruth just returned to take a few hacks in the old ball field.

Mutton Chops motions for everyone to remove their pins. "We've got a guest, gods' sake," he says, pulling his in bunches.

"Interfacing pins," Sofia tells me, softly. "Helps the connection."

"So, they... what, strengthen the signal?"

"Basically, yeah."

Does that mean Sofia once used them too?

"And all of you can communicate with objects?" I say, to the group.

"No, we're just the pretenders," an Asian woman says, twisting her hair into a slender braid as she answers. "Your wife's the only real-deal here."

Nearly everyone in the room bursts out laughing, as if they've finally alleviated a long-simmering tension over their sub-par skill levels.

Sofia's father clears his throat. "Time is short, people, and there's only one question for us to answer here this morning," he says, then looks at Sofia. "Are you going to help us, or not?"

The glow she exuded while greeting the others fades. "Depends on whether you're ready to apologize."

He grunts his disgust. "Goddammit Sofia, extremists are about to trigger a null. Get your priorities straight."

The way he's described it makes me remember: Sofia and Halston used the word 'advocates,' not 'extremists.' *Are they talking about the same group?*

Sofia seems confused too. "You mean extremist *objects*—the Leopards?"

The candlelight intensifies Anthony's craggy face as he steps closer.

"Forget the Leopards, you know exactly who I mean: the idiot Leopard sympathizers who used to be part of Amalgam," he says. "Sure, we tossed them, but now they're out there killing people every day, and building this apocalyptic nightmare because they think they can use the *scratch* to wipe out anyone who's trying to keep the Leopards under control. They're insane."

I'm taken aback. After worrying about human-hating objects for so long, it's startling to hear the conversation transform into what sounds like some sort of schism that's divided Amalgam's ranks.

"Pretty sure they call themselves 'Advocates,'" Sofia says. "Not extremists."

"Yeah, and terrorists call themselves freedom fighters. Same difference. These are the same idiots who support elements that, right this minute, are triggering attacks that are about to cascade into Asia and will probably escalate into the next World War."

"Even if that were true, creating a null would be an entirely different level of crazy... an existential threat to *all* beings, themselves included. That doesn't sound like something they'd want."

Anthony waggles a finger. "Well, this time it is. Florence, show them."

Frowning, she pushes her way through the group, disappearing into darkness. When she returns a few second later, she's carrying a scrubby plant no taller than a pencil. In the candle's glow, it looks like a bee: fuzzy black stems with yellowed bands, a few petal-less flower corollas eyeing its surroundings.

Turns out Florence has a small comb in her hand, which she runs against the plant's stem, collecting the fuzz against the comb's teeth. Soon she's built up a dandelion's worth of fluff, which she grabs between two fingers and smothers across her flattened palm. The fuzz sparkles, and sounds electrified.

Sofia unzips her belt bag and passes her sister-in-law a small pouch filled with the same type of acupuncture-sized interfacing pins I saw Mutton Chops remove. Without hesitating, Florence punctures her own fuzz-filled hand with at least a dozen of them, driving them deeper than any acupuncturist.

"She's interfacing with a zero-zero-three share, if we include the I-pins," Sofia whispers to me, as if that makes perfect sense. "The percentage of object-to-flesh immersion improves communication. I typically use a bigger share, but this is just a simple mood request, not a full interface."

"And the fuzz?" I say, trying to pretend I'm following.

"Air is an object, or more accurately, a community of objects: gas molecules, aerosols, pollen... all sorts of tangible stuff," she says. "The spores give her inanimate allies... sentient 'middle-men' to vouch for her, again facilitating better communication."

Pins waggle from Florence's palm as she "rubs" the sparkling fuzz into the air, giving the emptiness a circular polish. The "sky" she's creating turns a satanic rainstorm color I've never seen before, more shocking than a red but lined with darker highlights. If Florence had lived two centuries earlier, she'd have ended up one of my persecuted witch Melds for sure.

"Crazy number of components here," she says, studying the color, "but that's where they agree we're at."

"We've dealt with worse," someone behind us says.

"That's what I thought too," Florence says. "But watch what they say it'll look like by this time next week."

Sparks fly; the tinted red fades... but so does everything else. The entire room turns pure, dull white. I wait for something else to happen, but it doesn't. No colors at all, nothing but the looming, pallid air, smothering us from whatever lay beyond. The weird thing is, there's also a *déjà vu* component to it, as if it's something I should be familiar with.

Then I realize I *am* familiar with it. In fact, I've seen this before, and just recently.

It's *Outset*.

NINETEEN

J ust thinking about *Outset* claws at my consciousness, yanking my emotions in ways I don't understand. The filthy white palette gives me an odd mix of shivers and thrills. It's like the nothingness Florence is showing us, an entire world embalmed into a bleak, powdered void.

"What am I seeing right now?" I manage, trying to act strong though I'm frightened to my core.

Sofia's face tightens. "That," she says, "would be a null."

Everyone around her seems to agree.

"You're telling me *Outset* was an impression of a null?" I say. "It looks like a postwar holocaust."

Sofia's throat is dry enough, and perhaps clenched enough, that I can hear her swallow. "No. Something much worse."

"What's worse than complete annihilation?"

She closes her eyes. "Complete creation."

Her eyes remain shut while she draws me into a weary embrace.

"I know, creation sounds like rainbows and flowers," she says, "but when you're rebooting, so to speak, it's the most destructive act imaginable."

"Because the people creating the null will tear things down in order to rebuild?"

Anthony steps forward, lifts the candle flame straight into the pallid color, then sweeps left and right... wiping it away.

"You poor, ignorant man... it's so much more drastic than that," he says, as warm candlelight returns both the room's glow and its shadows. "Genuine emptiness, Beren, is way beyond a tear-down. It's more like a blank slate. Every bit of reality as we know it, melted away."

Sofia's reopened eyes look scuffed. Anthony, on the other hand, seems pleased, as if he thinks discussing this is yet another way to rub past decisions in her face.

"Think about it," he says. "Bomb everything, you still have rubble. True creation requires a void where people, objects, and land have dissolved into a generic substance."

Even though I'd heard Sofia and Halston touch on this earlier, it somehow seems more terrifying now.

"So, everything inside a null is just... *gone*?"

Anthony nods. "It's a miniature version of what the universe might have looked like on day one, and it's not easy to achieve."

"How 'not easy' are we talking about?"

"Years of preparation," he says. "It takes an exact combination of objects representing every universal property accounted for on the Periodic Table—and a few that people haven't yet discovered—to trigger it. All of them have to be gathered together at the same place and time, and then they need a triggering event."

He taps his bullhead cane against the concrete floor for emphasis. "Only sentient objects have that kind of knowledge. For the extremists to go so far as to work with the Leopards to gather everything together must have taken one helluva lot of interfacing—but I guess we shouldn't be surprised. I mean, the extremists are Leopard sympathizers, after all, and the Leopards want to see the rest of us wiped out."

I see several disgruntled looks, but I can't tell whether it's because of the bad news or because they disagree.

"Last night I was told a null is only the size of a neighborhood," I say, repeating Sofia's description. "Not the world threat you're making it seem."

His biting laugh tells me what he thinks of my assessment. "Yeah, it starts out the size of a neighborhood. Then it seems to get smaller, because the more material it breaks down, the more unstable it becomes, until it collapses in on itself. All that goop? It dissolves the ground itself, spreading unseen, eating away at everything beneath it."

He points to the cavern floor. "Eventually it gets into water tables, volcanic recesses, gas vents... dissolves its way through the planet's crust the way liquid travels across a paper towel. Over time, as tectonic plates liquify, you have a worldwide catastrophe."

He starts pacing, as if it helps him curb his stress. "The only way to stop that from happening is for someone to re-tool all of that goopy, generic material before it collapses—basically, stripping it of its fuel. But you can only engineer a null for a few people to survive inside, and even then, assuming they know how to work with the goop, they have only a few hours before it dissolves them, too. Last time this happened... well, let's just say we were only a few seconds from losing containment."

Wait—did he just say...

"The *last* time? You're telling me this has happened before?"

He mocks me with a cane-bump against his head, as if a lightbulb finally switched on.

"Five years ago. Now we're on the verge of another. Best-case scenario, the people working inside use up all the material by re-creating it into whatever they wanted it for in the first place," he says, "at which point what's left of the null dissipates into a small, toxic waste nightmare that takes decades to clean."

"And worst-case?"

He grimaces. "It collapses, dissolves everything below it, then expands beyond anyone's ability to control."

Sofia has her head in her hands, covering her ears as if everything he's saying is resurrecting too many unwanted memories.

"Given that it's happening in less than one week," Anthony continues, "we'll assume the necessary objects are already in place at some unknown location. Adding or subtracting components would prevent the null from occurring, so all we need to do is find that location."

He casts Sofia a scornful look. "I wonder if my prodigy daughter might have any thoughts on whether we might be able to *do* anything about that."

What an ass. Sofia, to her credit, keeps her cool.

"Plenty of good people here," she says.

Anthony lifts his eyes. "For simple spy data and all that cutesy, smoke-swirling-into-faces stuff? Sure. But you know you're the only one those things ever listened to when it came time for something significant."

Déjà vu: I heard a similar comment recently. But when? It hits me: Neil couldn't close the Melds deal because the people at Kelapa Materials wouldn't do anything without me. Now Anthony's suggesting that Amalgam's objects won't do anything significant without Sofia. *But they're just objects. Could they really value relationships the same way humans do?*

Sofia runs her fingers along my shoulder, as if touching me helps keep her thoughts straight. "Ironic, you saying Matt and I are your only option."

"I never said anything about *him* being an option," he says, his expression darkening. "Just you."

I want to lay into the guy, but I know family baggage when I hear it.

"It's not like you don't owe us," he continues. "None of us needs to interface to see the worldwide escalation of isolationism, inflexibility, and intolerance. We told you we'd lose control if you left, and that's exactly what's happened."

Sofia mock-smiles, stands up. "I can see nothing's changed. Flo—we're done here."

Florence doesn't move.

"One week," she tells Sofia. "That's all we need. If this null crisis can't be solved within a week, well, it won't be solved."

Sofia looks away. Everyone else looks away too, which makes me suspect they understand the sacrifice they're asking her to make much better than I do.

"Florence, really—" Sofia starts.

"Darlin', we all know your father's a royal prick,"—she glances at Anthony Alfaro—"especially compared to Rosemary, when she was still with us."

That name grabs my attention. Rosemary Coronado was Sofia's mother.

"But we're on the brink of a null," Florence continues. "It's a nightmare we *have* to prevent, and we desperately need to discover the location."

The group seems to hold its collective breath.

"No pressure," Mutton Chops says, clearly disgusted with Florence's approach.

She shrugs. "We've got a full network of loyal Flies in strategic locations, but we need someone who can find out what they've learned, fast... someone who is leaps and bounds better at it than the rest of us."

"Bollocks to that," Mutton Chops says. "We should just let the woman be."

"Yo, Spray: shut it," the twentyish male says, straightening into a threatening posture. "We already decided how this is going to be handled."

The two men nearly come to blows; several of the others have to hold them back.

"That's enough, Mike," Anthony says.

"That *is* enough, old man," Mike says. "We all know a lame duck when we see one."

Several heads nod, others are shaking in disagreement. I'm not sure what's happening, but the group definitely seems fractured.

Anthony returns his attention to Sofia. "As I was saying, we only need *you*, to interface with a few dozen objects and find out where the extremists will trigger the null. At that point, the team here will intervene."

Everyone stares at the floor, looking solemn.

"You don't even know that this null timeline is real," Sofia says. "They're objects, we're people; miscommunications happen."

"There's no goddamn mistake," Anthony says, indignant. "Except the one *you* made when you put us in this position by leaving."

"That's not fair to Sofia," someone shouts.

It's Doug Halston. I can't see him but I recognize the voice, apparently everyone else does too. He's somewhere in the darkness, at the back of the room. The others seem surprised, but I'm not. *I knew that guy wasn't leaving.*

"Oh, I think it's plenty fair to expect someone who can help keep six billion people safe—six *billion* people—to do so, whether they want to or not," Anthony says. "Ty does his part. Why can't she do hers?"

Most of the candlelit faces are looking everywhere but at Sofia, trying to pretend they aren't bothered by the tension.

"Well, what's it gonna be?" Anthony says. "Are you helping us, or not?"

She takes my hand, squeezes it tight as she lifts our joined fingers in a show of defiance, then mumbles something, too faint to hear.

"Aw for shit's sake, speak up!" he says.

I angle myself in front of her, fed up with what's happening here, but she nudges me to one side.

"I said *fine*," Sofia says, her voice stilted.

She gives me a devastated, apologetic glance, then looks at the room full of candlelit faces. "I'll help you, okay? I'll help you."

TWENTY

I'm horrified. *Did Sofia just give up her life for Amalgam?*

"Lily..." I start.

"It's okay. I can handle a week."

My hands clutch hers. "You said you could lose yourself."

"I won't."

"But you wanted normal. You wanted *us*."

"I know! You think I don't know what I'm giving up?"

My heart's pounding. I don't fully understand the ramifications of interfacing, but I haven't forgotten how determined she was to avoid it and I can't keep quiet any longer.

"You people are telling me millions could lose their lives?" I say, with a sweeping gaze at every face in the room. "Don't you understand that if that's true, you need to let them know there's a crisis so we can all get working on a solution, together?"

Everyone goes rigid, like they're anticipating a volcano blast. Anthony Alfaro curses, spits on his own floor, then moves so close to my face that his reddened cheeks fill my entire view.

"*Together*, you say? You dare say *together*? When your kind toss perfectly sentient beings into your trash can every day, you use the word *together*?"

He curses again, then rants, mostly about the payback he'd like to inflict on the objects' behalf.

"Ignorant people like you stomp on conscious concrete, smack the brainwaves out of baseballs, treat utensils like slaves," he says. "And *you*, in particular... savaging your way through thousands of elements... not for shelter, transportation, protection, not for *anything* important. No—you do it to make a bunch of shit no one needs!"

He shoves his bullhead cane right up to my chin. "So damn much that your work will strand millions of innocent elements in swirling trash heaps, out in the ocean. And now you dare stand there telling me objects will want to work together with *you*?"

Whipping the cane away, he unleashes another round of curses. Sofia clutches my shoulder, signaling me to stay quiet. She's livid too, but it's not her father's simple fury. This is deeper... loss-of-a-parent deeper, the kind of raw, heartbroken anger where the rage is only there to stem the tears.

"Like I said before, you and I are done," she tells her father, turning toward the stairs. "I'll give the rest of you one week, because of the bigger picture. After that, assuming we even succeed... I'm never coming back here again."

"Perfect, because you aren't welcome back here again," Anthony says.

Spray intercepts her at the staircase, offering a handshake and a hug. Then Florence leads the way upstairs. Neither of us looks at her, or says anything. We just trudge, one step to the next, downcast and overwhelmed. The three flights seem like walking up a dozen Eiffel Towers.

"Damn," escapes my mouth as we climb, dwelling on how much of a burden Sofia's had to bear from her father... from that life... from *me*.

"Yeah, well... nothing new," she says.

"I'm so sorry. I've caused you so much—"

"Don't," she says, as we scale the third flight.

"I'm just saying, you've had a to deal with a lot of—"

"Just... *don't.*"

Sunshine greets us at the top stair, peering in through The Tiny's living room window. It's already Sunday morning... a new week. *Our final week?* I find myself dwelling on the null... how orchestrating millions of events to bring thousands of objects together at one specific point in time sounds like a twisted version of what I do to create Melds.

"How exactly does someone re-shape that goopy material that's inside a null?" I say. "Will the Leopard objects inside be manufacturing components?"

It's the last thing Sofia and Florence want to discuss, but after an uneasy moment they acquiesce.

"I don't know the details," Sofia says. "But you've heard the baking expression 'making something from scratch?' The generic material inside a null is also called *scratch.* Apparently, anyone who is top-flight at interfacing—person or object—can reconfigure it into something else, so long as the null was engineered for them to survive long enough to do it."

"I've heard it's like sculpting," Florence adds, "but in this case your mind is as important as your hands."

I lean against a chair. "Wait... did you say a person *or* object can do this?"

Sofia's nod tells me I'm correct.

"So, it's not just the extremists we're up against?" I say. "We might have Leopards playing God right along with them, turning scratch into whatever they please?"

Florence heads down the hallway. "Wouldn't be the first time, sugar," she calls as she steps into the kitchen, out of sight. "But at least it ain't easy, creatin' one. So many specific elements needed at a single place. Sure, it's happened before, but the odds they actually nail it are pretty low."

But no different from the hundreds of ingredients necessary to make a single Melds line. Industry people insisted it couldn't be done. What if some extremist or Leopard equivalent of myself is out there, just as determined?

Florence is wrong. Outset seems all too possible.

Sofia takes my hand, but looks away. "Matt, I've been thinking about it and... I'm sorry, I can't interface with you staying here."

"You don't seriously think there's any chance I'm leaving you while—"

"I don't want you seeing how it happens," she says. "You'd never get that image out of your head. I can barely get it out of mine."

She passes me a canvas bag with our torn, wet clothes from yesterday. "Spray will drive you back to whatever's left of our house, so you can grab *Assembly Required.* Then get yourself somewhere off the radar."

She steps onto the front porch, then into the dirt road beyond. By the time I catch up she's tossing three pebbles into the air, one by one. I watch her juggle them, feeling helpless. Here she is, dragged into an unthinkable circumstance, the weight of family drama and the world on her shoulders, with a strong possibility she's going to lose the life she worked so hard to achieve... and there's nothing I can do.

She adds a pebble to the three that are already airborne, then tosses it away because it's too heavy. For an artist, she's got a pretty good throwing arm.

"Forget about me," I say softly. "I'm worried about *you.*"

She gives me a forced version of my half-smile. "I'll be fine."

"That interfacing process... don't pretend there's no risk. Do you have to stick pins into yourself too?"

She pauses the juggling to finger-brush her hair, away from her face. "Something like that."

"Pretty extreme."

"Yeah, well, talking with objects is pretty extreme too. Anything you can do to make it go faster, and clearer... that's what you do."

"And sticking yourself does that?

She resumes juggling. "Making yourself part-object is what does that."

I'd love to know whether dental fillings or artificial limbs work better than needles, but she's already walking away from me.

"Even if you find out where the null is being created, how can the Amalgam people—only what, three hundred of you, worldwide—stop both a null *and* a war in less than one week?" I say.

The finger-brushed hair tumbles back onto her shoulder. "Doug already told you."

"Yeah. *Doug.*"

For a moment I'm thinking one of those pebbles will come firing straight at my head, but she ignores my dead-stop at his name. "It's usually as easy as a diversionary text message, or making sure a launch button refuses to push. Other times you use a sequence: malfunction leads to radiation leak, which leads to truce."

"If it's so easy, then why don't you want any part of it?"

She's looking at the circling stones but I can tell she's seeing something else... a memory, maybe, something from her past.

"Interfacing's a joy," she says. "Engaging with beings you never knew existed, the chance to save lives. But you give up so much when your thoughts are joined. There's no way to keep the things in your head private... over time, your identity leaches away. It gets to where you can't tell where your thoughts end and theirs begin."

She's sweating.

"Then let's bring in linguists and scientists to help you work with the objects," I say. "Diplomats too, to start dialogues with the extremists, and with the Leopards... and hazardous waste experts, in case the null spreads underground."

I brush the fallen hair away from her face. "People can help if we give them the chance."

She catches the pebbles, one-by-one, then gently places them upon the ground. "We've been over this already. No one will believe what they can't see."

"But given the stakes they deserve the choice, even if they choose not to believe. You must understand that."

"What I understand," she says, "is that their safety is better handled by that small percentage of people with an innate openness to interacting with objects."

She takes a breath, upset. "You think you're the first person to make a pro-awareness argument? Not even close. But sentient objects like anonymity above all else. Expose them and it won't just be the Leopards coming after us. It'll be all of them."

Her eyelids are lowered, as if she's in the process of making a wish.

"I'll get in touch with you when I finish here," she says. "Now go. Spray's waiting."

I look up the road and see a blue pickup truck pulling up.

"Sofia Coronado deserves to remain Sofia Coronado," I implore, "no matter what the rest of the world needs."

I can see the scales tipping in her eyes; she's *this* close to agreeing.

Instead, she pulls me close and kisses me, a passionate, goodbye kiss if there ever was one. "I'm sorry... I have to do everything I can to help stop the null."

Her voice lowers to a forlorn whisper. "I hate it, and yeah, there's a chance I'll lose myself to it. But I'll always be grateful I had the chance to experience *us*."

This can't be happening. My dream relationship can't be ending like *this*.

She shakes her head. "You and your Melds, me with interfacing... we both understand the things we need to move on from, but somehow, we just can't do it."

"Maybe if I interface with you I can..." I start, through a tightened throat.

"No, my interfacing happens on a much deeper level than what you saw Florence and the other people doing with that stuff inside, and it uses a different method. It's something I have to do on my own."

She pulls away, then steps onto the front porch. Even now, with everything crumbling, I can't stop thinking there's something special about her, something I've never felt from anyone else... something I know I can't live without.

Which is why my breath catches when Doug Halston appears in the doorway, and the verbal knife digs extra deep as Sofia calls back to me.

"I love you with all my heart," she says. "I always will. But if you go public with what you know, Doug and I will make sure you fail."

The front door closes; she's gone.

Before I can even begin to process this gut-wrenching turn of events, another familiar voice calls out from the idling pickup. I look over but it isn't Spray. Instead, I see Anthony Alfaro sitting behind the wheel, impatiently rapping his fingers.

"Hurry up, asshole," he says. "I'm driving you the hell out of my daughter's life."

TWENTY-ONE

Anthony leans over, popping the pickup's passenger door wide open.

"No thanks," I say.

He glares. "*Get in.*"

"I thought Spray was—" I start.

"Spray couldn't make it."

He lets it linger, as if Spray's dead, which I don't think he is, but somehow with this guy I'm not sure. I glance in the cab before climbing inside, checking for bloody axes, but there aren't any obvious threats other than the crazy father-in-law behind the wheel.

He hits the gas before I'm buckled, peeling out the back tires and sending up a dirt cloud bigger than The Tiny. The pickup fishtails, which he seems to enjoy.

He's humming as we shoot up the dirt road, his body tucked so close to the steering wheel that I'm pretty sure an airbag deployment would fire him clean out the back window. Every now and then he lets go of the wheel to fiddle with something in the cab, even though the pickup is way too old to be self-driving, but we don't crash and he's the guy who started Amalgam, so maybe he and the truck have some sort of agreement.

I try starting a conversation or two, but I'm swatted down each time.

"Don't need to know you," he says.

The ride is awkward and unending, one nameless, scrub-lined dirt road after another since the flood apparently washed out the direct route. Since he clearly knows where he's going, I'm stuck hoping it isn't some ditch where my body will never be found. All of which is secondary to my prevailing thought.

Sofia's inside The Tiny, right now, with Doug Halston.

"Tell you what," Anthony says, after we've been driving for nearly half an hour. "I'm gonna end your misery sooner than I'd planned."

I find myself fingering my seat belt's release button... and discovering it won't push inward. *What? I'm strapped to the seat?*

Anthony rolls down the driver's window, clears his throat, then spits thick phlegm with such force that I can see it carry off, into the rocks.

"There's a junction with the state highway about a mile ahead. I'll drop you there instead of driving you all the way back down into the valley. How's that sound?"

"It sounds like there's a catch."

He grunts. "Well, my thinking is that making your way back will give you a chance to reconsider the way you choose to spend your time plundering resources. It matters, and it's wrong."

That makes me laugh. "You know what's wrong? Not being the least bit apologetic to your daughter, not even with a crisis at your doorstep. Flo was right about you being a prick."

He spits another gumball-sized phlegm wad, then turns back to me.

"I *am* a prick," he says, "maybe even a royal prick, and there's a very good reason for that."

"Which is?"

He grunts. "Which is none of your business. And not some-thing I'd share with some goddamn element abuser regardless, es-pecially when I need to focus on stopping a war."

I'm tempted to tell him he cusses to the point of meaningless-ness, but I stick with the more important issue. "You want to stop a war? Then go public. Tell people that everything around them is sentient. If *that* doesn't reset their priorities, nothing will."

He slams on the brakes. My seat belt feels like a hand, pinning me to the seat-back as the pickup skids along the dusty road. By the time it comes to a stop, we're already sitting amid the result-ing dirt cloud.

"Have you ever tried reaching out to your stuff?" he says. "Just once? A man with your insights... have you ever even *considered* looking and listening to the elements around you on *their* terms, rather than filtering everything through your notions of how you *think* an object should be?"

Damn right I have. My crappy, rudimentary interfacing still somehow connected me with robotic components at Fustian, household possessions whispering "Amalgam" into my ear, and my old sedan as it practically screamed its desire to help me and Sofia escape the Leopards. I could screech all of that, and more, at Anthony... but why? *Even objects are more forthcoming than this jerk.* Father-in-law or not, I'm not sharing with someone I don't trust.

He interprets my silence as guilt.

"So that'd be a 'no" then," he says, disgusted. "You're no better than the rest of them. They 'feel' when a traffic light is about to change, sense a forthcoming phone call, or recognize when some-one's lingering unseen. They just too stupid to put it all together."

He slides the pickup's transmission into PARK, apparently so he can shove both of his middle fingers into my chest instead of just one.

"Listen to me, dumbass: if you've been hearing everyday items whisper—and I know you have—then you're predisposed to interfacing as well," he says. "You already experienced a crude version when the car skidded toward you—everything went into slow-motion, right?"

Who told him about my stress blackout? I push his fingers away from my chest.

"Seems like a guy who knows so much could do better at distributing all that knowledge," I say, fussing with the seat belt, still unable to get it unbuckled. "You and your Amalgam friends ever think about *teaching* people to interface, rather than keeping it to yourselves?"

Frustration lines ripple his face, aging him twenty years.

"Let me teach you something right now, 'Melds King,'" he says. "Elements see all those outdated clothes Florence wears and understand she's re-using, to lower the need for more sentient resources. You? All they see you do is take, and abuse."

"Yeah, well all *you* do is keep secrets and burn bridges."

By now the dirt cloud has dissipated enough that I can see the junction he was referring to, in the distance. It looks like less than a mile, but in the middle of nowhere distances can be deceiving. Not that it matters; I'm still struggling with the seat belt.

"You credit *Outset* as the reason you suddenly noticed the sentience in objects, but you knew before that, didn't you," Anthony says, practically spitting the words. "You knew as a child, then tried to bury the knowledge—like the rest of them. What age—seven? Eight?"

He launches into another rant, about kids and how they all understand it, until they choose not to. "For the sake of being an 'adult' they turn away," he rages. "But then there's you: never completely burying what you noticed, just conveniently ignoring it until *Outset* shoved it in your face, so you could abuse all those sentient beings without feeling guilty."

"That's not true whatsoever!"

He looks me in the eye. "I happen to know that it is."

What? I'm not sure what this intolerant ass thinks he knows, but I'm convinced he doesn't know *jack*. He doesn't understand the skill, and the process, that goes into Melds. The pure joy of designing and manufacturing, of seeing your creation come to fruition. And then, watching the glow on people's faces when they hold that finished product in their hands... nothing malicious about *that*, either. Everyone knows that 'holding a Meld is like holding a piece of the Earth.' What's more heartwarming, more *human* even, than a piece of...

Oh god.

"Get the hell out of my truck," Anthony says, firing up the truck's ignition. "You can walk the rest of the way. Unless you're planning to cuddle up with that seat belt forever."

He knows I'm trapped. *Of course, he does.* Doesn't help that I'm still fumbling with the seat belt button.

"Oh, for shit's sake... don't *use* it, work *with* it," he says. "Avert your eyes, so you're relying on your peripheral vision."

"Why would I intentionally make it even harder to see?"

He leans back in his seat, giving me the once-over as if he's trying to figure out whether I'm worth spending any more of his time. "Think 'telescope.' Jupiter's a white blob until you avert your eyes."

"Okay, so...?"

"So, if you keep averting your eyes, you'll eventually notice the colored bands. After that, you see them right away."

And what, he thinks the same thing applies to working with objects?

"Well right now the seatbelt is the white blob, because I don't see anything."

"Goddamn quitter."

Frustrated, I try again. Nothing changes. Anthony's busy muttering gibberish about retinas, the types of light-detecting cells, how rods are set away from the center and more sensitive than cones.

"That's why averted vision reveals stuff that's forty times fainter than direct vision," he mutters, as if it's something I should already know.

For a moment I imagine faint, horizontal hairline markings, maybe three of them, materializing across my view of the seat belt, but they're gone as fast as they were there.

Then, a change: the button finally depresses when I push it, releasing the belt. Anthony grunts, seeing the belt release. "If it was up to me, I'd have kept you tied in."

I look at the seat belt, then him. Is he really suggesting I communicated with an object in some fashion? That it gave way to reward my efforts?

"Everyone has those innate skills, to limited extent," he says. "Embrace them, maybe you'll have more. Or keep raping the planet and ignore the truth. Probably too late anyway."

He points to the passenger door. "Now get the hell out. And let my daughter do what only she can do."

I jump from the pickup, more than happy to walk in exchange for some distance from Anthony Alfaro.

"Your people... they seemed divided," I say, wrapping my hands over the rolled-down window to shut the truck's door. "What was going on in that meeting?"

"Nothing good."

"Yet you think that splintered, ragtag group is going to stop Armageddon? All because they can... *maybe*... talk to objects?"

He cocks his head.

"If the gun doesn't want to fire," he says, "the war's over."

"Maybe if people know the consequences of firing the gun, it's just as over."

He mock-grins. "Yeah... good luck with that."

The pickup's tires peel out, the dirt cloud kicks my face, and he's gone.

TWENTY-TWO

The dust cloud takes its sweet time clearing. Once it does, I head toward the junction, a shorter walk through the warm, September sun than I'd anticipated.

My insides feel like *Outset*: a bleak void. Doesn't help that I'm emotionally numb and running on only two hours of sleep. Knowing Sofia's now been with Doug Halston for nearly an hour helps even less. She basically left me for *him*, but it's her threat that's still replaying in my head, again and again. The only good news: there's an idea germinating in there too, maybe even a plan.

The junction is just that: a meeting between my dirt road and an empty, two-lane, asphalt highway. At least a dozen worn tires are strewn along the roadside, plus the dilapidated remains of what might once have been a fruit stand, but far more interesting is the cellular tower looming near the horizon.

I pull out my waterlogged phone and, much to my surprise, it's not only updating headlines but showing enough cellular service to make a crackly, gap-filled call. Some ninety minutes later, with dawn's blossoming sun now ripened into an 11 a.m. sky, Neil rolls up in a black sport utility vehicle that I recognize as one of Fustian's company cars.

"Holy shit," he says, seeing my sleepy, disheveled appearance and the bag of torn, wet clothes I'm carrying.

"Yeah, seemed like a good time to cash in that favor you offered."

He thinks—and insists—that he's driving me to a hospital, which he isn't. Then he assumes he's driving me home, which he is, but first I have him cut across the hills, back to the site where I crashed the sedan. The area looks like Noah's flood hit, with mud all over the roadway and the shrubs ripped away where the reservoir water rushed through. Judging from tire tracks, rescue workers have come and gone. Below us, the moisture-glistened highway sports a silt-splotched cheetah pattern, the orange pylons washed away hours ago.

Neil recognizes the location from morning news reports. Apparently entire neighborhoods were deluged by the floodwaters, with millions in damage and dozens injured, but miraculously, no one died.

"And we're here *why*?" he says.

"Because I need to grab something out of my car."

Turns out the sedan's not where I left it. The flood was so strong it shoved my wreck over the hillside, leaving it at an angle between the road and the highway below.

"You survived *that*?" Neil says.

I nod without explaining, because it's not a story I'm ready to tell.

"Sonnova..." Neil says, shaking his head.

He waits at the top as I inch my way down the hillside, my feet sinking into deep mud. The car looks as if an allosaurus used it for playtime, muddied and riddled with deep scratches. Wrenching the passenger door open, I climb inside amid inches of water, trash, soggy seats, and plenty of leftover asphalt pebbles... but the real treasure is finding the sealed case that houses a tiny hard drive for the windshield camera system. Takes me two screwdrivers and a fair bit of fiddling, but eventually I get it removed.

"You saved us once," I say, to the car. "With this, you might just do it again."

Suddenly I'm one of those guys who talks to his car? Sure... why not. "I'll be back for you."

I leave a note with my contact information on the dash, in case the police show up before I get the sedan hauled to a repair shop. Cheerful sentiments billow from the vehicle, smothering every negative vibe rising from the nearby highway. *Greatest car ever.*

With the highway closed from the flooding, Neil drives me home using a circuitous route that takes us into the afternoon.

"This whole thing—the car, my condition—it stays between us until I can prove what I've seen, okay?" I say. "Speaking of which, I need the video from this hard drive. Can you get it to the people who restore damaged security video for Fustian?"

"I only owed you one favor. This strikes me as wishing for more wishes."

"I know, and I'm sorry. But it's crucial."

"Look, man," Neil begins, but I cut him off before he can say anything more.

"Not now, okay? I'll explain everything but right now, I'm too wiped."

"Maybe you should have Sofia help you instead," he says. "Where's your wife during all of this?"

"That's... complicated."

"Yeah. I'll bet."

I'm tired enough that even mustering a sigh takes effort. "Will you get the video for me, or not?"

He agrees... barely. *Getting him to believe everything I've learned about sentient objects isn't going to be easy. Still, tomorrow I'll try telling him. If I can convince Neil, I'll know I might be able to convince other people too.*

Not yet, though. Not without evidence, and rest. I have him drop me at the corner near my house, not far from the Stenders' melodious flowers but, hopefully, far enough away that he won't notice last night's disaster.

No such luck. The rubble out front is a big, obvious, smoking debris pile.

"The house *too*?" he says.

The garage, spare bedroom, and one corner of my living room appear crushed. Everything else looks the same as always, as if someone used a knife to separate the home into two sections. Red tags are posted all over the exterior, meaning the building department's already been there and deemed the place structurally unfit.

"You're not really going in there?" Neil says.

"Yeah, I need to check some things."

"It's not safe, man. Let the fire department get whatever you need. Better than risking your life."

"Can't. I'll talk with you tonight."

I can feel his doubts, his car's too, as I watch him drive away.

There's no sign of city building inspectors, but several lookie-loos are pointing to the dirt rectangle that used to be my concrete driveway. I'd rather not call attention to my visit, so I go around back instead.

The sight that greets me as I open the back door takes my breath. My carpet is covered in dirt, splintered drywall, and framework shards. The ceiling's sagged in on one corner, opposite the kitchen. The furniture is filthy, tattered, and tossed.

Does a homeowner's policy cover sentient object attacks? I'm guessing not.

Scrambling over furniture and around debris, I reach the entry hall then let out a startled gasp.

Assembly Required is gone.

I didn't expect to find it on the splintered wall, but it isn't on the floor either, or in any of the nearby debris piles. Maybe looters came inside the house? But nothing else is missing, not even our loose cash and jewelry. It certainly pales in comparison to what's happening with Sofia and the null, but I'm still devastated that it's gone.

After a much-needed bathroom break, I change into a fresh tee and jeans—once again transferring Agnes between pockets—then make my way back to what's left of the living room. Even with the place a disaster, being home feels like a reprieve. Part of it is the warm, whispered vibes I'm getting from my stuff: relief that I'm here again, regret for what transpired, eagerness to help, concern that Sofia isn't here with me.

Sofia.

My wife, who is now off... *interfacing...* with Doug Halston. The thought tears me apart. There must be—

Something's moving in the kitchen.

I look but it's already gone, then register that it's not actually gone, it's just reappeared off to one side, barely within my field of vision. Turning my head for a better look, it vanishes again. The only place I can see the movement is...

In my peripheral vision.

Averting my eyes, the movement resumes, only the "motion" isn't an object. Instead, it's something materializing from the ether... the same faint, horizontal hairline markings I saw in Anthony Alfaro's pickup, only this time they're darker. If I look at them directly, they vanish. With averted vision they darken and extend, resembling slatted, translucent window blinds superimposed over the cabinets, the appliances, everything.

Everything looks pleated.

The pleating vanishes. Staring, angling my eyes... nothing helps.

Give it time, I tell myself. *This is already way beyond hearing simple whispers.*

But there's so much I want to know, including why I need to avert my vision when Sofia doesn't. Maybe, eventually, I won't either? Is it a matter of adjusting how your mind interprets the information it receives from your eyes, like Anthony suggested?

Sofia wasn't kidding about interfacing being a touchy-feely method for communication. Thinking about the ways my 'world' has changed of late makes my head swoon. Discovering that objects are sentient... that a fraction of them hate organic life... that my wife already knew because her family not only communicates with those objects, but uses them as spies... and that she once did the same thing, better than anyone else.

And now, learning that an extremist Amalgam splinter-group plans on detonating matter in just such a way that it creates some sort of void.

Just your run-of-the-mill week.

The house still has electricity; the TV works. *Hey, the sofa works too.* It's a dirty mess but so am I, so I pounce onto it for a few seconds of channel-surfing. There's nothing on but old movies and a multi-channel, breaking news update about three Asian conglomerates accused of financing the drone attacks that have killed hundreds of people in several nations.

Hold on...

This could be the doomsday scenario Anthony and Florence were worried about: an escalation of threats that begins in Asia, then dominoes into a massive war. From what I'm seeing, the TV report is based on nothing but rumors and unnamed sources... but what if hubris and internal politics means certain world leaders won't see it that way?

I continue watching, or at least, I try. Between the all-nighter and last night's sentient object chaos, it turns out I need downtime more than I need breaking news, if only for a moment.

Make that three hours.

That's how long I doze off. When I wake, late-afternoon sunlight is streaming in above the windowsill, the TV's tuned to a ballgame, and I'm really tempted to stay overnight. Then I remember the frightening reason the house is such a mess. I drag up, part of me wishing I could still relegate my things to dumb, lifeless objects the way everyone else does. *Is it wrong to miss the simplicity?*

That's the mentality I'll be up against if I try exposing the null crisis. Deep down, even an intelligent guy like Neil won't want to shift from the standard mindset—it's more comfortable that way. But things aren't simple, they never were. How am I going to get people to accept that?

I duck into the bedroom and immediately spot Sofia's wedding ring on the nightstand. *Left intentionally, knowing she might see Halston?* I pocket her ring, and her favorite paintbrush, for the next time I see her. Between those, my phone, my wallet, and Agnes, my pockets are nearly full. It's crazy, keeping a Meld with me, but other objects don't give me warm fuzzies the way Agnes does. Does the emotional component come from subconsciously sensing an item's sentience?

My phone vibrates from an incoming call.

"Matt, get out of the house," Sofia tells me.

"How did you know I'm—"

"Go, now! They have the place monitored, and they have a plan."

I head toward the hallway. "*Who* has it monitored?"

"The Latchkeys," she says. "They're micro-drones that—look, I'll explain later. Meet me at our spot. You know where I'm talking about, right?"

"Yeah, but…"

"Go straight there. I'll be waiting for you."

"What about…"

"Just get over there! Doug and I already learned more than we expected. We know the where the staging site for the null is, and we've confirmed the organizers are close to pulling it off… *really* close, maybe as soon as tonight. I think I've found a way out of this mess, and it might even convince the Leopards I won't try to fix my big mistake, but I have to move fast because—"

A massive boom sounds from Sofia's side of the call, strong enough that it reverberates my phone.

"They know where I'm at—I have to go," she says. "I'll see you at our spot."

She ends the call. So much crucial information, and that terrifying boom, yet I'm dwelling on her mentioning Doug Halston. I grab a jacket then head toward the front door. Dirt and destruction aside, the living room looks normal. The kitchen too, except for an odd shine on the tile floor.

Shine?

The carpet suddenly makes a gushy, squishing sound as I walk. Startled, I look down. It's sopping wet, which it wasn't when I was watching television. The kitchen floor is covered too, a good inch of liquid puddled throughout. I trace the water stain to our guest bathroom and find the toilet apparently never shut off after I used it.

I turn the water valve until the hum stops. *Is there any connection to what happened in here last night?* If so, I don't see it. Sofia's warning prods me toward the door, but then I remember: the television is still on, and I won't be coming back for a few days.

Tiptoeing across the squishy living room, I can't see the screen or hear the broadcasters but somehow, I know that the game is in the second inning. Compliments of my television? If so, I wish the remote was as forthcoming. *Where is it? I just used it when I turned the TV on!* I give up searching and turn the set off by hand.

There's a micro-second before you do something stupid when you realize it isn't a good idea, but your brain doesn't have time to make your body change course. This is one of those micro-seconds. My pointer finger's probably one toothpick away from the TV's power button when I recognize that this is an electrical device, and I'm standing on water-logged carpet, wearing soggy shoes. Touching the silver button, which might be metal, isn't a safe course of action.

But that understanding comes too late. As my finger makes contact, I'm hoping the button is just plastic, that it doesn't conduct, that my finger's not still wet from messing with the water valve. Even as I hear a strident, sparking pop, and feel electrical current threading into my finger and across my entire body, I'm holding out hope that it'll just be a momentary thing.

It's not. It's searing pain, a life-threatening electrocution that vibrates my teeth, jolts my heart, and makes my entire, three-plus decades of memories flicker before me. It also makes me think there's more than a button and some water at fault... that it was a trap.

Then, it makes me not think at all.

TWENTY-THREE

The most frightening thing about losing consciousness is waking. That's when you understand that until a moment ago you had no thought processes, no awareness, no individuality, no nothing. You didn't exist in any intellectual manner, meaning your body was an empty shell with a head that might, or might not, have ever refilled. Seriously, is there anything as scary as a mental time-out?

Not for me, there isn't. My living room isn't pitch dark, but it's close enough that I can't see anything. *Wait—it's never this dark inside my house, not even in the middle of the night.* The white noise is different, too... there's a faint, ongoing whirr, and the ambient smell is much heavier on carpet fumes.

This isn't my house! Where am I?

I blink my eyes, unnerved that I also have no idea how much time has passed or whether I'm still in danger, understanding only that I have so little energy that eye-blinks are the most strenuous activity I'll undertake. I'm on my back, prone atop what feels like thin, rough, indoor-outdoor carpet. No pain, though my hand—especially the pointer finger that got zapped—isn't happy when I try moving it. A quick feel of my chest and legs tells me I'm still wearing my jacket, T-shirt, and jeans.

Reviewing what happened amounts to remembering that I was an idiot. But that remote... did I truly misplace it? If my electrocution was pure chance, the answer is yes. If it was part of a planned attack, then somehow the remote was shoved out of sight or else I would never have considered touching the television's power button.

What was it Sofia mentioned about tubes that roll, and so forth? Could the couch cushions have created enough of a gap to hide the remote? Did the toilet flood the carpet by design? Shouldn't I consider the possibility they were Leopards, especially since Sofia had just phoned with a warning?

Sofia! She wanted me to meet her right away!

I bolt upright, feeling the way I might have expected to feel after being fried: stiff and sluggish. My hand aches something fierce, and I get the idea it's probably scarred with burns, but the room I'm in—if it's actually a room—is too dark to tell for sure. A sudden thought sends my other hand darting to my pockets; Agnes is still inside, along with Sofia's stuff, but I can't find—

An underground rock song blasts my ears, launching my heart into my brain as I see my missing phone on the floor, ringtone blaring. It's right next to me, lighting up my corner of a small room, so I'm able to grab it without moving. The volume's not up very high, but in the quiet room it sounds like the band's right there, playing the music live. I send the incoming call to voicemail, though according to the screen there *isn't* an incoming call. It's just blank.

A door opens, broadening a narrow shaft of exterior light until it fills the room. My heart pounds. Squinting, I watch an angular-headed silhouette lean inside.

"Hey, keep it down, will you?" I hear.

That voice, is it... "Neil?"

"Yeah, give me a few minutes, we'll talk when everyone goes home," he says, his thread-like goatee lit by fluorescent hallway lighting. "For now, you need to lay low."

"I'm on the floor. Can't lay much lower."

"You're a riot," Neil says. "You weren't so funny when I hauled you in here."

"In *where*?"

"Fustian. Now hush up or I'll ignore your wife and toss you out."

I perk up, hearing him say that. *Sofia knows I'm here*? Neil closes the door before I can ask. I switch my phone to vibrate, then peek at the screen to check the date and time. It's still Sunday but just after seven at night, meaning I lost about three hours. But now that I have a light source...

The phone's flashlight exposes two small bookcases, one shoved against the wall next to me, the other leaning backward against a dilapidated desk chair.

"The storage room," I mutter.

I helped clear this room for remodeling. The walls are thick, but I can hear Neil chatting with our department managers during their typical, late Sunday hours. They're discussing product lines, production details... all the stuff I miss.

Regret sweeps over me. Creating the Melds that millions of people love is my calling. The thought of possibly giving it up...

Was I really abusing another form of life? If so, can I ever make that right?

The voices die down. Rising slowly to my feet, I expect Neil to pop back in but he's taking his sweet time. Finally, just as I'm about to let myself out, he shows.

"You already owed me one, this time you owe me a hundred," he says, flicking the lights on as I shield my eyes. "Your wife said you need to meet her by 9 p.m. or the world cracks apart. That gives you less than two hours... and she wouldn't even tell me where you're supposed to find her. Said you'd know."

He looks irritated that she wouldn't tell him. "So where are you going? And by the way... how do you feel?"

I offer a wan smile. "Like crap. How did I get here?"

"By ignoring my advice about staying out of your house," he says. "But if you mean *here* here, I got a call from Sofia begging me to get to your place fast, claiming you were in trouble. I recommended 911, she insisted you were into something so deep you just needed out, no questions asked."

He gives me the once-over. "From the looks of it, she was right. What happened back there? The house looked like *another* bomb hit it. You too."

For the first time, I glance down, at myself. My right hand's swollen, blackened, blistered, burned. The jacket, tee, and jeans are sooty, but intact. The rest of me seems surprisingly okay for an electrocuted man. I ask Neil what he saw when he found me.

"You mean aside from a condemned building?" he says. "Just you, passed out in your flooded living room, next to a melted, smoking TV. And I mean, that thing was *way* melted. You lost a good screen, that's for sure."

Yeah, but I could've lost a lot more than the TV. Unless... A crazy thought hits me. Did the television hinder the electrical conduction by melting? Is it possible one of my favorite objects gave its life to save mine? A couple days ago, I never would have considered such a possibility. But now...

"Look Matt," Neil says, "you know I've been trying to help you and I have nothing but respect for your wife. But your place was trashed. Whatever you two are up against, it's time to get help."

"Tell me about it."

"I'm serious. I pulled you out of there and stuffed you in an empty room, exactly as Sofia asked and against my better judgment. But I don't need to tell you how messed up all of this is. You've dragged me into something bad here, and this is as far as I want to go. Understand?"

I pull Agnes from my pocket, figuring I can use the morale boost she always gives me, then push her back inside. "So then, no one else knows I'm here?"

"Just you, me, and the bookcases."

He's being flippant, but mentioning the bookcases reinforces just how hard it is for me to go anywhere unnoticed. It also underscores the jam Sofia and I are facing—possibly worse than she already knows. If Leopard objects were monitoring the house, then they heard me talking with her. They'll know she wanted me to meet her, and even though I never said the location aloud, if they've been in that household long enough then they'll know where she had in mind. Which means... *they'll be waiting for her, same as they were waiting for me.*

"How long has it been since you talked with Sofia?" I blurt, tapping her number on my phone, operating left-handed because my right hand's too sore and swollen.

Neil shrugs. "Two, maybe three hours. Took me some time, you know, dragging you out of that house. And then pulling you in here without anyone noticing, that was—"

"I know—and thank you, but we need to go. I hope it's not too late."

Maybe it's adrenaline but suddenly I'm pacing around the room just fine... still sore, but I'm limbering up fast. I check the phone. Sofia's not answering. *Dammit!*

"What about your hand?" Neil says. "Looks blistered, you need a doctor."

"Not right now I don't."

"Great, ignoring my advice yet again," Neil says. "I'm telling you, it's time you look in the mirror and admit—"

"Can you take me, or not?"

"I'm headed to Indonesia in the morning, remember? I don't have time for this."

I position a finger near a rideshare app on the phone's screen.

He utters an exasperated sigh. "Like I'm going to let some stranger haul you around in your condition. Let's go. But you still haven't told me where."

My eyes rove the room, wary of... everything. "I'll tell you once we're outside," I say, motioning for us to get moving.

Meet me at our spot, Sofia had said. Truth is, we have a bunch of special spots. There's the street corner where we shared our first kiss, the theater where I proposed... the list goes on. But *our spot*... there's really only one location in the entire world that we consider our spot. It's the place where heavy wooden planks steered my feet toward her canvas, and therefore to her easel, which directed my attention to her paint, her brush... her beautiful face. It's the place where I first saw Sofia Coronado, and watched her bring *Assembly Required* to life. The place where we eventually got married.

"Get us to Buttercove Pier," I tell Neil, as he helps me stagger out to the parking lot.

No company SUV this time. Instead, we climb into his tricked-out van. The engine coughs to life, rumbling my seat like someone just lit a match under an old rocket nozzle. We're zero-to-fifty before we reach the end of the short block, and whipping around a corner leaves skid marks and squeals. It's not stealthy, but what a ride, and at this point fast is probably better than subtle anyway.

Ten minutes into the drive, Neil still hasn't said a word. He probably just wants me and my craziness out of his van and out of his life, which makes a lot of sense. Dumping the craziness actually sounds pretty appealing to me too. I suddenly remember that the last time we talked before he dropped me at the house,

I'd asked him to have someone restore the video from my car's windshield camera system... footage that should show asphalt pebbles somehow flinging themselves through the air, and the other bizarre events that happened on the freeway.

"Did you get the hard drive to someone who can extract the video?"

He nods. "It's in bad shape, but they think some of the video's intact. We'll know more tomorrow."

I glance at my watch, angling it so I can see the dusk-smothered numbers telling me it's nearly seven-thirty. Meaning, ninety minutes until whatever Sofia thinks will happen at nine. Traffic to the pier isn't bad, but some sort of red-yellow-blue emergency lights are flickering up ahead. *Please let it be a fender bender* crosses my mind, but the lights are too bright. Already I can make out a mix of fire engines, police cruisers, and maybe an ambulance blocking the roadway about three blocks ahead of us, right in the middle of a narrow downtown street.

"I know a way to horseshoe around all this," Neil says, breaking our silence.

"I don't mind walking, it's only about four blocks."

"Uh-uh. After hearing your wife sound so life-or-death serious and with you not even close to tip-top shape, I'm making sure I see you walk onto that pier before I leave."

Somehow, the van whips around tight corners like they're roller coaster turns. A minute later, we're past the downtown hub, a block away from Buttercove Pier... which is cordoned off by emergency vehicles on this approach as well.

"What the hell?" Neil mutters, pulling over.

"Red zone," I say, pointing to the curb.

"Don't care," he says. "Let's get you over there. I'll deal with the ticket later."

I nod my appreciation as we climb out of the van. My heart's beating fast; all these police and fire units surrounding the pier where Sofia wanted to meet... something can't be right. My determined stagger becomes a fast-walk, then a flat-out run as my worry turns to panic. Neil's footsteps tell me he's running too, his feet mashing empty candy wrappers along our path as he attempts to keep up.

Ahead, glaring lights from police and fire vehicles are flickering off the single-story souvenir shops. The dusk is seven minutes deeper than it was when I checked my watch, too dark to see beyond all the emergency trucks, but I know we're close. No one's blocking our way, so whatever's going on up there must be happening right at this moment, and it must be big enough that the police need *everyone*. I slink between the fire trucks then stop dead in my tracks as I see something I never anticipated.

Buttercove Pier is collapsing.

Huge, wooden planks are plummeting into the sea, vanishing beneath plumes of ocean spray. Worse, the entire structure is sagging away from the beach, each of the vertical, wooden supports splintering, as if some leviathan is trying to tug the entire pier out to sea.

And is that Doug Halston charging away from the falling pier?

The guy disappears into a crowd before I can tell for certain. Emergency teams are scrambling, connecting ropes from their vehicles to what's left of the beams, trying to buy time as their colleagues help several people who are stuck on two sagging wooden platforms—the only thing left of the pier. Fire crews have ladders extended horizontally over the debris, so they can hoist people up and over the disaster. Closer to shore, police officers are in the water, pulling people from the shattered wooden walkway. Other rescuers are farther out, fighting wind-driven waves as they swim people to safety.

But the worst part is what I'm *not* seeing: the far end of the pier.

"Holy fuh..." Neil says, pulling up short behind me. "It's gone. The outer half of the pier... it's friggin' gone!"

The implication pierces my chest, my head, my spirit. I'm whipping around, looking in every direction, hoping to spot Sofia somewhere on shore, but there's no sign of her. My heart feels like lead, my fingers turn numb. The far end of the pier... that's where the food vendors and carnival rides were located, but more important, at least to me, was the "Artist's Alley" of tables and easels that lined the north side. Now all but a tiny, splintered section of it is missing, apparently sunk beneath the waves.

My knees buckle and my leaden stomach nearly heaves as I realize *"our place,"* the special spot where I first met her, where I was supposed to meet her tonight, where she created *Assembly Required*... it's gone.

And most likely, so is Sofia.

7:56 p.m.

Sunday, Sep. 6

Notifications

NEWS

* Aircraft carrying 336 people struck by missile over the East China Sea

* Authorities: "Survivors unlikely."

* No one claims responsibility; governments condemn attack.

* Four nations redeploy naval vessels, preparing for possible skirmishes.

* Japanese air squadron evades missiles from undetermined source.

* Nine tourists cancel, 86 remain as spaceplane *Resnik* readies for launch.

BREAKING:

California pier collapses after drone "swarm" reported nearby.

Press HOME to unlock Screen Time, Reminders, and Purchases.

TWENTY-FOUR

aybe she wasn't on the pier.

That's the only thought keeping me going right now, a single, neuronal cling to the edge of an emotional cliff. Losing Sofia, even with our relationship in shambles, would be horrific. Losing her with the world teetering on the brink of disaster would be even worse. To say I'm devastated doesn't begin to address the concept of losing her.

But maybe she wasn't on the pier. That's all I've got, but at least it's something. Until I know otherwise, I'm clinging to it, odds notwithstanding. Just offshore, an approaching rescue helicopter settles into a hover, spotlight activated, scanning the choppy sea. I scan it too. One glimpse of Sofia and I'll dive in, waves and rip tides be damned.

I must be telegraphing the thought; two police officers yell for me and Neil to get back, behind the fire engines. We're about to comply when a makeshift guy-wire extending from the beach to one of the pier's remaining support posts yanks taut, then snaps, sending the closest of the two "islands" into a Tower of Pisa lean.

Three people stranded on top scream. The two officers use their feet to stop the guy-wire from dragging across the beach, then grab onto it. Neil and I do the same. The four of us plant our heels, engaged in a tug of war against a heavy pier post that's determined to topple into the ocean. The post is winning, yanking us across the sand, but firefighters are already swinging their ladder over the leaning pier island. Soon the three stranded people are up, and safe.

We let go of the cable. It shoots over the sand, then slides through the surf as the heavy post, and then the entire pier island, plunges into the waves. My eyes follow the splash, a massive plume of water that showers onto the now solitary, remaining island—which, I suddenly realize, isn't just some random segment of the pier.

It's a section of Artist's Alley.

The thing's sagging, but its resplendent, fenced edge is still there, angled above the waves like the raised bow of a sinking ship. *Because the post leaned on purpose, to create the splash, which would make certain I saw the fence... that I saw the last island was Artist's Alley.*

There's no way I could know such a thing, no way it could even be true. But I'm suddenly hearing whispers, and seeing faint, hairline markings deepen into pleats when I avert my eyes, so...

"There's something on that fence," I say to myself, forgetting Neil is within earshot.

"So?" he says.

"So, whatever it is, it's for me."

It's at least fifty yards away, so there's clearly no way I could see any such thing, but I say it with such confidence that he doesn't even question it.

"Then go grab it," Neil says, snatching my jacket, then waiting as I wriggle out of my other clothes, leaving only my boxers as ersatz swim trunks. "I'll deal with the cops."

I go; he deals. Even as other people are jumping from the island, trying to escape the imminent collapse, I swim through the frigid, angry surf and climb onto it, ignoring the buckling motions, the shouts from authorities, the freezing wind, everything but the understanding that I need whatever it is Sofia left for me on that fence. *It's the last thing she did before she died.*

Walking atop a wobbly, collapsing structure is about as easy as it sounds. The helicopter's spotlight is on me, so that helps, but my feet are breaking through weakened boards and the pier is so much lower than usual that I'm being slammed by icy, rogue waves. Reaching the fence, I'm hit with something much stronger: feelings of warmth, welcome, and joy. There's no one here, just me, a fence, and a buckling pier, but it's suddenly as if Sofia is standing right here, arms open, smiling.

My mind again flashes to memories of the night I met her... to the way the lights near the ocean drew my attention to the creaky pier boards, which then seemed to steer my feet to the fence-side spot where I could see her sitting, painting *Assembly Required...* and the way the painting seemed to hold me there until she noticed me.

And then it hits me: this is the same spot.

Somehow, this one, tiny, fragmented section of Artist's Alley is the only part of Buttercove Pier that's still standing.

"You knew I'd come," I say, to myself but also, if I'm being honest, to the fence and every hunk of pier timber nearby. "You waited."

The pier is with me—that's what Sofia would say. Suddenly I'm smiling, like I've reunited with an old friend in the midst of chaos. "*Our place*" isn't gone after all... at least, not yet. Then I see the reason I'm there: a sheet of paper, rubber-banded to the fence post. The corners are flapping in the wind, in fact one of them is missing, but as I un-band it I can tell the rest is holding together.

It's a crossword puzzle page.

What? Why would Sofia leave me one of her crosswords?

I fold it tight, then use the rubber band to attach it to my wrist. It'll still get soaked, but if it makes it back to shore with me in one piece that's good enough.

"Thank you," I say to the fence, feeling silly but also knowing it's coming from the heart. "All of you—crossbeams, posts, walkway. Thank you for everything."

Another new sensation: like someone's aiming a heater in front of my face, but instead of heat it's gracious appreciation.

"Is she gone? Have I lost her?"

The sensation changes from appreciation to uncertainty. Does that mean they're uncertain she's still alive? Or that they don't have an answer? Or that I'm just not skilled enough at interfacing with them to understand?

The pier island shudders, then gives way. I leap off the edge, hoping the collapsing structure won't topple in my direction. For one amazing, beautiful moment I'm weightless over the ocean, separated from the collapse, the noise, the raging waves, the spotlights, everything. Then, as I fall, a big wave smashes into me, shoving me into deep, cold, dark water.

My blistered hand throbs from the cold, but I have bigger problems. I'm head-over-heels, completely disoriented, trying to keep what little breath I'm still holding. Swimming won't help, I can't even tell which way is up. Floating might work, if I can hold my breath long enough, but—

The water ignites all around me, bubbles sparkling like stars, particles glowing yellow, everything so bright I have to squint. *From the helicopter spotlight?* Something bumps the back of my head. Buried fears surface, tied to dubious tales about helicopter sounds attracting sharks. *Seriously? A shark?* Swirling myself around exposes something long, and dark, matching my every surf-bob. *Nurse? Great White?*

No, a small fence post from the pier... a post with a life pre-server attached. *The pier is still with me.* I grab on, lungs begging for air as the turbulent currents shove me forward, down, back. Illuminated by the spotlight, on the verge of letting my held breath loose, I feel myself rising—meaning I finally know up from down. Kicking violently, feeling like my chest is about to burst, I breach the surface, gulping an air-surf mix until a hand grabs onto my collar.

"Let go of the post!" I hear, over a deafening beat of helicopter rotors.

Not a chance. I use my good hand to grab onto whoever's got me from above while the other arm keeps hold of the floating post, knowing both of them just saved my life. A stout firefighter with a mustache drags me inside the helicopter, none too pleased that I didn't ditch the post. I'm grateful to him and his team... but I hang tight to the post regardless.

They drop me and four other soggy souls at the beach, where every one of us accepts a towel but declines paramedic checks. Not sure why the others decline, but me, I've got a crossword to salvage. The police are there, so is Neil, and there's talk of citations. I keep myself agreeable, avoiding the worst of it, and I can tell Neil's already let them know my wife was supposed to be at the pier and is now missing, which softens the reprimand.

"Did you get it?" Neil says in a hushed voice, when we finally get a moment away.

"Right here," I say, showing the soggy, folded-up paper that's rubber-banded to my wrist, then explain what she left me.

"A crossword? That's it?"

"Weird, right? I need to take a closer look, there must be more to it. But I'm drenched and that sheet of paper will fall apart if I pull it off too fast."

He scowls. "This was a waste of time. Plan B, then."

I have no idea what he's talking about. Behind us, a subdued "Ooooh" erupts from the gathered crowd as Buttercove Pier's final remnants crash into the roiling waves. The emergency spotlights dim as the debris sinks under, like an old circus act going dark.

"Sonnova..." Neil says. "The entire pier, gone."

"What's Plan B?"

"Sofia said if we couldn't find her at the pier, I'm supposed to drive you to another place... but I'm not supposed to tell you where until we're a block away from it. You two always this cloak-and-dagger with your marriage?"

"Keeps things fresh. Do you think there's any chance she's waiting there instead?"

"Not sure. She just told me to take you there if things didn't work out here."

Meaning she was already suspicious, I decide. If she knew Leopard objects were watching me at the house, she must have also known they might look for her at the pier. My spirits nudge higher. Is it possible she stayed away altogether, or made only a brief stop to leave the crossword before heading for the backup location? And what about Doug Halston? If it really was him that I saw leaving the scene, what was he doing there?

"Look, Plan B or not, we should wait while the rescue crews are still searching for... well, for survivors," Neil says.

He says 'survivors,' but I understand what he means is 'bodies.'

"No time," I tell him. "Besides, there's still a chance she's somewhere else, right? I can come back later if... if things don't work out."

I can't bring myself to say the words my mind's stifling. Doing so would somehow make it real, as if I'm the one sealing Sofia's fate. The possibility she wasn't on the pier is still the only thing keeping my head in one piece.

Neil and I look around, see that no one's paying attention to us anymore, and head back to the van. I toss the post, life preserver still attached, onto the back seat. As I change into the clothes I'd left with Neil, I notice two things: the Agnes Meld and Sofia's stuff are still inside the jean pockets, and my burned, blistered hand actually feels a little better. Maybe the saltwater did some good.

"Now let's see what this is," I say, stretching the rubber band and slowly, gently inching the folded paper up and out.

It's dripping, and wet as a sponge, but I resist the temptation to wring it out. Instead, I climb inside the van, shut the door, and slowly peel the paper open atop the dashboard. To my relief, the printing isn't washed out once it's finally unfolded.

"You gotta be kidding me—it's blank?" Neil says, leaning in for a closer look.

He's right—almost.

"There are two words filled in," I say, pointing. "See, one horizontal, one vertical, both in her writing. She always adds little eyes inside her b's and d's."

Neil flashes me a "wow, are you whipped" look. I shrug. *Guilty as charged.*

"Hit the interior light, will you?" I ask him.

He does, and both of us lean in, studying the crossword. The paper's thicker than newsprint, so she either printed it from a website or tore it from one of her books. The horizontal word is harder to read, so I try the vertical one first.

"It's 'required,' see?" I tell Neil, then freeze. Could the horizontal word really be...

"Assembly," I mumble.

Assembly Required.

TWENTY-FIVE

ll this effort for *that*?" Neil says. "Either of those words mean anything to you?"

I explain that it's the name of the painting she was working on when we met.

He shakes his head. "So why did she leave you the name of that painting?"

Good question. Thinking about it makes me even more upset that the piece was stolen from our collapsed home. My gut tells me the crossword is her way of sending me to the Whitmore Center, the local art mecca— and the place where she and I spent hours discussing the unusual connection I've felt with *Assembly Required*, ever since the night she painted it. Even now, I can visualize the mesmerizing, introspective, raven-haired woman: the mosaic skin that's puzzle-pieced together, the sense that this vibrant individual is emerging from some cosmic location, that she's a freshly minted human being. But how does it connect to my relationship with Sofia, or with anything that's happened here tonight, or even with everything happening big-picture?

I tell Neil about the Whitmore, with a caveat that "it's entirely possible I'm missing something."

He scoffs. "Maybe *both of you* are missing something," he says, tapping a finger against his head as if I didn't already get what he was suggesting. "Get your seat belt on, I'll take you to her Plan B first. And if the seat belt talks to you, I don't want to know."

He pulls a three-point turn and drives us out of there, headed away from the coast, back through the pine-covered hills that run west of the valley. Wherever this Plan B location is, it's nowhere near the pier.

"Just understand this," Neil says, suddenly indignant. "There isn't a Plan C. I'm taking you to the only other place that came up. We get there, I drop you off. Got it? Because if Sofia's Plan B location can't resolve whatever it is the two of you are dealing with, then you don't need me, you need the police. Or someone else. Not me."

His concept seems so quaint: *just call the police.* A couple days ago, I'd have said the same, naive thing.

"What about that video from the hard drive? I really need it."

"You keep forgetting I'm leaving for Jakarta tomorrow morning. The business card for the guy who's working on your hard drive is in the glove box, right on top. It'll be ready tomorrow, just tell him I referred you."

I pocket the card, figuring there's nothing left to say. Problem is, there's so much left to say, so before he can stop me, I give him the one-minute bottom line about Amalgam, Sofia's involvement, and the imminent, potentially worldwide disaster.

"So, thank you for not walking away the moment Sofia phoned you," I tell him. "What you're doing...it means *everything* to me, okay?"

Neil's eyebrows arch as I wrap up a speech that I hadn't intended on making. He shakes his head, and I suppose he's thinking *you need mental help*, which reminds me how much my relationship with my best friend has deteriorated. But he's also aware there's a good chance I lost my wife tonight, and I'm guessing that's holding him back.

"Let's just get this done," he says, staring at the road, careful not to look my way. "Up there, on the hilltop. That's where we're going."

I glance up the narrow, pine-sided road and see an iconic, spiral terrarium the size of a modest skyscraper.

The Whitmore? But that means...

"Guess your gut was spot-on about the crossword," Neil says. "This is where Sofia said to bring you if the pier didn't work out."

A world-class art museum, the Whitmore Center is a three-year-old landmark named after the late software magnate Maurice Whitmore, who did what most retired magnates do with their money: shed their guilt from decades of environmental transgressions by creating an endowment to build and maintain an iconic, artistic hub. Sofia doesn't like Whitmore, but she loves the museum.

But I heard someone else mention the Whitmore recently: Florence, who said Anthony Alfaro had sent Ty there on some sort of assignment. *That can't be a coincidence.* Does it mean Sofia planned on having me meet with *him* too?

"It's Sunday night, isn't the place closed?"

Neil swings the van around a tight curve. "That's what I thought, but your wife claims it's open until nine for some sort of evening exhibition."

I check my phone: it's already 8:30, meaning they'll start ushering people out in about fifteen minutes. *Definitely cutting things close.*

"Where am I supposed to find her?"

Neil shrugs. "She didn't say. Just gave me some mumbo-jumbo about museums being 'institutional expressions of magical thinking,' places where... how'd she put it? Where 'objects are given reverence that doesn't disengage with the residual presence of what inhabited the object in the past.' She seriously said that.

Guess you'll have to do your cloak and dagger bit again to figure out where she'll be."

He pulls the van into the entry driveway. The clear, spiral terrarium towers before us, as if the art gods dropped a pin to help us find the place. Behind it, the museum itself is a group of four travertine-sided buildings, each crammed with exhibits ranging from the Old Masters to the Modern Experimentalists.

At the security kiosk, Neil informs the guard he's doing a drop-off then pulls up to an adjacent curb as instructed. Several yards away, people are entering a serpentine, triple-wide escalator designed and painted by street artists—and billed as the tallest, most scenic moving stairway in the world, connecting visitors to parking lots at the base of the hill, some two miles below. The Center's illuminated stone walkway connects both the escalator and the drop-off with a sloped pathway leading to the massive, glass terrarium.

"Look... you understand this is a long-shot, right?" Neil says. "I mean, I hope I'm wrong, but she's probably not in there and if she isn't, well... that's a pretty devastating thing to have to face on your own, you know what I'm saying?"

I open the passenger door and jump out, conscious that I'm up against a clock. "It's an art center; I can always find Sofia in a place like this, whether she's here or not."

He still seems bothered. I'm not sure why, until he backpedals from his earlier, hardline stance.

"Maybe I'll swing back here in half an hour," he says, passing me my jacket as if it'll dry my soggy underpants. "Get you set up someplace for the night."

"Just take care of my pier railing. God willing, I'll be back for it."

I shut the door and head up the hill, toward the pathway. Behind me, the security guard is telling Neil he needs to move along.

Without looking back, I hear the van's engine growl, then some faint tire squeals as Neil navigates the center's horseshoe driveway. A moment later all's quiet, a sobering silence that lasts only a few seconds but allows far too many of Neil's valid points to linger in my mind.

That silence comes to an abrupt end as an ear-splitting, mind-jarring explosion rocks the terrarium, the museum, and the entire hillside. It's jet-engine-loud and earthquake strong, which is why it takes me a moment to process a horrifying truth.

Something just exploded inside the Whitmore Center.

TWENTY-SIX

The explosion's deafening rumble echoes off the travertine wall tile, then subsides. Whatever happened, it probably wasn't in the terrarium since the glass spiral looks intact. The spiral and pathway lights are on, so I know the museum didn't lose power. Ahead of me, people are streaming from the terrarium's exits, seemingly uninjured.

But there's a distant glow in the sky behind the spiral... a sickening, fiery glow... and some sort of chemical smell hangs in the air. Screams sound from elsewhere in the museum complex, along with several faint fire alarms.

I race inside the terrarium, which doubles as the museum's foyer. The place is an urban fairy's dream, with pinprick-sized lighting and floral arrangements lining walkways that follow the spiral architecture to the structure's apex. Everyone is running in the opposite direction, straight into me. It occurs to me that this is the second site linked to Sofia that's suffered a disaster in less than two hours.

Someone grabs my shoulders, whips me around.

"Halston?" I say, both shocked and irritated to see him standing there in his dark suit. "What the—is Sofia okay?"

His eyes dart side to side, as if someone's in hot pursuit. "No time to talk, you're needed inside. Look for what speaks to you."

I grab his arm before he can run off. "Is she alive or not?"

He yanks the arm away, then sprints toward the parking lot.

"What about Ty? Have you seen him?" I call.

"Just get in there—and fast!"

I'd chase after him, but if there's any chance Sofia's in that burning building... Halston has already disappeared into the fleeing crowd anyway, same as he did at the pier—and I'm more convinced than ever that he was at the pier.

Darting forward means dodging everyone headed the other way. At the far end of the terrarium, the Center's massive, roll-away glass doors are wide open. Scores of people are elbowing their way out, urged on by security and a line of docents. I'll never get past them, but I've been here several times so I know there's a barely used side entry... and in the chaos, I doubt anyone's had time to lock it down.

Sidestepping the herd, I take an exterior path that bisects the museum's front buildings, then follow a winding, garden stream to its lily pond origin. A bridge spanning the pond gets me to the side entry... and sure enough it's wide open, and unguarded.

Inside, the museum's ground floor is a vacuous, glass enclosure with towering sculptures rimming the perimeter, a horseshoe desk at its center, and two huge, glass staircases spiraling to the upper floors. So many visitors are exiting that no one notices me bounding up the closest staircase, looking for someplace with an overview of the Center's other buildings. If the explosion was connected to Sofia, then that's how I'll find her—and if she actually needs help, I might still have time to make a difference.

The glass steps are spaced for seniors, wide but shallow, so I can leap three of them with every bound. A staircase sign indicates a rooftop garden on level three; several bounds later, I'm greeted by dense, potted palms and a landing with a view of the museum's three adjoining buildings. One of them is a charred, smoking steel skeleton.

What scant structure remains is engulfed in massive fireballs. Even through the glass, I can smell the acrid stench. The remaining buildings look like they're swimming, which tells me the heat from the explosion is so intense it's rippling the air.

If Sofia was in that building...

But she might have been on the pier too, or we both could have died in the reservoir flood, or on the freeway. I steel my emotions, telling myself there's no use dwelling on it until I find out for sure. That's when I hear someone whispering to me from a hallway to my right.

Only there's no one there. The hallway is chained off, and a sign on the ritzy, gold chain decrees the Harrison Wing closed for the night. But that same sign has an exhibit list, superimposed over an image.

I gasp. The image is *Assembly Required.*

Sofia's painting isn't on the list, nor is her name, but it's definitely the same artwork I've enjoyed in my home for two years... the one I saw her create right before my eyes on that pier. *Did she copy some famous artist's work without me knowing?* It doesn't seem possible.

Regardless, Halston said I should look for what speaks to me, and nothing speaks to me more than *Assembly Required.* Stepping over the chain, I race down the corridor. Since I'm almost certainly on camera, I'll only have minutes, maybe seconds, before security is on me.

The corridor takes me to a set of closed, double-doors with "Segerstrode Gallery" engraved onto their brushed-steel veneer. Small windows in each door are no help, their reflective glass preventing my attempts to peek inside.

A faint *snick* issues from the doors. *Did someone just unlock them?* I pull the handle and the door swivels, smooth and silent. The hinges are architectural overkill: three narrow, metallic arms connected by multiple joints. No one's in the gallery's entryway, but a banner on the wall trumpets "The Early Mind," with an explanation that "Everything human-made began as a thought in someone's head." The contrast between those thoughts and their physical realization is apparently the focus of this forthcoming exhibit, and the banner, like the hallway sign, makes it clear the organizers selected a single image to represent it.

Assembly Required.

The exhibit itself begins a few paces past the doors. I see never-developed tool designs along one wall and tools created for now-obsolete tasks on the other. Other displays center on early, unrecognizable versions of simple items, from square coffee mugs to noodle-shaped ovens. A futuristic section offers concepts for brain-implanted game controllers, a sand-grain clock, and a "bar-less shark cage."

The larger exhibits center around a snub-nosed, 1935 industrial truck that was converted into an early snowplow. The plow's double-rear wheels are taller than my legs, and the rusted plow blade could shovel up a dumpster as easily as a drift. Snowplows bursting from the fog of a snow-packed road are scary enough; the thought of this ancient behemoth heading my direction gives me the creeps.

Far above the plow, I see something I actually recognize: a Meld.

Wait—a Meld, here?

It's from the "Souls for Sale" line, specifically Johann Georg Faust, the sixteenth-century magician who claimed to be in league with Satan. Stranger still, it's sitting atop a ceiling-mounted neon sign that spells out the word "EAT," probably a relic from some roadside Mom-and-Pop diner. My thoughts flash to Doug Halston and Anthony Alfaro, condemning the things people create with the limited materials we're given. *Is that why someone stuck a Meld on an "EAT" sign?*

The gallery is as silent as the door's metallic hinges: no one on the walkway, all viewing benches empty. Even the strange whisper that beckoned me here is gone. Maybe I imagined the whole thing? But no, *Assembly Required* was superimposed over that exhibit sign, that can't be a coincidence. I'm not seeing the painting anywhere in the gallery, only odd things like the wooden "lawn prod" that I find near a nineteenth-century laundry tub. *Maybe because it's still an unfinished, forthcoming exhibit?*

Footsteps, then voices sound from behind the gallery's entry doors: people moving up the corridor, probably security. *Did Halston send me in here to set me up as a bombing suspect?* I glance around the room, see small cameras mounted, each with tiny, glowing red lights resembling cat eyes.

Cat eyes... *Agnes.*

From the moment I remove Agnes Waterhouse from my pocket, I'm questioning the motives behind the exhibit signs that led me here. Probably simple marketing... but what if it was in fact *targeted* marketing? Nothing, literally nothing, would have caught my attention better than *Assembly Required*... and then the doors let me in. Are they Leopard objects, out to get me? Or is it the opposite—concerned objects that drew me in here to show me something important?

And does any of this sudden brainstorming have something to do with me holding Agnes? Sofia would probably claim Agnes' lantern also sheds light in non-literal fashion. After everything I've seen lately, I might agree with her.

The approaching voices are close to the entry doors so I pocket the Meld and race through the exhibit, hoping to find another exit. Behind me, guards are tugging and banging on the entry, and a commanding voice is telling me to open up. *Why don't they just walk in, like I did? Unless... they can't?*

Maybe the entry doors are with me? I find another set and give them a push, but they're locked. *So much for the doors being with me.* I ram my shoulder against them, but the rumors are true: a desk-jockey can't bust through solid steel doors. No way to smash them; nothing but a wall-mounted water dispenser nearby. I'm trapped.

Ignoring the sinking feeling in my stomach, I return to the gallery's entry doors and confirm what I already suspected: they're locked too. The cantilevered ceiling is vaulted, far too high to reach, and there's no sign of duct access anyway.

That leaves placebo magic, better than no magic at all. I pull out Agnes Waterhouse again, and right away my mind flashes to *Assembly Required*, clearly superimposed over the exhibit signs. *An exhibit that I never would have entered if I didn't see Sofia's painting. So why isn't it in the gallery?* Were the signs left as bread crumbs, or... *bait?*

Or is that just Agnes talking? Soon as she's back in my pocket, the suspicions settle down... but the hair on my neck rises. I spin around, convinced someone's watching—not just whoever's monitoring the security cameras, someone *in the room.* There's no one here, and yet...

The EAT sign cracks loose from its ceiling mount. Instinct sends me diving off the walkway as the massive thing plummets. I crash into a laundry tub then bounce up. Joints twist and muscles pull but I'm moving, angling to my left, eyeballing the displays around me as if they're wolves ready to spring.

At the far end, near the locked back doors, I finally stop. Glancing back, I see the EAT sign upright on the exhibit walkway, motionless and mostly undamaged. *Could it really fall from a vaulted ceiling without taking damage?* Now that it's no longer mounted, I appreciate its true scale: three times my height and more than half a garage door in width. It's still illuminated too, even though I don't see an electrical connection.

Huffing as I catch my breath, I search the walls for an intercom or a functioning camera, anything that might offer some help.

"Matt?" I hear.

I freeze mid-step. *That was no intercom.* The voice came from somewhere behind me, near the EAT sign. It sounds raspy, feminine, possibly straining for oxygen, and yet oh-so familiar because...

It's Sofia.

TWENTY-SEVEN

The woman I love, if it really is her, gasps convulsively, like she's trying to breathe after having the wind knocked out of her.

"Sofia?"

"Yeah," she says, barely.

"Where are you?" My voice is equally strained, from the fear that this, like the whisper and the sign, is just another setup.

My eyes are darting display-to-display, but none of the objects have moved or responded in any way to the sound of another person in the room.

"Other side..." I hear. "Behind... sign."

My heart's pounding. How do I know it's really her? The voice is similar, but if it's Sofia she sounds like she's been run over by a truck. *Maybe some Leopard object can mimic voices?*

I cut to the exhibit's far right side, keeping close to the wall while climbing over a display case filled with obsolete phones. An aisle on the other side of the case not only leads me around the back side of the fallen EAT sign, it offers an angled approach that shows me what's over there without having to get too close.

Two paintings are wire-hung into a corner hidden behind the sign. Someone's housed them in narrow, gilded frames, but I'd recognize them anywhere: *Outset* and *Assembly Required.* Our stolen painting was taken *here?* They're mounted on separate walls, forming an intimate corner display I couldn't see earlier.

The whispers I heard, calling me to this gallery… was it the paintings? I've heard them 'call' me at home, and in Sofia's studio, but never like this, from afar. The fallen EAT sign nearly crushed them. But how could they be in here at all? *Assembly Required* was just stolen last night, and Sofia didn't tell Doug Halston to return *Outset* until after our car was totaled. Then again, that was more than twenty hours ago… plenty of time for someone to bring them to the Whitmore.

"Matt." It's the raspy, feminine voice again.

Something's crumpled on the gallery floor, just below the paintings. At this distance, with my imagination already running wild, it looks like a vintage, human-shaped robot wearing rumpled blue rags and covered in multiple antennae. Or it could be…

"Sofia!"

I rush over, then pull up short. It's her, sitting up but slumped, with crucifixion-sized, rebar stakes jammed into her shoulders, arms, and legs.

"Oh god…" escapes my mouth, an involuntary, visceral reaction. "Sofia, what the hell… what *happened*?"

Whatever I considered horrific up until now, it wasn't. Seeing my wife, punctured with at least a dozen jagged pieces of rebar… my chest feels tight, and my stomach's twisting as if it's cramped. My temperature soars, then drops as if I've just died, and my knees buckle. Next thing I know, I'm crumpled on the floor next to her.

She's the one who's been gored, yet I'm feeling as if I've been run through as well. I take several deep breaths, trying to keep from gagging at the sight, the severity, the implications. A few seconds pass before my mind processes details initially blocked by shock. First: there's no blood anywhere. How can she have injuries that severe without any blood loss? There's also no sign of trauma other than her difficult breathing. Aside from a rumpled blue blouse and mussed hair, she looks fine. And somehow, she's not in pain. All of that rebar shoved into her, and she's not feeling anything?

That's when I notice: her entire body is lightly coated in the same type of electrified fuzz that Florence combed from the flower stem during the Amalgam meeting. *Was she attacked while in the process of interfacing?*

Sofia forces the half-smile. "Hard... to breathe."

"Who did this to you?"

"Doug..."

So, it *was* Halston. "I knew we couldn't trust that guy."

"No... we *can*," she says, gasping.

I'm flabbergasted. *What will it take for her to stop protecting him?*

She locks a hand onto my arm, squeezing so I'll listen closely. "Null site... is this room," she says, barely. "Outer museum, dist... distraction."

"The explosion was a decoy?"

She nods. "Trigger... evac."

So that this gallery would be in total lockdown, with only the specific objects needed to create the null *inside.* As a man who routinely assembles hundreds of Melds ingredients, I can't help but be impressed by the scale of what I'm seeing. There must be tens of thousands of items in here.

"They're *all* part of the null plan? Even our paintings?"

Consternation ripples her face. "Not sure who installed... paintings. But Matt..."

She struggles for a breath, then momentarily holds it before continuing. "Latchkey attack... studio, pier... ... gone."

Her art studio's gone too? "What about Ty, is he here?"

"No, left... few minutes..."

Which might place him near that adjoining building just before it exploded. Are he and Halston both *in on this?*

"There are security cameras all over the gallery!" I say, still aghast by the rebar spikes. "The Whitmore should have sent help as soon as you were attacked."

"They never saw. Leopard cameras..."

Her voice trails, but she musters strength and adds, "But rebar's mine. To interface with elements... like I-pins, at Tiny. Maybe I can... stop meltdown."

Is she suggesting she *wanted* these horrific things embedded into her?

Her eyelids dip as she grips one of the gruesome spikes. A few seconds later she moves on to the next one, then another, as if she's extending handshakes to them. *She actually thinks being impaled can help her stop a matter-dissolving null.* I gingerly touch the rebar protruding from her shoulder and limbs. Each stake is more than a foot long and narrow as garden fence posts, but they're also steel so they weigh a couple of pounds apiece. From what I can tell, each was pounded at least two inches into her body.

Removing them here doesn't seem like a good option, so I grab her by the armpits, gentle as I can, thinking I might be able to slide her toward the gallery doors then figure a way to bust them open. The strain on her face tells me I'm only making things worse. I'm desperate to call 9-1-1, but my phone still has no service and text messages just sit on the screen, marked 'Undelivered.'

"I'll find us a way out of here," I say, hoping she believes it more than I do. "Putting *Assembly Required* on the gallery sign, to draw me in here... that was genius. I just hope the extremists—"

She shakes her head, as if everything I've said is wrong, then inhales. It's a deep, raspy effort, but a few repeats seem to give her the air she needs.

"Not extre... *Advocates*," she says, then pauses to regain the breath she needs to finish the thought. "And not... lure you. Lure *us*."

Wait... someone wanted both of us inside the gallery where they're creating a null? But why? They'd know we'd try to stop it. And why is it Anthony considered "extremists" and "Advocates" interchangeable, but she doesn't?

She holds up her left hand so I can slide her wedding ring onto her ring finger. I'd forgotten about it—*did it whisper to her, letting her know I'd grabbed it from the house?* She seems so happy, seeing it, that I pass along her favorite paintbrush too, knowing it means even more now that her studio's been destroyed.

Her next breath comes much easier, but only because it's much shorter.

Love you, she mouths. Her head's bobbing, her eyelids fluttering. The only thing I understand about any of this is that she's saying goodbye. My chest feels like a garbage bin just landed on it.

"Lily, whatever's going on, whatever you're trying to do, we'll find another option, okay?" I say, my voice weak, and shaking. "I'll keep your family's work a secret... hell, I can kill the Kelapa deal if that's what it takes to get you back to yourself, I don't care."

Wait—did I actually just say that? Would the Meld King really end his own innovation—his dream product? The idea scares me, but in thinking about how much Sofia means to me, along with everything I've learned... it occurs to me that I'm voicing a shift I've subconsciously contemplated for a few days.

"Whatever you need, I'll do it," I add, as if speaking the words constitutes some sort of contract with myself.

She smiles, but it's a placating, believe-it-when-I-see-it substitute.

"No, I mean it," I insist, with a pleading tone.

"Avert... eyes," she says, barely.

First her father, now her? Even if I see a few markings, like earlier, what good would that do us now? She circles a finger, insisting, so I placate her with an averted glance... then stiffen.

The massive EAT sign is ribboned in far more than faint, hairline markings. These are more like accordion pleats, each vacillating between translucent and opaque, exposing a bizarre stew of objects compacted within each pleat. Worse, the sign's pleats are covered in glassy, pea-sized eyes, worn like beads, as if a billion hapless souls are peering out at me through past and present, life and death. They soak me with emotions as eyes do, but they're also looking past me, or maybe... askew, same as me.

Is it possible they have the same trouble seeing me as I have seeing them? I shift back to standard, straight-on vision, gasping. My wife is pierced with rebar stakes yet somehow, it's not the most terrifying sight in the room.

She circles the finger, like before. I'm afraid to try again.

For good reason. An extended, averted stare exposes minuscule body pieces streaming along the sign's edges, like blood through veins. One accordion pleat alone has protruding nails, wiggling fly wings, and smashed dog paws.

Same with everything else in the exhibit: the obsolete phones transform to accordion-pleated insects, each slowly emerging the longer I stare; the shark cage and the noodle-shaped oven are jam-packed with pumice, rotted apple cores, and crushed cockroaches. It's like scrutinizing a rainforest for spiders: you fail until you learn how to spot them, and then you see them everywhere.

Only *Assembly Required* and *Outset* look the same as always. The framed paintings feel like lighthouses amid a storm, anchor points for me to tether my mind.

Sofia sucks another breath.

"See... easy..." she says.

No, terrifying, I want to say.

"This... interfacing," she says.

"I don't *want* to interface. Not if this is what I'll see every time."

She nods. "*Assembly*... will help us... has info..."

That grabs my attention. She's never before tied her interfacing to *Assembly Required* or *Outset*.

She stops, then points to the rebar driven into her body. "Fix... this way... using a ninety per... leave mistake be... remember now... can finally..."

I get that she thinks she's somehow giving herself a chance to correct whatever mistake she made a few years back, but something about the way she said "this way" while pointing at the spikes bothers me. It's as if she thinks I've seen something I haven't, something about—

About her.

What if Sofia wasn't telling me to avert my eyes from the *exhibit*? What if she was telling me to shift them... from *her*?

My stilted breathing catches. I'm surrounded by a scrap heap worth of camouflaged, possibly conscious *somethings*, but I'm more afraid of what a sideways view of my wife will reveal. Terrified, I force a breath, avert my eyes, and discover...

"Sofia... my god, Sofia, what's happening?"

My beautiful wife, the woman who I so dearly love... she's covered in accordion pleats too.

TWENTY-EIGHT

My gasp is more of a scream.

The pleats extend all the way from Sofia's waist to her feet, loaded with the same bizarre stew as the gallery objects. Worse, the fuzz spread over her skin is now frothing with a dusty, ashen material, and parts of her look superimposed, as if she's a phantom being forced to materialize. Even more confusing, her slumped figure periodically flickers, spikes and all, contorting into something with a translucent, origami appearance for just a split-second before flickering back.

What?

I'm panicking. Sofia needs paramedics, *now*, but there's no phone service, the steel doors are locked, the security cameras are probably working against us, and the gallery's full of...*what?* Leopard objects, along with ash, and object-loaded pleats that only averted eyes reveal? How do I report *that*?

And... crap, how long do we have before this whole place turns into a null?

I give myself five seconds to come up with a plan, because even though I don't know what's going on, it's clear Sofia doesn't have much time. *Four, three, two...*

Too long. The ash on her waist shifts color, from black to ruby. I'm expecting the worst, something insane, and I'm right. The bubbles shimmer, then burst, showering her in tiny, glowing embers. She's not alone: everything in the gallery—dozens upon dozens of objects—is suddenly spewing embers.

Patting doesn't smother them; squashing them with my wadded jacket doesn't either. Sofia whispers as I kneel next to her, but between her strained voice and my cursing, all I catch is the end.

"...and thank you... for normal."

She winks as more ash bubbles shimmer and burst, adding another layer of embers. They're on *me* too—if I avert my eyes, I can see them, and feel them tingling as they cool to gray cinder. That's when I notice Sofia's are different: they don't cool. They're ruby colored, and fiery, and stay that way. *Why are they staying lit on Sofia?*

I run to the water dispenser I saw earlier, then use one of the attached paper cups to shower Sofia's left hand, expecting sizzle and steam. Instead... nothing.

As Sofia waves me back I notice her embers, though warm and fiery, are only burning the flesh near the rebar spikes. I scoop a handful and pour them on my arm, testing. Tingling aside, nothing happens; the embers turn to ash. Hers, by contrast, remain so fiery that she resembles a glowing, Vesuvius mummy.

My hands are at my head, trying to figure out what to do.

"Didn't want... to cross this line... but couldn't have it... both ways," she says.

Something splatters, and pops: more embers shower over her. Sofia's caressing the rebar wounds, but rather than easing the stakes out she's holding them inside. She lets out a groan; her eyes roll sideways then dilate, and though she's still conscious it's clear she's losing coherence.

"Mess with these two," I suddenly hear, from behind me, "and every one of you will have *me* on your hides."

Whirling, I see Ty Coronado, staring at the exhibits as if his eyes are firing grenades. His clothes look dated as always, but it's his face I notice most of all, moist with sweat, skin splotched in falling ash as if a black eye somehow spread across his cheeks.

After a prolonged stare-down with the EAT sign, he brushes fallen embers from his shoulders then stands straight, his chin raised, resolute.

"Ty! Thank god, we need to get Sofia out of—"

He holds up a "shush" finger. "You can see the crimps? The menagerie?"

The crimps. If that's what he's calling the window blind shapes I'm seeing, then the 'menagerie' must be…

"You mean those eyes and all that creepy stuff between the crimp lines?"

"Yeah, the relics of each object's prior existences. You're the same: a sum of phases from an eons-long life."

"You're not making any sense. Just tell me how to help her."

He gives Sofia's situation a once-over.

"She's here because she's carrying the only elements that can stop this null at such a late stage," he says, unmoved by her pleats, shimmers, and groans.

What is he talking about?

"It's the rebar," he continues. "At this stage, adding those stakes into their mix is the only thing that can prevent the objects in here from creating a null. That's why Sofia's interfacing with each stake: to help form a joined consciousness between them and the gallery objects—a connection that'll spoil the brew and prevent the whole thing from happening."

The same way the spores helped Florence form a connection with air. Is Sofia the "middle-man" this time around?

"How long do we have?"

Ty casts a nervous, averted-eye glance around the gallery. "A few minutes, maybe? At that point the embers will ignite every item in here, triggering a null.... unless Sofia's rebar stakes melt *with* them, spoiling the brew and preventing the whole thing from happening."

A few minutes. That's all the time we have? My fists clench.

"Why would a bunch of rebar prevent—?"

"Think of it as a poison pill," he says, brushing ashes from his hair. "The stakes were specially formulated for this exact emergency. Their presence here in the gallery, combined with the cerebral connection that Sofia's facilitating, means the embers would still ignite the gallery but the components in the rebar would dissolve all of the objects."

"Meaning no null, right?"

"Right. Problem is, Sofia will dissolve along with them, and there's no way I'm letting my sister sacrifice herself to stop this thing."

No argument there. "Good, then let's yank the rebar and get her out of here."

He kneels next to Sofia, distraught as he glides a hand across her cheek. "You think I wouldn't have done that if I could? We can't just 'yank the rebar,' as you put it—not without a medical team and some extensive surgery. The things were precision-placed using sentient object knowledge acquired by... well, by someone very close to her."

He looks away, knowing damn well I've understood he's telling me the "someone" was Doug Halston. "Besides which... the method I used to get in here is connected to my job, and isn't available to the two of you. So, we have no way to get her out."

Another mystery, one I'm too exasperated to explore. "Fine, we'll bust the doors open and start carting her and some of the objects out of the gallery," I say, brushing ash from my face.

"Then these things won't have their perfect mix and the embers can't ignite them into a null."

He takes a long look at the exhibit.

"These items," he says, his voice lowered, "would never let us do any such thing, doors included. But you're right: there's another option that will save her life."

"Well then hurry up and tell me!"

I stare at him, watching him methodically formulate words for whatever information he's trying to give me, knowing that if it requires this much effort it must be a doozy.

"You had a hernia procedure two years ago."

"Yeah, I'm aware. So?"

His face tightens.

"So... doctors left a tiny pair of surgical scissors inside your gut."

"*What?*"

"Yeah, it's common. Instruments are left inside patients every year. Hospitals always assume it's because the tracking nurse screwed up the instrument count... because it couldn't possibly be the instruments themselves, right?"

This is crazy. "Even if I believed that, what does it have to do with getting Sofia out of here?"

He joins his hands meditation-style: fingertips touching, palms separated. "If I'm right, the scissors would counter the effects of the rebar."

That's even crazier. "You're telling me we can save Sofia because the scissors in my gut are an antidote to the poison pill that Sofia's feeding the extremist objects?"

He takes a long, desperate look at his sister, then nods.

"Not buying it," I say. "How could something be in there without me having any pain, or getting stopped at the airport? And how would *you* know they're there?"

"Because they're telling me, right now. Also, they're polymer scissors, not metal, and medical tools often go unnoticed inside patients. In this case, I'm sure the scissors themselves had a little something to do with remaining undetected."

Suddenly, *crazy* turns to *horrific* as my mind processes what I think I'm hearing. Given the fear I feel rising inside me, I'd almost rather that he keep quiet. But he doesn't.

"I'm sorry, Matthew," Ty says, "but the scissors in your gut aren't just some random pair. They're, well..."

"Just say it," I mutter.

He drops his voice to a whisper. "They're one of the Leopards."

TWENTY-NINE

Things must really be bad, since at this point I'm actually wishing the scissors are simply the result of a ghastly surgical oversight. The alternative Ty's suggesting—an appalling violation by an extremist, sentient object—seems far worse.

"For two years, you've been carrying a counteragent to her poison pill," he says. "Seems someone was so convinced that Sofia would put a stop to the null that they used your hernia procedure as a fallback. Use those scissors and we save Sofia... but since they'll counteract the rebar, the null will end up forming."

I'm hearing him but I'm not, preoccupied with the terrifying understanding that I have a human-hating object *inside* of me. *Could it kill me internally, on a whim?*

Besides... Sofia's life is on the line! Am I really supposed to care whether someone creates this insane null?

"How do I use the scissors?" I mumble.

"If you interface with the gallery elements, even at a novice level, those embers that are glowing on Sofia will start glowing on you too. The skin near the scissors will then melt clear through, exposing them to everything in the gallery."

He offers a sympathetic look. "It's a rough process—Sofia's going through something similar right now. But if the scissors are exposed as the embers ignite the gallery, her rebar will have no effect and the resulting explosion will trigger the null."

"But then the explosion will kill her instead of the rebar! And won't I die too?"

He caresses Sofia's shoulder, looking shaken by her condition. "You'll both be fine. The embers coating you are made of a substance that should buy you enough time to get out. I wouldn't stand around taking pictures, but as long as you hustle, you'll make it out okay."

That strikes me as guesswork.

"Did... did she know?" I say, unable to keep from stammering. "About the scissors?"

"At first? No. But over time? There's no way a woman so sensitive to the sentience around her could miss an unwelcome inanimate inside her own husband."

"And neither of you told me? For *two years*?"

"Sofia's wedding ring told us not to," he says with a guilty look, then stands. "And why wouldn't it? Your rings are committed to the two of you having the longest possible time together. Someone turning you into an unknowing means of keeping Sofia alive was another way to achieve that."

I head a few paces up the walkway then turn back, considering what he's saying. "There are *millions* of objects in this gallery, how could one pair of scissors—?"

"I would think a man who has made a career mixing thousands of elements knows all too well that one ingredient—just *one*—can make all the difference in the world."

He gives the gallery a despondent gaze. "Though, as I said..."

"It means I'd be letting someone create a deadly void," I say, finishing his thought.

Outset immediately springs to mind. That bleak, barren visage didn't look like an environment I'd want to have a hand in creating, especially if the extremists could then use the void to their advantage.

"You actually *want* me to let this null happen?" I say, suddenly uncertain.

"No, I don't *want* it! But I don't want to lose my sister either, and I'm pretty sure we can contain it... keep it localized, so it doesn't become a worldwide catastrophe."

I'm shaking my head; the whole thing sounds like a terrible gamble. "Sofia told me there is no worse possible outcome than a null."

"She's not wrong. But if we want to save her, this is the only option."

Wonderful. I kneel next to Sofia, wishing I could get her thoughts, but her eyes are still rolled sideways.

It comes down to a horrible choice. Saving Sofia means helping the extremists—or 'Advocates,' or whatever they are—achieve their deadly null. The alternative, allowing her to prevent it, means letting her die.

Lose the woman I love so dearly, who feels almost like an extension of myself? A woman who creates art that feels as if it's filled with our souls? No chance. We'll find another way to dismantle the void.

"Wait—if I do what you're suggesting, we'd be here when the null forms," I realize. "Won't we end up inside it?"

"Again, the embers should buy enough time for the two of you to get away."

"The 'two' of us? Don't you mean 'all' of us?"

His face clouds. "I wish, but no. We're facing a two-headed monster, remember? My father asked me to stop the war that's about to break out in Asia; to do that I'll need to get back to the cleanup site right away, so I can interface with some objects that could help."

"How about you tell your father to go to hell."

He gives a half-hearted smile.

"Believe me, there are days," he says, walking toward the sand-grain clock. "But listen, seeing *Outset* and *Assembly Required* in here is a good sign. I'm told they're preserving vital information for you and Sofia."

I'd love to know more, but Sofia's breathing is getting worse. Kneeling, I check her pulse. It seems normal, but her breathing isn't.

When I look up again, Ty's gone. No door sounds, no good wishes, no nothing; he's just vanished. Averting my eyes, I spot movement through the pleats near the clock, maybe from Ty, maybe not. Right now, I'm too worried about Sofia to figure it out.

Her body's jerking side-to-side, spasming. I grab her hand, to calm her. An averted look reveals an ember blizzard, with piles of them mounded on her head and body... and if I listen closely, I can 'hear' their jumbled whispers. Only the rebar stakes and the surrounding punctures remain free of the piles, the glowing embers instead cratered around the scarred, exposed wounds.

But something's different about the stakes. Their edges are undulating like molten glass, as if an artist pulled it from a kiln and began reshaping it into—

A vigorous twitch moves the skin near my abdomen... or at least, I think it's a twitch. If it is, it's the most violent twitch ever. Looking directly at it shows me nothing, so I try an averted look instead.

The ember blizzard is all over me as well, shimmering and bursting like a witch's brew, but unlike before, they're glowing. It's the same ruby color I see on Sofia, and on pretty much everything in the gallery, piling ash everywhere I look... except for my abdomen, where they're beginning to crater—the same way they're cratered around the rebar puncturing Sofia's body.

Oh god... is Ty's description really happening?

I stretch the waist of my jeans, needing a look. Sure enough, the embers have somehow penetrated my clothing and affected the abdominal skin, stretching it so thin that I can see a bubbled, finger-length shape. Brushing the embers, I rest a finger atop the shape and feel something solid.

My blood turns ice-cold as I probe what must be the scissors. The pointed tips feel like they're spread open, with the springs now slowly returning them to a closed position. *Or are they simply moving of their own free will, attempting to send the blades slicing through my skin?*

I want to scream; maybe I do. But I also want to stay with Sofia, because if Ty's information was correct then I might be able to get her out of this mess alive. Odd sounds echo across my mind as every color in the gallery, from wall paint to lightbulb hues, suddenly smear together. My consciousness feels as if it's being propelled into that same, smeared space. Objects whisper; the muscle twitches intensify, and I feel myself collapsing.

Next thing I know, I'm groggy, confused, and lying prone next to Sofia on the gallery floor. Checking my condition is a mistake; the glowing, abdominal embers reveal a blackened pair of scissors, which are exposed yet held tight by my skin, the points and one of the finger loops sticking halfway out.

There's no blood or pain, but the sight of those scissor tips amid a glowing, ashen miasma makes my stomach churn. My subsequent gasp jars Sofia into awareness. She angles her head, her glazed eyes searching until, seeing the scissors, her eyes widen.

"Get them... out!" she utters, and it sounds like she needed every bit of oxygen she could inhale to say it. "Out of... gallery! Ruining... everything..."

"That's the idea."

She's looking at me as if her worst nightmares have come to pass, but with the scissors now exposed they ought to begin counteracting her poison pill—or at least, that's my hope. Because otherwise I'm back to—

The ashes falling on my arm… they're glowing.

The particles that were already coating my arm reignite as well, transforming from ash to glowing embers. Did exposing the scissors actually change something?

I hear more popping, see the ash bubbles shimmering, bursting, and pumping out dense ember clouds. Sofia and I are glowing, looking like fire demons, and for all I know that's what we're about to become.

Her eyes plead with me, then her voice does as well. "Please… disaster…"

She grits her teeth, inhales once, twice, three times, desperate for enough air to speak. "Toss them… out… gallery."

"Can't. I'm not letting you die."

The embers on her skin flatten into larger segments, and their ruby glow shifts to lavender, like a mood ring gauging a finger. In mere seconds she looks completely different, her face covered in continents, with fault-like splits forming across the hardening segments and her hair turning a rich, raven black.

Stunned recognition hits: Sofia Coronado is now the woman from *Assembly Required.*

The painting is wired to the wall above, the woman it depicts is slumped below. Both are spitting images of one another. I want answers so bad, for why this is happening and to what end… answers I may never get because the fleeting moment fades.

Sofia's puzzle-pieced body and the embedded rebar begin dissolving.

What? But Ty said…

What's left of her flesh is bubbling and fizzing, looking carbonated as it unravels into vapor, which in turn is streaming into the gallery's other objects.

"No! Lily... this wasn't supposed to happen!"

I'm vaporizing too. I've been so preoccupied with Sofia that I never noticed everything happening to her was also happening to me. It's painless but my skin feels taut, like I'm covered in plate mail, and did gravity just double?

I push my fracturing body against Sofia and embrace her. Her shoulders sink to mush, then to something altogether untouchable, yet she's right there, within my arms, and we're staring into one another's eyes.

In that brief moment, our consciousness feels mixed. She *is* me, and I am her, a joining so thorough I can finally understand why *Assembly Required*—a depiction of the moment leading up to this—might carry such an intimate connection.

Then our combined, vaporizing selves rip into the Early Mind exhibit, tearing off so much debris that the air's clouding with disintegrating crimps, objects, and eyeballs. The surgical scissors dissolve too, glowing like a fiery angel. Something in the gallery issues guttural screams, sounds you'd imagine hearing if you tore the beating hearts from a million living horses. As the shimmering intensifies to blinding proportions, the bubbles swell several magnitudes larger.

For a moment, everything stabilizes. My skin softens, the vaporizing subsides.

Then the bubbling embers explode. I'm enveloped within a white-hot wind, everything's glowing blue, my body has a smell that I can only describe as reality burning...

And deep inside, I know I've done something very, very wrong.

9:16 p.m.

Sunday, Sep. 6

Notifications

NEWS

* Political fallout from drone attacks on aircraft intensifies.

*Nations, extremist organizations continue to deny responsibility.

* World leaders threaten war: "We will not chance further incidents."

* Foreign submarines spotted in domestic waters.

* Authorities promise "decisive" response.

* Borders close worldwide; 14 nations void trade, discontinue relations.

* "Doomsday Clock" reaches 30 seconds to midnight, first time in decades.

* Spaceplane *Resnik* remains set for Monday launch in Mojave.

BREAKING:

* China blamed for drone strike at Swedish nuclear plant.

* Chinese officials deny involvement.

* Nuclear core stability still unknown; diplomats among hundreds trapped.

BREAKING:

* Whitmore Ctr. blast kills dozens, building is "minutes" from toppling.

Press HOME to unlock Screen Time, Reminders, and Purchases.

THIRTY

Four bursts. That's the way I experience it.

The initial burst swings into me like a baseball bat, right after the ruby bubbles explode, and oh, does it hurt. All I see is color: loosened up, ripped from the world, spraying straight at me. Feels like a rockslide, only the rocks are paint dollops plowing through my body, ripping my pigments away as they pass through. My clothes, my skin, my dirty fingernails... every piece of me wrenches apart, the colors leaching away, zipping into the distance with the rest of life's palette.

I can't see myself. I can't see *anything*. Fade to white.

The sound burst hits next, loud and angry. It's every bulldozer growl, drunken laugh, leaf tap, horse gallop, and more, all rolled up into a big sound ball that bowls across the world in one final crescendo, then dies away. My eardrums swell three times their size, or at least that's the way it feels.

The fragrance burst hurts more than you'd imagine, a noxious brew slamming my sinus cavities, knocking me out. I'd beg to smell again, but never to smell *that* again.

But all of it pales compared to the sensation burst: an onslaught of strikes and slams, buffeting me as one passing force, stripped from the world. The good sensations were mixed in there too, and they were strong. But the others... too much.

Now, everything's blank. Me, the ground, the sky, it's all vanished. *Assembly Required* and *Outset*, the paintings that meant so much to me and Sofia... gone. Nothing but white, everywhere.

Almost everywhere. I'm stumbling away from the EAT sign's shimmering remains, nothing left but the cracked "T" crumpled near my whitewashed feet. The remaining eyes from its crimp menagerie are gazing at me through the bleach, like they can't pull away from the only discernible object, like they know something I don't.

Patting my body—because I can't see it—gives me pertinent information: I'm whole. The scissors are gone, dissolved maybe, and my abdomen seems different now... firm, if that makes any sense.

I fall to my knees, which I suppose hurts, but who can tell. I sooooo need to feel, to see, to hear. I'm reaching around, trying to find Sofia, to make any sort of finger-finger, finger-hair, finger-clothes contact.

My depth perception is gone; everything's so stripped of color that outlines are all that's left. A thin, charcoal line might be the edge of a building, the leg of a crumpled body, or the rim of a cliff. Color now comes from within, my mind streaking the milk, replaying experiences from an obsolete palette. My muddled brain tempts me with my past, trying to convince me that that the world of five minutes ago isn't gone, that I didn't blast civilization into one massive, blank void.

But I think I did.

The eyes within the EAT sign go dark, but they're the only things that do. Everything else is blank, pallid, stifling. Sun, sky, land, objects, all filthy white. This is life, embalmed... drained of its pigment, numbed from all feeling, a world muted into some kind of powdered void. Surprise: white makes things bleak, not bright. Sterile in a toxic way. No day, no night, no shapes, no nothing. I can't even distinguish *myself*.

The thought kindles understanding. I know exactly what this is, where I am. I should have known from the moment I watched all color ripped from the world.

This is *Outset*.

This is the hell-void that Sofia and Florence described, the place where nothing—

Agnes.

I check my clothes. They feel tattered, but Agnes is still inside... my wallet and a dead phone too. My shirt's hanging from my arms like a sweaty towel. No smell, though. Nothing smells anymore, but it's the quiet that gets you more than anything. All those little sounds I took for granted, missing; no breeze, no birdsong, no buzzing insects.

The loose scrabble I'm sitting on feels like sand that's coated in gel, then mixed with flour. My fingers are too numb to sense much of the difference, so I'm left wondering whether you're still who you think you are when you can't figure out where you end and the empty space next to you begins.

A blind-man-grab at my immediate vicinity pays off: my hand collides with something solid. *An arm, maybe?* Flesh feels no different from wood, or stone, and there's no visible outline around the arm. But it's Sofia's—I can tell from the wiry wrist and the way we each tense, then relax, as we make contact. She touches me back but neither of us speak, probably because we're both completely freaked out.

One, maybe two minutes later, I have to say something.

"You okay?" I whisper, my voice hoarse.

No answer.

More minutes pass. At least her breathing sounds steady, an improvement from whatever was happening to her before the explosion.

The explosion. Ty said the embers offered protection. Is that why we're still alive?

"Never thought I'd see another one of *these*," Sofia mumbles.

Hearing her voice break the smothering silence feels like seeing your country's flag hoisted in the midst of a pitched battle.

"Lily, thank God," I whisper, checking her injuries. "And you're breathing normally again... wait, I don't feel the rebar stakes."

"What'd you expect?" she says, her tone bitter. "Because of you, everything I was interfacing with was just wiped away, stakes included."

"Not everything. Why weren't we wiped out too?"

"I don't know! Give me a minute to figure all this out, will you?"

So many other questions spring to mind but it's clear she needs me to back off. We sit amid emptiness, on scrabble we can't see, connected only by our numbed, interlocked hands. Nothing in my life has prepared me for such a terrifying situation.

I watch Sofia's outline studying the void, overwhelmed.

"Not even the paintings," she says, despondent. "I poured everything I am into those pieces. Purged emotions and knowledge I barely remember anymore, right into the canvas. All lost."

I squeeze her hand in comfort; turns out it serves as a reminder.

"Damn you, Matt, I had it handled. Now... *this.*"

Suddenly, the blank void doesn't seem so blank.

She makes an irate huff. "Adding those scissors—even though I told you *not* to. You gave the elements what they needed to ignite the null. You just *gave* it to them!"

Her words pierce far deeper than the dying, staring eyes did. "Damn right I did, and I'd…"

My voice trails. Finishing with "I'd do it again" doesn't feel right, not with scores of people, irreplaceable artwork, and an entire architectural landmark gone. *Maybe everything else is, too?*

"I knew *exactly* what I was doing," she says, frustration lacing every word. "Not only would I have survived and stopped this null from forming, destroying it would have convinced the Leopards I'd never try reversing the mistake I made. Now that's all gone to hell."

Even numbed, I feel like throwing up. Looking at her, or at least the whitewashed object shaped like her, I can't help but worry that's all we are now: outlines of our former selves.

She shakes her head. "I love you Matt, but you're an idiot. Those Leopard scissors triggered the null. *You* triggered the null."

"Yeah, to keep you alive!

"*Alive?* We've discussed this before: inanimate, animate, living, dead… they're just different stages of our overall lifetime."

Again, with that craziness from earlier. "I don't know about that, but I do know I prefer you in *this* stage. Besides, you and Ty knew about those scissors for two years and didn't tell me!"

Her surprise feels tangible. "It's… complicated. My ring—"

I can't stifle an embittered laugh. "Oh right, the wedding ring. Are you kidding me? Two years with an extremist Leopard inside of me, and you didn't think it was important I have it removed?"

"It never occurred to me that you'd actually use the scissors."

"I never knew I could! If not for your brother showing up…"

That grabs her attention. "Of course… naturally, it'd be Ty."

"Don't give me 'of course.' Halston's the one who was murdering you with those massive stakes, not Ty."

Amid the whiteout, there's no way for me to dodge the shove that accompanies her reply.

"Doug wasn't 'murdering' me!" she says. "Those rebar stakes were the heavy-duty equivalent of the I-pins you saw people using at The Tiny, for deeper interface connections. They only affected the gallery elements, not me."

I run my hands through my hair, confused. "But Ty said the stakes would kill you."

"Yeah, I'll bet he did."

Ty lied? But why wouldn't he want me to save his sister's life? And yet there's Sofia, looking at me like I'm a donkey thinking the carrot that led me into the pen was a prize.

"Ty played you," she says, as if I haven't already absorbed as much. "He and Dad wanted this null. They're the ones who built it."

What? Sofia thinks her father and brother built something that could wipe out humanity? That defies all common sense.

"They probably engineered it so I could survive for a short time," she says, "but they also knew I'd try stopping it, so Ty conned you into stopping me instead."

"Your father said only sentient objects have the knowledge to assemble and trigger a null. That doesn't seem like something he and Ty could—"

"Well, they apparently did. The elements at The Tiny and the pier filled me in."

"The *elements* told you? Seriously? Even you said interfacing can be hit or miss."

But she clearly believes it. "Much as I might wish otherwise, it's true," she insists. "Dad and Ty are responsible for this null."

She starts filling me in on what happened from the moment our phone call got cut off, explaining that the pier started collapsing, and that all of this was taking place just a few minutes after she'd tacked the crossword to our spot in Artist's Alley.

"There wasn't time for me to grab it," she says, "and by the time I was sure the null was being assembled at the Whitmore, I had no way to warn you or Neil to stay away."

"Why not just call me again?"

"Same reason I shouldn't have called you in the first place. Smartphones are the most corrupted elements out there."

She takes a breath, trying to regain her calm.

"Look," she says, pushing herself to her knees after a long, uneasy silence, "I know interfacing with rebar isn't easy to watch. I never wanted you to see me doing it."

I manage to give her hand a gentle squeeze through our numbness, figuring it says more than any spoken answer.

"We need to go, the null won't be stable for long," she says.

I get to my knees as well. "You dad's probably already inside, working to contain it. Or if not him, maybe the extremists."

She sighs. Maybe she just doesn't feel like answering, but my sense is that something about what I said is bothering her.

"I need to clear something up," she says. "First, I'm sorry to get so mad at you when you were just trying to help me—really, I am. But mostly, I'm sorry for not being more open... for trying to forget my past by burying it, and for not telling you the truth about my dad, my brother... about *all* of them."

Now I'm even more on edge than before. "What truth?"

She pushes her face close enough for me to see the sketch-like, charcoal outlines. "You already know my dad and Ty are with Amalgam, but the reality is, Amalgam's no longer the same group it was back when my parents started it. They're hardliners now, determined to subjugate sentient objects rather than work with them."

She pauses a beat.

"Dad's only pretending to be a hardliner so he can keep running Amalgam," she adds. "That way he could engineer the void, unbeknownst to the rest of the group. Like I told you, it wasn't the people they're calling 'extremists,' it was Dad and Ty."

I stare, dumbfounded.

"But if a null is as deadly as all of you said, why did your father and Ty want to build this thing so badly?"

She hesitates, anguished over whatever she's about to tell me, then mutters words I'll never forget.

"Because... they made the null for me."

THIRTY-ONE

S ofia gives her lower lip a nervous lick. It's quivering.

Mine is too. My wife, who claims she was trying to stop this existential threat to everyone in Canoga Springs... if not *everyone*, period... is the reason it was created in the first place?

"They made the null... for you," I repeat, because I can't quite process it.

She takes a breath. "Against my wishes... but yeah."

I grab a handful of scratch, because there's nothing else to grab and I need to feel *something* as I sift through the ramifications.

Her voice shakes as she continues. "It ties to what happened five years ago... to my mistake, to curbing my interfacing. Dad and Ty think I can use the scratch inside this null to correct what I did—and they're probably right."

All of this chaos is happening because she curbed her interfacing skills with elements, and her family disagreed? I'm no fan of the people-hating objects who want Sofia dead—and who want the guy who makes Melds dead, too—but this terrifying null does make me understand their mistrust.

"Even if you could make this correction they want, why would they think you'd have any interest? You left Amalgam. You're no longer a part of anything they're working on."

She lets out a frustrated yell. "Exactly! Not only did I leave, I made it clear I was done... that I wanted a normal life with *you*, that I'd *never* support them making this nightmare!"

Not only that, I realize, but why would they think she'd tamper with things when the Leopards are are so dead-set against it that some of them are willing to kill her to make sure she doesn't do it?

Sofia pushes close to me. "I swear Matt, I told my father over and over that I'd stop the null before he could make this happen... and dammit, I would've! I had the thing stopped in its tracks, it would've ended this mess once and for all, if not for..."

If not for me.

An uneasy silence ensues. The surrounding whiteness sifts, shudders, and slides, like clouds turned to pouring sand. My insides feel more blank than any of it, as if what's missing now isn't just the world but the comfort zone that I created to make my way through it.

Knowing the null was custom-made for Sofia explains why we didn't disintegrate when it formed—or at least, why *she* didn't. Ty probably knew the ember coating would do the job, even though he made it seem as if he was just guessing.

"How did touchy-feely Amalgam become a bunch of hardliners?" I ask.

Her eyes narrow. "The usual way: over time, a splinter movement gained popularity by pushing control over cooperation," she says. "The hardliners said it was time to stamp out the Leopards. Then they branded *us* the extremists for advocating diplomacy instead."

"And your father's so determined to stay atop the group that he pretends he's a hardliner when he's not?"

She nods. "They're on to him, though—you saw that, when some of them got up in his face at The Tiny."

The more I learn, the more twisted this mess becomes.

"Where does Florence fall in all of this?"

"Dad and Ty don't know this, but Florence, Doug, and a handful of other Amalgam members are actually Advocates—the people Dad has falsely branded 'extremist Leopard sympathizers.'"

I can't help but laugh. Maybe Anthony's lie stuck, but I love hearing that a few Amalgam members are still trying to take sentient objects' views and needs into consideration.

Details I'd thought irrelevant suddenly come to mind... moments when I attributed events to the extremists and noticed Sofia and Florence sharing uneasy glances or remaining mum, letting me assume whatever I wanted. Ty had done much the same. And Sofia was visibly unhappy whenever her father used the word 'extremist.' The clues were there the entire time.

"Now Dad will insist the 'extremists' created the null, when it was really him," she says. "He and the hardliners will use that, and the resulting deaths, as 'proof' of how extreme the supposed Leopard sympathizers are."

The void shudders. Sofia's right; this place isn't stable. "We'll discuss this later. How do we get out of here?"

"How do you think? We find the edge."

Finally, an obvious solution. "How big is this thing?"

"I didn't engineer it, how am I supposed to know?" she says, heading us into the fog. "Let's just get moving."

We grab hands so we don't get separated, then step forward, into the nothingness. Her fingers feel heavy and wooden, same as my emotions. Around us, scratch is sliding and dropping. I keep thinking we'll stumble across leftover walkways, curbs, or low-profile places standing defiant to the white, but they're gone. *And to think snowy landscapes used to seem magical.* The void's bleached terrain feels oppressive.

"Wait—other people are probably looking for a way out of here too," I say, stopping.

"This is a null. There *is* no one else."

Hearing her say what I already assumed makes it even worse. *Everything and everyone... wiped clean.*

"Can you try interfacing, to make sure?"

She sighs. "Matt..."

"All those people, Sofia... because of *me*. I need to be certain."

She thinks it over. "Fine, I'll see if there's anyone out there to connect with."

Her outline jostles as she removes the pouch of I-pins from her belt bag, inserts three of the pins into her left forearm, then stiffens.

"You found someone already?"

She waves me off, trying to concentrate. I may not know much about interfacing, but I know when something's bothering my wife, and that's the vibe I'm getting right now.

After more time than I expected, she pulls the pins.

"No one," she says. "Just bottles, car parts, hodgepodge stuff."

"You seem pretty worked up about random leftovers."

She looks away as we resume walking. "I swear, there's no one else. But yeah, I did find something."

She goes silent.

"Lily, please... what is it?"

More silence, trailed by a resigned sigh.

"It's the paintings, okay?" she says. "Somehow *Assembly Required* and *Outlook*, they're both still in one piece, somewhere out in all this cotton."

Learning the paintings somehow survived the null exhilarates me more than I care to admit. "Ty said they're preserving information for us. Is that true?"

"Probably. What I don't understand is how *Assembly Required* was in the gallery to begin with."

"Someone stole it. It wasn't at the house when I got back."

Her eyes widen. "Dad must have arranged that too. He wanted me *and* those paintings in the gallery when the null formed."

"Why would he want all of you together?"

She shakes her head, still frustrated. "Because everything he wants me to know is inside of those things."

Another tremor hits, knocking us to our knees before I can clarify what she means.

"All this white scratch is brittle," she says, scooping a handful of it. "Everything's breaking down. Once the few remaining objects dissolve away, then Dad and Ty will come in here and use this stuff as raw material to create whatever they want, fast as they can."

She sifts the gel-like grains between her fingers.

"Because if they take too long, the scratch changes beyond anyone's ability to contain it?"

She nods.

"What could they make with this... goop?"

"Their element network told me the hardliners want Dad to craft it into more of the Flies and Latchkey micro-drones they've been using to trigger the war in Asia."

"Spies and drones are enough to trigger a war?"

"Sure, because governments escalate against other nations as unexplained attacks mount. No one ever suspects the objects."

Those news updates I chalked up to fear-mongering suddenly seem ominous. *Maybe Amalgam really could orchestrate a war without people ever knowing.*

"If Anthony and Ty can play God with the scratch," I say, "then maybe we can too."

She doesn't sound happy, hearing me suggest such a thing.

"That," she says, "is exactly the carrot Dad's dangling. But sorry, Matt, I left Amalgam before Dad engineered this thing, so I have no clue how to do that. And I... I don't want to know."

Clear words, but... *she doesn't sound convinced.*

We plunge through the nothingness, hoping to find a border. The ground feels gushy, the whiteness curling around us. Walking on unseen, whitewashed terrain is nigh impossible, especially with numbed legs that feel sluggish. Twenty steps in, a huge, bland sheet drops away from the deeper white, sliding in our direction, avalanche-style. We spot the motion in time to sidestep it, then watch as the falling material pushes the scratch mounds into massive, snowdrift-like piles that hurtle past. *Just barely*, I think, grateful we were lucky enough to dodge the avalanche.

Except maybe we didn't. Something rumbles, both audibly and through bass reverberations that feel very different from the quakes we felt earlier.

I lower my voice. "Thought you said there's nothing in here."

"There wasn't," she whispers, her hand against my chest to slow my pace. Her tone makes it clear she doesn't think it's someone coming to our rescue. I don't either; the Early Mind exhibit was loaded with unfriendly objects, so if anything managed to survive the explosion...

More reverberations hit, vibrating the scratch. Whatever it is sounds like it borrowed Lucifer's throat. The rumbles ramp to drag racing levels as I search for the falling piano that I can't see, the scurrying I can't hear, the knife blade I won't feel. If only—

A massive, rectangular contour forms out of the whiteness, headed for us. There's no time to sidestep so we swivel and dive, hoping it helps.

It doesn't. The enormous object rises, dips...

Then it smacks straight into us.

THIRTY-TWO

Our clasped hands separate as the massive silhouette bulldozes us into a mounded, rolling debris pile that's heaving up around me as it's shoved forward. It's enough of a wallop that even here, I feel muted pain from the impact.

Holding my breath keeps me from choking on scratch as I dig like a madman, trying to escape the debris before I'm crushed. But the momentum shoving me forward is too strong, and too fast. Sofia's nowhere in sight, but not much else is either—just the thing that hit me. Its wide, shrouded outline looms from behind, resembling a colorless ping-pong table that's been turned on its side and thrust straight at us.

Can't breathe, there's too much debris. Can't move either. I can hardly open my eyes. The rumbles change resonance, sounding strained, as if the rectangular shape is as desperate to escape as I am. A split-second glimpse shows me the outline of a battered vehicle with a shovel-shaped blade.

The vintage plow truck, from the gallery? The rusted thing already looked menacing as a museum display. Now...

"Matt, get out, the truck's tipping over!"

Sofia's voice is far enough away that I know she's gotten to safety. I'm fighting to do the same, knowing I'm finished if all that weight lands on top of me, but it's too late. My shoulder rams something that hasn't finished disintegrating into scratch. The rest of me feels smushed and tossed in multiple directions. My final moment is a no-win debate: shut my eyes, or keep them open to the very end?

The plow's end, as it turns out. To my astonishment, a sheet of null material slides into the vehicle from the side, knocking the plow away but also acting like a vegetable slicer, passing clear through. The rumbling goes silent as millions of tiny, diced-up truck and plow pieces flutter upward, then disintegrate, momentarily shading the whitewash.

Flailing, I manage to punch through the scratch, gulping air as I surface.

I'm alive.

Sofia scrambles over to me, gushing about how lucky we were, that there wasn't much left of the plow truck when the avalanche hit it. I mumble something about how we need to get going before any more scratch drops. That fantasy lasts until I sit up and realize I've underestimated how badly I was slammed.

"Another minute," I manage, feeling woozy.

It's more like fifteen, during which I find myself wishing for simple things, like a breeze, or sunlight. Hell isn't a conflagration, it's emptiness.

"We're breathing, so this can't be a true void." Me, babbling.

She mulls my observation. "If I'm remembering right, oxygen is the last thing to go. In case it's needed to repurpose scratch into biological life."

I hear an odd fluttering sound, not loud yet maddening, a wing-like noise in my ears. You want to swat it, but you want to see it even more. We spot something tiny, far away yet parting the milky white because it's flying and... *it's yellow?*

There's *a color* inside the null?

Leaping to my feet, I yell for Sofia to follow me, but the truth is I'm so locked in on that yellow speck I don't know whether she's behind me or not. The thing's bobbing up and down as it flutters, and I can't help but think of those fish that use a lighted appendage to lure prey in the pitch-black oceans. But I'm almost on it now. It's...

I stop. My heart sinks. I don't know what I was expecting, but it isn't this.

A simple butterfly.

I watch it bob, searching for nasturtiums it will never find. Then it's gone. The yellow color winks out, or at least that's how it appears. I collapse to my knees. The butterfly will be back; it probably dipped behind some chunk of scratch. But does it matter? The thing that seemed like life or death is *a butterfly*.

That's what I've been reduced to, a desperate charge through oblivion for a butterfly.

My eyes are tearing and yet I feel laughter welling, the deep, angry, finger-pointing laugh you utter when you meet yourself and you don't like who you find. Looking up, I search for sky, furious when there's only more whiteness. Slamming the ground with my fists makes no sense but I'm doing so anyway, probably bruising myself, or worse, but I can't feel anything, and whatever I was is gone anyway: no features, no name, no community, nothing. Maybe God turned everything pallid because he didn't want me to be able to find his home cloud.

The fluttering returns, but this time I don't even look. Only my heartbeat, pounding in my ears, carries any appeal. Life's rhythm, once an orchestra, now *a cappella*... until I sense a second heart.

Sofia is beside me, easing my despair. Opening my eyes, I see the butterfly. It's sitting arm's length from my nose, atop the gray outline of who-knows-what, motionless but for a few V-to-horizontal wing-fans. I extend my index finger; the butterfly launches, circles, then lands. My eyes soak in the wondrous colors. Butterflies are inherently captivating, but in the midst of nothing... *wow*.

"Why does it have color when we don't?" I say, as it sits there, fanning. "For that matter, how is it alive inside the null?"

Sofia leans in, for a closer look. "She's probably freshly repurposed scratch. My guess is Dad and Ty are testing their skills by creating something simple."

"Or," I counter, "when your dad engineered this null for you to survive, he created it to help you somehow."

"Well, she *is* going to help, because she's following air currents we can't feel, which will lead her to one of the 'exit gales.' They're like umbilical cords that feed repurposed null objects into the world outside."

"You didn't mention that earlier. Can we use them too?"

"Yeah, but they're called 'gales' for a reason. They're the scariest windstorms you'll ever find, turbulence at the places where null scratch comes in contact with the physical world."

The butterfly flutters off my finger, lands on Sofia's, then takes flight. We charge after it, our feet colliding with all sorts of unseen scrabble. Fifty, maybe sixty paces forward, the faint, gray edges of our arms look a shade darker... enough so that they have defined lines. But that's nothing compared to the other change.

"A breeze?" I say, hardly daring to hope.

It doesn't seem possible but cool air is brushing our numbed cheeks, strong enough to make my ragged shirt flutter. You'd think we just discovered heaven, the way we start whooping it up. The whistling wind seems like carnival music to our sound-starved ears.

Something flickers. Our whitened world turns pink, then returns to white. Another flicker shades everything in blue, then orange, before reverting to white. I let out a joyous scream. "The color's returning!"

"No—it just means we're close to the null's edge."

A flashed, purple-tinted glance at our surroundings doesn't show much: just open wasteland and splintered material ripped loose from... somewhere. The gusting wind is becoming so loud that we have to raise our voices to hear one another. That's when we notice the butterfly is gone.

"Probably carried off by the wind," Sofia says.

Meaning she made it through the exit gale?

The hopeful thought makes scrambling forward easier than before, especially since the scrabbled terrain now has thicker outlines. The wind picks up, to the point where we're having trouble keeping our feet on the ground. As the roar grows louder, I have the uncomfortable sense that as we're approaching the gale, the gale's approaching us.

And then, suddenly, we see it.

If a tornado spun sideways in multiple colors, with dust-devil tentacles lashing out on all sides, it might look similar. I can't help but think of a wildfire: it's chaos, yet you feel a consciousness at work with every movement, like maybe the exit gale is yet another sentient being. There's scratch and debris swirling inside, from bookends to boxes, but it looks freshly manufactured—presumably created by Anthony and Ty.

"This is the place!" Sofia shouts, over the roar. "The gale will carry us outside!"

It's hard to imagine how such a thing could be an escape hatch. The flickering, insanely fast funnel is only a few yards away, headed our direction. Sofia and I, still clutching one another, lean closer together. As the gale closes in, she puts her mouth to my ear so I can hear her.

"Thank you for saving my life, back at the Whitmore," she says. "I love you for it, and now I'm going to return the favor."

"What are you—?"

"I didn't want this damned null, but now that it's here... seems Dad and Ty were right about me. I can't ignore this one last chance to go back and correct my mistake."

Her lips brush my ear, for just an instant.

"I'm heading to the paintings," she says, breaking our embrace. "And I'm heading there alone."

Before I can react, she gives me a hard shove.

"Lily! No!"

Tumbling backward sends me head-over-heels into the gale. For one brief second, I spot her perched on her hind end, using her arms and legs to reverse-scramble away. She mouths something I can't hear, her cheeks damp as another round of flickers hits. Everything turns void-white.

No!

By the time the colors return, I'm whipping around the gale's perimeter, caught within the whirlwind like the other dirt and debris, and a cannon couldn't shoot me out any faster. The flickering colors reach strobe-speed as an ear-splitting squeal tears into my head. My teeth vibrate, my spine aches, and everything shakes like a snow globe in a monster's claws.

And then I'm gone.

THIRTY-THREE

For a few eyelid-blinks, everything's perfect.

The wind, the noise, the flickering, it all stops. I squint; wherever I'm at, it's crazy bright and colorful things are moving—but it's a continuous, rich color, the way I used to take for granted.

Have I left the null? I call Sofia's name, but there's no answer. *Because she stayed. What was so important, or dangerous, about As-*sembly Required *and* Outset *that she felt she had to go to them without me?*

As my eyes adjust, I see what's moving: butterflies, clouds of them. After so much time in the cotton, they're riveting—and scented, too, with a citrus aroma. That's when I register that I can *smell* again.

I glance at myself; no cuts, no bruises, no rips in my clothing. It's like the whirlwind decontaminated me before sending me on my way. *Or was it the fluttering wings?* They suddenly blur into dizzying, kaleidoscopic patterns... too dizzying. Swoon begets collapse, except I don't fall, because... someone's holding me? Still squinting, I glance over my shoulder, hoping it's Sofia, disappointed when it's not.

"Neil?" I blurt, startled.

"Yeah. Come on, I'll help you up."

We're on a cobblestone walkway, next to a hillside road which curves between pine trees. The opposite side has no walkway, just terrain, and the box-hedged landscaping along its edge looks familiar. It's the Whitmore Center's entry road.

"I'm parked just down the hill," Neil says. "We should put some distance between us and that void."

I'm completely confused. "How are you here—and how do you know anything about the null?"

He points. "You mean *that*?"

I look up the hill, and gasp. The Whitmore and its magnificent spiral terrarium are gone, but there's no pile of smoking rubble. Instead, the entire hilltop is nothing but blurred, swirling air, shaped like a miles-wide, toppled decagon that's tinted in the same unique color I'd never seen until visiting The Tiny.

The null, as it looks from outside.

Around it, pure chaos: streams of detritus, from tree limbs to street signs, even massive sidewalk chunks, bounding across the decimated terrain before disappearing into the void. It's as if they're caught in a windstorm... yet there's hardly a draft.

"Emergency crews go in, they turn to mush—their stuff does too," Neil says. "There's a three-second headcam clip circulating that'll blow your mind. I'm looking forward to hearing how you managed to survive."

Knowing my actions helped create this horror is one thing; seeing the disaster right in front of my eyes is another experience altogether. At least a dozen news chopper fleets are hovering, their loud, incessant rotors a sickening score. Aerial and land-based drones are everywhere, scouring the area for survivors.

"Not too far," Neil says, grabbing my arm as I step toward the chaos. "You've already seen how that thing tugs stuff like a magnet, and it's not gentle about it."

He's right; just up the road I see a car yanked straight in, as if it weighs nothing. One of the drones is also skittering across the pavement. Its aerial counterpart, which is shaped like a skeleton key with wings, manages to veer away.

"How long was I in there?"

"Been eleven hours since I dropped you off," Neil says. "It's Monday morning."

He skipped the Indonesia trip? I'm grateful that he waited, but startled since he was so adamant about going.

"Never mind the trip," he says. "Did you find Sofia? Is she still alive?"

It occurs to me the last time we talked, Sofia was missing and I was on my way into the Whitmore in hopes of finding her. I quickly fill him in on everything that happened, or at least do the best I can given how crazy it all sounds.

"Hold on—did you say you talked to some guy who was racing out of the museum after the explosion?" Neil says.

"Yeah. Why?"

"Because the same thing happened to me when you were out on that collapsing pier. And, the guy I talked with mentioned the Whitmore as a Plan B if you couldn't find Sofia. Since she'd already told me to do that anyway, I decided to drive you there."

What? Sofia had wanted me to meet her at the museum because I was in danger at the house... but who was at the pier, pushing Neil to get me to the same place?

"All I was told was that getting you to the museum would give you the chance to find find Sofia," Neil says.

"Told by who?"

"By *that* guy." He points, and sure enough I see Doug Halston several yards away from us, suited as always.

"You *know* him?" I say, to Neil.

"Not by choice. Guy's an ass."

Neil sounding like Neil offers an iota of reassurance. If Halston was running away from both the pier *and* the Whitmore, was he responsible for both disasters? Moreover, had he been steering me to the museum by design, making sure the surgical scissors were at the exact place and time to guarantee Anthony and Ty could create their null?

"He said not to tell you I spoke with him—and yeah, I should have questioned it, but I didn't," Neil says, as Halston notices us and sprints in our direction. "Then he saw me looking for you after the museum blew and told me where you'd show up if you survived. That's how I knew to find you right here."

"You just did what some stranger told you to do?"

He looks sheepish. "He wasn't a total stranger. Remember when I told you I checked into those web links you sent? This is the guy who brought me up to speed on the research."

Now I'm *really* confused. Doug Halston, the guy who hates my career, was helping me get reinstated at Fustian?

He approaches us as if he's charging in on horseback. Grabbing him by his tie, I yank him up against me, eyebrow-to-sagging eyebrow.

"This piece of work hammered rebar into Sofia," I tell Neil. "It's a miracle she's alive. He probably took out the pier too."

Terrified screams ring out from up the hill. I feel sick to my stomach as I see a firefighter and two paramedics tugged across several yards of broken asphalt, then snatched into the void. Halston uses the distraction to wrench himself from my grasp.

"Enough of your B.S.," he tells me, smoothing his tie. "I didn't mess with the pier, or the museum. I went to the pier after I heard the drones got it, figuring the pier's connection to you and Sofia wasn't a coincidence. Honestly, I was worried the Leopards had gone after the two of you."

I'm not swayed. "Very thoughtful for a guy who stalks my wife."

He smirks. "Think what you want. She was *my* fiancée long before she was yours."

My chest freezes.

"Oh, is that a detail she kept from you?" he says. "Well, touché: I never knew about *you* until she announced she was getting married. That's Sofia for you, right?"

I'm bristling, but he's not wrong. "Doesn't explain how you just happened to be at the museum when one of the buildings blew up. Or why you told everyone you were leaving The Tiny, then stayed."

He removes his suit jacket, slinging it over his shoulder as if he's at a country club. "Sofia *asked* me to stay. We worked together for years, so I'm the only one she trusts to insert inanimate elements correctly for the full-scale interfaces. That's why I was at the Whitmore: those stakes needed precision placement."

A cocky smile spreads across his face. "So no, it's not a miracle she's still alive. It's because of *me*."

He lets his horn-tooting sink in before continuing. "As for that first explosion, the man you're looking for is her brother. Ty and Anthony needed to isolate the collected null elements to trigger it correctly. Their solution was to evacuate the building. If I'd known their plan sooner, I'd have stopped them."

His smug grin reinforces my disdain, but nearly everything he's said fits with Sofia's version.

"Okay, this is as settled as it's going to get," Neil says, positioning himself between us. "Let's get the hell away from that *thing*."

We look up the road, where the Whitmore should be. An old computer monitor and a garage door skitter-bang their way toward the null, then disappear inside.

I step away from Neil and Doug. "You two go ahead. I need to get back in there."

"*In?*" Neil says. "You just got *out* of that hellhole."

"Only because Sofia tossed me. She's headed to the paintings, and didn't want me in danger. But I'm not leaving without her."

Halston shakes his head. "You might have to. There's a good chance you'll turn to scratch if you're pulled in from out here."

"Maybe," I say, checking under my sleeves to doublecheck that my skin still looks ashen, "but I'm hoping whatever those embers coated me with will still protect me."

They try talking me out of it, but my determination to help Sofia isn't wavering. As I head uphill, I feel the void's tug growing and can't help but think I'm being grabbed by invisible tendrils. Seeing debris pulled inside, hearing panicked, desperate yells... it's almost more terrifying than the way I ended up in there the first time. Portions of the null's tinted exterior now appear blank. Am I seeing it differently because I'm averting my eyes?

To my surprise, Halston jogs up next to me.

"I know I'm the last person you want to hear this from," he says, keeping a wary eye on our position, "but this is a bad idea. Getting dragged inside will probably scrape off your ember protections. Hours of safety will shrink to... I don't know, maybe minutes."

"Then I'll make it fast."

He heaves an irritated sigh. "Even if you survive, the odds you and Sofia would have enough time for the paintings to reveal how to repurpose the scratch, which I'm guessing is what she's hoping to learn... let's just say it's not a good bet."

I stop, startled. "Are you saying the paintings can tell her how to use the null?"

Now *he* looks thoroughly confused.

"Sure—they have the information *she* embedded," Halston says. "One interface and she'll be able to repurpose the scratch."

His patronizing tone tells me he thought I knew all along. "I know she's done her best to forget stuff, but are you telling me she doesn't even remember *that*?"

I shrug. "Apparently not."

He swears. "Look, Anthony specifically engineered the null to give Sofia a shot at repurposing the scratch—because he's playing both sides, right? He pretends to be a hardliner so he can run Amalgam, but all along he's arranging things so she can get inside a null, connect with the paintings for instructions, then use the scratch to fix some big mistake she made."

That jibes with what Sofia said. It probably also explains why Anthony had Ty purchase *Outset*, and stole *Assembly Required* from our home: to get all three together inside the null, figuring she'd never be able to pass up such an easy chance at fixing her mistakes from five years ago.

If so, then that's why Anthony shifted from his anti-Leopard, hardliner guise to telling me I should interact with objects on their own terms. Sofia was right: some of that hard-case bravado was just for show.

Halston shakes his head. "The kicker is, Sofia wanted nothing to do with this stuff. She had no contact with her dad, left Amalgam without knowing he was making this null for her, slammed her father when she found out what he was doing. Then she did her best to forget everything she ever learned—which I guess is why she needs to interface with her paintings to find out how to reconfigure the scratch."

I can practically feel gears turning inside my head. "So, just to be clear, you're telling me that *Assembly Required,* and *Outset...*"

He nods. "They're about to give Sofia the chance to play God."

7:36 a.m.

Monday., Sep. 7

Notifications

NEWS

* U.N. calls emergency session as nine nations declare war.

* Three nations hit by overnight bombings; leaders refuse further talks.

* 17 countries deploy ground troops to "strategic locations."

* "Doomsday Clock" now a scant 15 seconds to midnight.

Press HOME to unlock Screen Time, Reminders, and Purchases.

THIRTY-FOUR

I'm trying my best to ignore the terrified squawks I'm hearing as a murder of crows vanishes into the null, followed by the cloud of black feathers they left behind during their struggle to escape its pull. But what's bothering me more is what Doug Halston's just told me.

"I know it sounds nuts, but it's true," he says. "All those people who were in the museum during the explosion? She could use the scratch to reassemble them, but also to tweak their innate composition... heighten their awareness of sentient objects."

I have to replay what I just heard inside my head before answering. "You can't be serious."

"Hey, that's dozens of people who would suddenly notice inanimate life, more than enough to eventually make the knowledge go viral. It's a pie-in-the-sky idea, but we used to bat it around whenever the null concept came up."

Neil lumbers up, looking like Halston just claimed water runs uphill. "This guy actually expects us to believe your wife's not only planning on raising the dead, she's doing a 2.0 on them?"

Halston shakes his head. "You can't raise what didn't die. They're in a broken-down state right now: the scratch. If Sofia can get the information stored in the paintings, she could re-form those people, with the... *adjustments*... that I mentioned. It's literally a fraction of one percent difference."

Neil laughs, and I can certainly understand why.

"Actually, Halston might be on to something," I tell Neil. "Sofia considers our living or dead periods different stages of our overall lifetime."

Neil laughs again.

"On the other hand," I add, this time turning to Halston, "she sure never mentioned anything about *reassembling* anyone, and she wanted sentient objects kept secret, not exposed."

"Don't be so sure. I don't know what her big mistake was, but I do know it had something to do with Amalgam's early, pro-awareness days... and she and her father have never fully given up on the idea of correcting whatever she did."

"Thing is," Halston adds, "even if she decided to give it a try, I don't think..."

He hesitates for so long, I have to prompt him to finish the thought.

"Well, from what little she's told me about those paintings," he says, "I'm pretty sure she's wrong in thinking she can repurpose the scratch on her own."

I let out a huff. "You're thinking she needs *you*."

"I wish, but no. I'm thinking it's *you* she's going to need. I don't have the right connection with the paintings."

"And you think *I* do?"

"Absolutely. They aren't just exhibits, they're sentient collections: canvas, paint, and framing, with their own knowledge and opinions. Those attributes are shaped by the heart-and-soul emotions that our favorite surrealist poured into them when she fashioned them into *Assembly Required* and *Outset*... emotions specifically tied to the two of you."

Good—I wouldn't have left her alone in there anyway. "So, if I don't help her interface with the paintings before the null collapses..."

Halston's face tightens. "She loses everything. Maybe we all do."

Up the hill, a geyser shoots skyward in the spot where a fire hydrant stood just seconds before. The water arcs, then streams into the void, showering the sod, gophers, and torn-away curbsides that are also being tugged.

Given the null's state I'm not liking my odds, but I've already made up my mind.

Neil has already made up his as well. "Time to ditch this nutcase," he tells me, using his lip balm tube to gesture at Halston. "The rescue teams are on this. If Sofia's in there, they'll find her."

He's forgetting the rescue teams dissolve into scratch the moment they set foot inside the thing. An awkward pause ensues. This is hard enough for *me*; I can only imagine how insane all of it sounds to Neil, who has no context for the possibility that Halston's outlandish claims might be real.

Another round of chilling screams sound from the hilltop; this time I can't look. Desperate for a distraction, I focus on the sound of a jumbo jet that's ascending in our general direction, yet so high up that it's little more than a speck.

"Here's the thing," I say to Neil. "Whatever's going on here, crazy or not, I need to be at Sofia's side. I can't bear the thought of anything bad happening to her without me being there to try helping."

He seems to understand. "Then do me one favor. When you're in there and these Amalgam whackos try to sell you on yet another bill of goods, ask yourself what I would do. Because you know I'd be giving it a long, hard look."

He jabs a thumb in Halston's direction. "Especially if it's coming from this guy."

Halston nods, as if he actually agrees.

"And Matt," Neil calls. "When you and Sofia make it back, look for me—I'll be here. No way I'm missing my chance to get you two as far away from this as I can."

It's an unexpected, concerned gesture that prompts a half-hug between us. Resuming my uphill speed-walk now seems twice as hard... especially when Halston continues to escort me. For the first time he looks worried rather than smug, especially as we draw closer to the looming, pallid null. Its magnet-like tug exerts random grabs that make the steep grade seem nonexistent. I pat my pocket, reassuring myself that Agnes is still in there. If this isn't the time for a good-luck charm, I don't know when.

"Look for a butterfly when you and Sofia are ready to leave," Halston says, like a coach bringing a player up to speed. "They're part of the design, to make sure people can find their way out. And don't forget: at some point her father and brother will be in there too. Maybe they already are. They're desperate, and that makes them dangerous."

Scratch chunks roll past us like tumbleweeds, hitting the box-hedges below, sagging them into sallow mush.

"It's losing stability," Halston says, as we break into a run. "If it ruptures, the two of you are finished and all that unused scratch turns this whole region into a toxic waste dump. You saw how bad the site in the valley was, and that null was a whole lot smaller than this one."

The site in the valley. I cringe. I'd never considered that Ty's real job is cleaning up the aftermath of the null that Anthony and Sofia mentioned... the one they barely managed to contain.

A scraping sound fills the air as the null drags a large rowboat across an asphalt lot and yanks it into its midst—*a boat,* even though I don't see water anywhere. Above, the skeleton key drone I saw earlier is also getting tugged but manages to move higher, zooming off in the direction of the jumbo jet that I heard a few moments ago.

"Why haven't we been pulled in? It's tugging heavier stuff than us, from farther away."

Halston nods. "It's like earthquake damage: random."

But ongoing. The null wrenches a motorcycle straight into the void, followed by a yelping, wayward coyote.

"If I can't find Sofia, fast..." I start.

"Then it's over," Halston says. "And Matt..."

He looks away, as if whatever he has in mind can't be said face-to-face. "For what it's worth, she's always going to love me. But she's always going to love you more."

It's sincere, but unnerving since it also tells me he's convinced I'm about to die. He heads back down the hill, but only makes it a few steps before an ear-splitting explosion rocks the area—and it's not from the null. It's from... the sky?

Startled, I look up, see a fiery contrail, and realize the jet I heard earlier isn't some ordinary passenger plane. It's a space-plane—one of the new jumbo versions, presumably loaded with tourists headed for the thermosphere. Except now, it's in a nosedive.

Straight toward the null.

THIRTY-FIVE

So many things happen at once.

The void's pull suddenly doubles, as if hooking the plane's mass somehow boosted its range. The enormous force yanks my feet out from under me, dragging me forward, legs-first. I'm not alone; everything that isn't nailed down gets yanked away.

Halston too? There's too much chaos to tell.

Above, the spaceplane's still dropping. Its central fuselage looks like someone took a giant arrowhead, molded it around a rocket, then strapped the whole thing onto a grid-shaped mother ship with three standard aircraft engines on either side. But smoke and flames are spewing from the rocket's posterior and the mother ship's engine casings are bursting apart. Worse, though the pilots have managed to level the plane out of its nosedive, there's hardly any distance left between it and the null, which looms like a mountain.

The pilots attempt a desperate swerve, to no avail. My mind fills with the din of scorched, roaring engines and imagined screams from the terrified passengers as the null drop-skids the spaceplane onto the Whitmore's asphalt parking lot, dragging it across the blacktop in a deafening hail of sparks and explosions.

The aircraft's viewing windows explode into a billion projectile shards. One of the starboard engines rips clear off, smacks against the ground, then rolls alongside the plane, bowling ball style, until a speedbump sends it bounding into the void. I'm whisking toward the null as well, feeling like I'm strung to a race-car bumper and hoping I won't be crushed by the debris. Being tossed like junk settles any remaining doubt: though human, I'm just another object.

The spaceplane hits the null boundary and winks away.

There's no crash, no explosion, no nothing. It's just gone, all the more terrifying since I'm now hitting the boundary too.

Enveloped within the familiar, white-hot wind I experienced when embers ignited the null inside the Whitmore, I spot the crumbling aircraft. It's hurtling through the sallow void, but it's also disintegrating. The spaceplane's exterior colors fragment, then spray into me, ripping my own pigments free until there's nothing but terrifying, blank whiteness. Sounds die next, snuffing the rocket's roar, followed by the sensation burst, where every punch and slam buffets you as they're stripped from the world.

But as my consciousness flickers—*and pleats when I avert my eyes, for just an instant*—I do my best to ignore all of that and focus my mind on a single thing: *Outset*.

The flickering, and *everything*, fades away.

––––––––––––––––––

When I come around, however long later, so does a heart-wrenching thought: *All those passengers—are they gone?* There's certainly no sign of the spaceplane. The void is mushy this time, sloshing beneath me like sun-beaten snow. Pushing myself out of the waist-high, vanilla goo, it's clear this null isn't going to last much longer and Canoga Springs will be left with another wasteland like Ty's toxic cleanup site.

I may not last much longer either. True, the cinders coating my skin and clothes are reigniting, which is good since it's transforming from ash into the cool, glowing embers that protected me earlier. But my arms look puzzle-pieced, exactly like they did right before everything went to hell at the Whitmore. It's not happening as fast; maybe the embers are helping slow the process. But it's clearly only a matter of time before the segments harden into the same fault-like splits that nearly dissolved me the first time.

How am I going to find Sofia in time? Interfacing seems like my best shot, so I try averting my vision again, hoping it'll trigger my mind into seeing the crimps, and eventually offer some sense of where she—or her paintings—might be.

It doesn't.

Calling her name isn't helping either. The void is too big, the sounds too muffled. That leaves blind wandering, with crazy-low odds for success. Tapping my toes in various directions, to feel out the terrain, doesn't help either.

Then, something taps *me*.

"What the hell, Matt!"

Whirling, I see Sofia's outline next to me.

"Interfacing with the paintings to find me?" she says. "Really? After everything I did to get you out of this place?"

That's when I notice: she's in front of a *visible* object that's hanging on one of two erect, gallery walls... the only structures standing.

It's *Outset.*

I'm astounded. Focusing on the painting actually worked. *Assembly Required* is there too, hanging on the adjoining wall. Their colors aren't crisp and the paint seems blurred, but they're forming a bizarre corner installation in the middle of a void.

Sofia's gray, sketch outline folds its arms. "Dammit... I wanted you somewhere safe. Why would you risk coming back?"

"Aside from the fact I love you?"

She places a hand to her heart then leans in closer, so I can see more than just outlines. "Don't you get it? The Leopards were right, wanting to kill me. They'll keep trying."

Her desolate stare seems to coordinate with the null. "I never wanted to see another null, but now that it's set up and the paintings are right here for me, I'm going to tamper with everything again... fix what never should have happened... and I suppose, deep down, I always knew I'd do it if the opportunity arose."

She grabs my shoulders, distraught. "You need to steer clear of this whole mess."

I place a hand against her cheek, caressing it. "Not if you want your plan to actually work."

Her mouth drops open as I tell her there's a chance that interfacing with the paintings requires *both* of us. After a contemplative pause, she breaks into a thin smile. "Explains why I've haven't had any luck connecting with them."

"They haven't told you anything?"

"Only that Dad engineered an object mix that included my cells, so I could temporarily survive in here—your cells too, along with Ty's, and his own. But I still have no idea how to work with the scratch, and... Matt, there's something else that I haven't..."

Her words trail off as we hear scuffling nearby. The scratch clouds shift and we see Anthony and Ty, arguing. This is no spat; their faded outlines are in the midst of a vicious fight.

Rushing over, I pull Ty away, tossing him into lumpy scratch. He comes up slugging, but Sofia grabs his arms long enough to get him knocked flat by a roundhouse from her father.

Then Anthony turns to me. He's surprisingly agile in this setting, and I haven't been in a fight since grade school, so the old man's serving up a beating. *Doesn't he know he needs me working with Sofia?* If so, he's too subservient to his temper to stop. He's maybe one punch from knocking me cold when his legs inexplicably buckle, and he collapses.

"God-*damn* it," he says, flailing but unable to get back up.

Ty pushes himself far enough up to show us a syringe. "Got him right before the two of you showed up."

Drugged by his own son?

"I had to," Ty says. "Florence's life is on the line."

Sofia places a foot on her brother's chest, knocking him prone again. "What are you talking about?"

He shoves her foot to one side. "Mike and a couple of the other hardliners have her. They'll kill her if I don't follow their plan for the null."

I feel sick. *Is Florence truly in danger? Or is Ty lying yet again?*

"And what's their plan?" Sofia says.

Ty gets to his feet, but it's pretty obvious his bell is still ringing. "They want me using the scratch to create a substance that's toxic to Leopard objects—or to any objects."

"You can literally play God"—Sofia gestures at the null—"and *that's* the best they could come up with?"

He rubs his swelling cheeks. "Don't kid yourself. It's a lot of power over some very malicious objects. But I'm also supposed to let the null collapse, so they can tell the rest of Amalgam that the resulting toxic waste and deaths were the extremists' fault."

Meaning, they're using the same tactic Anthony used. The hardliners will accomplish their main objective—keeping objects subordinate to humans—while blaming the atrocity they used to achieve it on the people they falsely labeled extremists.

Anthony scoffs. "And the dumbass was going to do it."

"What else *can* I do?" Ty says.

I'm on my feet, barely. The fact I'm still woozy, even though the null blunts sensations, tells me how hard Anthony battered me. Looking over, he's still crumpled.

"If you have *any* influence left with Amalgam, now's the time to use it," I say, to Anthony. "Get back there with Ty, round up the entire group. Make it clear that Florence is in danger, that it's because of Mike and the hardliners.

He looks doubtful.

"It's still *your* group," I say. "This is your last chance to retake it from the people who corrupted it."

Ty swears. "And what—we just leave the null sitting here?"

"No. You leave it to the woman who's better at handling this than anyone."

Sofia shakes her head at what I'm promising. "Matt..."

"I mean it: the paintings are here, and so am I. You have everything you need; you'll take care of the null. Or maybe I should say, *we'll* take care of it. Together."

No one seems convinced; Sofia looks numb. "I don't know..."

"Yeah, well I do," Anthony says, his words sluggish from whatever Ty drugged him with. "And goddamn if this loser isn't making sense."

He pushes himself to his feet, sedatives be damned, then addresses his daughter. "He calls this my last chance? Well, it's your last chance too. I've spent four years on this null, put myself through things I never thought I could do, because I needed to give you this opportunity to reverse a well-intended but life-defining error."

His legs wobble, but he manages to keep himself from falling. "Fix the big mistake, honey. It's what we both wanted before we decided you shouldn't have to remember everything. And for what it's worth..." He glances at me, like he wishes he didn't have to say anything more in front of me. "The Melds King isn't wrong when he says you're better at this than anyone else."

For a moment, no one speaks or moves. Then Sofia and her father hug. It's brief, and silent, but I don't need an interface to know it's also healing.

Anthony points at Ty. "Help me out of here, *now*."

Ty swears, then puts an arm around his father. They're walking away until Ty suddenly turns to look at me.

"You're a solid guy," he says. "I'm sorry I had the scissors implanted, but I swear, Flo's in real trouble."

"Yeah, yeah... *I'll* make them set her free," Anthony says, as they trudge off.

He sounds like a man with an ace up his sleeve, but I'm preoccupied with what Ty said about the scissors. He'd lied about most everything back at the museum, but apparently one thing was true: someone *did* intend the scissors as their trump card.

Him.

Meaning he probably planted the Leopard objects in my home, too. Between those, his interfacing ability, and maybe some of Amalgam's Latchkey drones spying from afar, he could easily have timed the alarm, the window crashing down, the water leaks... even the driveway concrete slamming into our living room. *Because of me? Or was he a hardliner pawn then, too, trying to keep Florence safe?* I'll probably never be certain.

Then, I suddenly remember...

"Sofia, there's a crashed plane in here," I say, realizing we never had a chance to discuss it. "It's a spacepl—"

"I know. Amalgam's Latchkey micro-drones took it down."

She tells me they figured adding the plane's millions of elements would boost the null's gravitational pull, which would then draw even *more* elements inside.

"But it won't matter," she adds. "I should be able to help everyone from the plane and the Whitmore at the same time as—"

I hear aggressive whispers, inside my head and yet not.

"More Latchkeys," Sofia says, looking up. "Hundreds of them... somehow airborne here in the null."

She's right: when I avert my eyes, the same skeleton key-shaped micro-drones I'd seen earlier materialize from the murk, loaded with missiles and inexplicably undamaged. The null seems to magnify their gleaming, tar-like exterior, odd since it should have stripped all the color.

Meaning they were created from the scratch, probably by Ty, for the Amalgam hardliners. Passing overhead, they resemble a flock of ravens, hunting amid a cloud-choked sky, pleated with an eyeball menagerie.

"You think they're looking for the spaceplane?"

Sofia's face contorts.

"No," she says, downcast. "I think they're looking for us."

THIRTY-SIX

My stomach's twisting, watching the drone swarm carry out search patterns meant to flush us out of hiding. We're ducked down, but we're also between the only two walls still standing in this place, so we might as well be next to a beacon. Maybe we are; the null is so broken that a faint sunlight shaft is beginning to beam in from outside.

"They're Amalgam's drones, and you're Anthony's daughter," I say, as I remove *Assembly Required* and *Outset* from the walls and wedge them into the goopy scratch at seemingly haphazard angles, attempting to make a shape we can hide under. "Maybe it's a rescue."

Sofia offers a wry smile, and air quotes. "I'm a 'Leopard sympathizer' trying to dismantle the null, and they're the hardliners' drones. This is no rescue."

We tuck ourselves beneath the angled paintings, digging our feet and legs under the frames. It's the worst camouflage ever, but the drones are close, the scratch is determined to dissolve me, and this place is falling apart, so it's better than nothing.

The paintings call out to us, as close to audible as paint on canvas can get. They seem cognizant of the drones, the unstable null, and our dwindling odds.

"They're right; we need to interface with them, now," I say. "Find out how to use the scratch before the drones spot us."

Sofia nods. "But there's something you need to know."

She takes a breath, apparently searching for the right words. "When I painted them, I put so much of... *myself*... into them. Things I once understood but needed to bury, in order to have *us*. Interfacing with them will mean reconnecting with all of that."

Her bottom lip quivers. "Which means we could lose *us*."

I place a hand against her cheek. "*Us* is what's going to prevent that from happening."

We share a brief kiss, but I can tell something's still bothering her. When we pull away, she inserts her I-pins into her left shoulder with lightning speed. To my horror, she grabs a tiny corner of *Assembly Required* and tears it off. Pointing, she has me do the same with a corner of *Outset* before using her final needle to prod the two painting pieces into the same shoulder, wedging them just beneath the skin.

"Hold still, and avert your eyes," she says, planting herself deeper into the scratch. "I'm starting the interface."

Shifting *Assembly Required* and *Outset* to my peripheral vision, I can't make out much of their subject matter beyond a few crimps until Sofia's muscular interface kicks in. The paintings encompass us, as if they've become a virtual-reality stage. She and I are sitting within them, not in a single location on the canvas but in *all* locations, as if we're the paint that forms the images.

But it's not the visuals that engulf us so much as the emotions they convey. I'm deluged by impressions from Sofia's lifetime: her concentrated knowledge intertwined into her most personal observations and desires. Similar knowledge also exudes from dispassionate sources: the canvas, the paint, and the framework.

What seemed like whispers whenever the paintings reached out to me in the past now sound projected by a bullhorn, rendering them so garbled and tone-deficient that I'm not able to interpret the meaning.

Thankfully, Sofia removes us from the jarring, intrusive contact after only a few seconds. The paintings seem to stretch inside my head, then rubber-band outward, back into their frames until we're no longer encompassed.

"Got it," she says, her voice barely audible as she curbs our interface.

"Already? You found out how to use the scratch that fast?"

Sofia offers me a weary, doe-in-headlights glance. "Yeah, I saw what we have to do. How we play God."

She hesitates, as if the challenge is even bigger than she expected.

"Well?" I prompt.

She takes an extended, deliberate breath. "We do it by interfacing with the entire null."

What?

"The null is a bunch of muck," I say, exasperated. "What are we supposed to interface *with*?"

Sofia grips my forearm. "It's not 'muck,' it's billions of objects in a collapsed form. But in concept, they still have substance and sentience, no different from us except they've been reduced to scratch."

Billions of objects? She might be an interfacing ace who managed to connect her consciousness with every sentient object inside a packed art gallery, but trying the same thing here would be comparable to holding a conversation with every human being on the planet, all at once.

She can't possibly think that's feasible.

"You really think you can do that?" I say.

Her face brightens. "No. But I'm sure *we* can do that."

She senses my hesitation.

"Look, the most difficult interfaces require the deepest of bonds," she says. "That's why I wanted Doug with me at the gallery, and it's why I need you here with me now. If we want to give all those people a chance to continue living their human phase... and make them just a bit *better*... it'll take both of us."

I tell myself not to worry, that I'll find a way to help her, though I don't see how—especially knowing the Latchkey drones are getting closer to us.

"So, we're supposed to connect with every scrap of scratch in the null," I say, as we again shield ourselves behind the angled paintings, "then try convincing all those particles to work with us, so we can... what, re-form the people who died in here?"

"They didn't die. They're just—"

"Yeah, in a different phase of their overall life. You, Ty, and Doug have all made that clear, but..."

"Then you're also clear about the one tiny difference: we'll make sure they keep an innate awareness of objects' sentience."

By now, I know her well enough to sense she's holding something back.

"Whenever we've discussed your interfacing skills before," I say, "you were pretty insistent the objects would be furious if we did that."

"Yeah," she admits, "and some of them will be. The ethics on this are... questionable. But that, and the mistake I need to correct... you need to know that we're both—"

I stop her mid-sentence. "I don't care, okay? Because there's one thing that I believe in more than anything else." My nervous swallow makes this moment more awkward than I'd anticipated. "It's you. I believe in *you*."

She utters an exhausted mock-laugh.

"I'm serious. You created these amazing, sentient paintings—my first hint that objects might be something more than inanimate *things*."

Her taut face softens.

"*Your* art kindled that," I continue. "Your heart and soul, even if only subconsciously, wanted me *aware* of the sentience in those paintings."

Another nervous swallow, but this time it's hers.

"Am I wrong?" I press. "Because if so..."

"You're not wrong."

"*Because if so*," I repeat, needing for her to hear the complete thought, "then there's no reason for you to second-guess yourself. Whatever you think is best, I'm on board. If that means scooping goop in a null so I end up aware, or doing it to be sure *no one* is aware, I trust your judgement. I'll do whatever it takes to support your decision."

I think it over, then add, "But not just for some world-saving plan. For *us*. To bring us a step closer to building the normal life you've always wanted."

She looks horrified. "Stop..."

"I'm just trying to tell you that—"

"No! Not another word." Her eyes turn red. She starts to speak, collects herself when her voice cracks, then resumes. "This is what I've been trying to tell you, Matt: forget what I said before. We *can't* prioritize me having a normal life."

My heart stops. "Why not?"

She shakes her head. "We just can't. Not even if it's to preserve *us*."

Her cheeks are tear-streaked, something I've rarely seen. "How can there not be some way for us to accomplish both?"

"Because," she says, "it's part of the mistake I need to go back and fix."

I'm trying to figure it all out, but there's no time because, in the corner of my eyes, a swarm of dark, key-shaped objects soar from the mist. The null must truly be failing, because I can feel my blood chill at the sight.

A sickening peach flash lights up the whiteness, so bright we have to cover our eyes. As it fades, we see the Latchkey drones gathered together in the upper null, linked into an odd, hovering, tube-shaped formation. Then we notice two glowing dots the size of distant streetlights, not far from the drones but traveling away from them, fast.

Missiles, created and fired by the drones.

And they're headed directly toward us.

THIRTY-SEVEN

Double-death approaches, a twisted, compelling sight.

The twin missiles resemble gargantuan bullets, their heat-seeking noses wobbling as they close in on our location. I should dive, run, shield my wife, *something*. Instead, morbid fascination paralyzes me.

Agnes, still in my pocket, suddenly projects whisper-filled vibes on a scale I've never felt. In response, a lead weight slams into our ears... or at least that's how it seems, as what sounds like an entire city's worth of voices call out from behind us. I whirl: nothing there but more null. Then I get it: I'm 'hearing' because I'm still interfaced with Sofia and the few other remaining objects, like Agnes and...

The spaceplane? Or more accurately, whatever's left of it. Did my lucky Meld somehow catch the fallen aircraft's attention?

A broad warmth emanates from the same whitewashed region as the voices, so strong that even *I'm* noticing. It really is the plane's pleated remnants... or more specifically the objects, *thousands* of them, that form the aircraft. The arrow-shaped fuselage is only a short run behind us. From what I can tell, it's in the same situation we are: stuck in an empty void, deteriorating.

Sofia's interfacing skills so outdistance mine that she can fully understand what sounds like the whispers I heard from my bedroom furnishings. "My god... you don't have to do this," she says, a barely audible mumble.

Her emotions surge, gratitude projected at the aircraft. By now, those wobbling, incoming missiles are so close they could explode in midair and still wipe us out.

"Move!" she says, yanking me further underneath the paintings.

From somewhere behind us, the aircraft's rocket engine fires up, zero-to-full-throttle with a massive roar and an intense heat blast. Both missiles swerve, their heat-seeking sensors leading them straight toward the ignited rocket.

The subsequent explosion seems to ignite the null itself. Even through the scratch, there's no missing the fireball that blazes upward, propelled by impact velocity, explosives, and two aircraft wings full of fuel. The entire void looks like a supernova.

Some sort of blast wave hits, knocking me into the suffocating mush, rattling my brain. Gasping, I paw at the scratch until I find Sofia and pull her up, fighting my hardening, puzzle-pieced skin the entire time.

The rising plume envelops scratch clouds, undefinable null clumps... and hundreds of dark objects shaped like winged skeleton keys. The micro-drones tumble, spin out of control, and disappear.

Am I hearing secondary explosions? Are the Latchkeys really destroyed? The fireball blasts are too loud, and the scratch wisps too prevalent; there's no way to be sure. I am certain of one thing: by making themselves decoy targets, those spaceplane components—those *objects*—just sacrificed themselves for *us*.

Memories surface, of our car, the rope bridge, our TV, and several other objects that did the same. But also, of news reports about chimneys holding burglars until police arrive; coat zippers saving children from electrocution; bathroom pipes shielding kittens from explosions. Good fortune, yes... but why didn't I ever consider whether the objects might deserve some of the credit?

The fireball dissipates, sound and colors fading. Only *Assembly Required* and *Outset* remain, still shielding us as they lean against their battered gallery walls, looking reasonably intact— Anthony must have really done a number on them. Otherwise, the void is once again a void... and yet, for one beautiful moment, right here in the midst of emptiness, I'm feeling a sliver of hope. Sofia motions for me to look around.

"Do you realize what this is?"

All I see, and hear, is nothing.

She pulls me close. "It's *Outset*. The painting wasn't an image of emptiness at all. We were looking at *us*... at this moment where we either finish, or fail."

"Then let's finish."

We climb out from underneath the paintings, then re-hang them against what's left of the gallery walls, out of respect.

She gestures at them. "This is going to be very different from interfacing with the paintings. The null is so big I'll need to extend our reach massively further for us to have a chance."

Her mind seems to grab my head, as if it were a third hand. Her liaison skills transform my meager connection into a pleated, menagerie-filled world where finding sentient objects would be as easy as hearing mosquito wings in a darkened room. But the eyes embedded within these crimps are nothing like the ones I saw earlier. They're narrow and bloodied, horrific things that look like they've witnessed, perhaps even triggered, the worst events that life has to offer.

Everything tangible drops away: no images, light, or sound. No smell, or touch. All that's left is consciousness, enlivened by brief, organic phases that quickly crash back into a range of inorganic states. It's exactly what Sofia and Ty have been telling me all along, that humanity is simply a stage amid time, fleeting and precious within an eons-long, inanimate existence.

No wonder she tries to forget. Who wouldn't do anything to keep such petrifying impressions from interfering with their brief, human phase? I pull us into a bear hug, each breath a push against visions I'll never un-see. We calm as we hold each other, reassembling where we are, and why... grabbing onto anything that might fend off the insanity. It's the psychological equivalent of choking back an urge to vomit.

Our interface sends us beyond the crimps and their menagerie, our thoughts and emotions bursting through the void, disseminating everywhere. Sofia's no longer visible, she's just *there.* Everything's there... and nothing's there.

My heart's palpitating, so maybe I still have one. The sallow void smears into a gallery of new, nameless, breathtaking colors— including the one we saw when Florence interfaced at The Tiny. If the universe had an art studio, this borderless existence would be the place: no land, sky, or space, certainly no individuality.

Then, out of nowhere—or is it *everywhere*?—a gentle, pervasive warmth washes over us. Everything is on hold as strangers meet and assess, cautious. Suddenly, it's clear that this seemingly vacant, bleak place is nothing of the sort. This null, just as Sofia claimed, is an assemblage of sentient objects on a massive, influential scale. I've misjudged the scratch, same as I misjudged my digital clock, the sculpture garden, and the aircraft, because few human beings—certainly not an object-abusing Meld inventor like me—would ever guess that a collection of *things* could be a set of *someones*... and bright, wondrous someones at that.

Bright enough to understand the possibilities. The null probes our intent, our passions, the depth of our commitment. Sofia and I give our best pitch, describing what we hope to do, and—most importantly—the reason this only works as a collaborative effort between humans and objects.

An answer comes quick, and there's really only one way to describe it.

The null is with us.

Our minds and ambitions joined, we feel the ambient intellect surrounding us and allow our deep-seated instincts to kick in. Soon we're tugging at the mush with blazing speed, winding it around us like a thread around a spindle. Working with the scratch, a marvelous, pliable material that responds as much to the mind as the hand, we reformulate the human DNA lost within the void, altering it just one fraction of one percent—which is all it takes to modify, and thus transform—the hundreds of people we're returning.

More warmth. The null scratch is with us, indeed.

Sofia's outright joy feels palpable as she applies her talents to an entirely different canvas, employing her "brush" on a celestial scale, reveling in a vast palette of new, nameless colors, pulling from her soul, my soul... *our* collective soul. The artist I love is finally operating on the level she deserves. Doug Halston once said she could use one item to stop a war, and I'm now convinced that item is her mind.

Except... something's off about all of this. The ease with which we connected; how quickly the scratch signed on to our plan; Sofia's comfort level, working on a seemingly overwhelming scale as if...

As if she's done this before.

She freezes. The null seems to ice over as well, its color palettes no longer swirling, the scratch no longer pliable. An additional, ominous consciousness burgeons, a component that's been joined with us all this time but hidden... stifled, even... more of a subconsciousness, maybe... and there's something familiar about it.

"What's happening?" I utter, in my mind and yet echoing everywhere, a declaration of my proliferating awareness more than an actual question.

As if I've done this before, too.

Because I have?

The subconsciousness screams: —*Yes, and you were here with Sofia! Just like now, only... only the goal was very different.*—

The mood of our connection dampens, the ambient colors darken. No one speaks, because they don't need to. The knowledge is here, shared between us, undeniable.

Not all of the human beings in Canoga Springs are ignorant or insensitive to sentient objects—or at least, they aren't supposed to be... and they didn't used to be. The only reason they're that way now is because they were violated.

The atrocity happened five years ago, in the previous null. For some inexplicable, god-awful reason, someone used the scratch to strip people of their ability to recognize sentience in objects.

And that someone was me.

THIRTY-EIGHT

I did this?" I say, to Sofia but to every ounce of scratch in the null as well. "*I'm* responsible? Everything that's transpired in this community for *five years* is history that I set in motion?"

My existence feels empty, as if I've lost a piece of myself. Now I understand: the subconscious thoughts I'm hearing are my own, confirming the horrible, shared truth: Sofia didn't make the mistake. *It was me.* With Sofia's help, I tweaked the innate composition of every human being in Canoga Springs... tailored genetic instructions from null scratch and allowed our unique creation to propagate through groundwater as scratch naturally does. We stood by as it entered the drinking water supply, infiltrating bloodstreams. We delivered our instructions to neurons, which then rewrote the code governing sensory function.

We robbed every sentience-sensitive individual of their awareness of sentient objects.

That was the secret Sofia buried, the mistake she wanted to correct... and it wasn't even her mistake. It was mine.

A green-hued flash illuminates the null, then fades. *Missile fire?* No, the rocket engine downed the drones. *Then what is it?* Our interface conveys horrified cries from decimated elements. Has some distant section of the compromised void crumbled?

"Voices" erupt within our minds, a chorus of scratch elements taking advantage of our shared link. Many are engaged in a heated debate about whether I deserve to have any part in this interface. The comments from Melds, insisting their very existence amounts to serial exploitation, are the most crushing. It's such a contrast to everything I feel from Agnes, but I'm not surprised that object-phase viewpoints would be just as diverse than our own.

Most of the chorus consists of elements giving us their rundown of events from the past few years... and it's a mind-blowing account. The community they depict is supposedly Canoga Springs, but I have no memory of anything they're sharing: landscapes sporting wondrous geometrical shapes, office buildings utilizing interactive architecture, cars navigating via human-object interfaces. The sky above their idyllic town is tinted in glorious, unknown colors, and ambient birdsong fills the air, rich and detailed, as if master composers are streaming their melodious brainstorms throughout the environment.

Because of the collaborations, I hear, the voices of thousands somehow joining to produce the same sentiment. *Because in the years before your "mistake," Amalgam helped transform a portion of Canoga Springs into a unique enclave where elements and sentience-sensitive people worked together.* Organic and mineral, liquid and gas, active and inert, all were treated as what they are: life stages that every being experiences at some point during their existence. Variations in consciousness and capabilities were celebrated and comingled, resulting in fusions of physics, biology, empathy, and ideas.

But eventually, an inexplicable shift transpired: people began claiming a hierarchy, suggesting the most active, mobile, "intelligent" individuals are *meant* to take the lead on decisions and actions, whether elements approved or not.

Another green flash illuminates the null; again, we hear cries from decimated elements as more sections of the compromised void crumble.

There's no time for history lessons. "Why did I rob people of their awareness?" I say, "and how do I fix it?"

Sofia's voice coalesces within my ears. "We wiped everyone's awareness because the Leopard objects insisted," ripples through my mind, though it's garbled, as if she's passing through a tunnel. "That previous null Dad told you about, the one Amalgam barely managed to dismantle five years ago? A group of Leopards created it. If we didn't dampen people's awareness, they were going to use their null as a genocide weapon."

The Leopards' plan, she adds without having to speak the words aloud, was to prevent the human hierarchy movement from ever spreading to sentience-sensitive people outside of Canoga Springs.

I don't remember *any* of this. *How much of my past am I missing?* What could have caused such memory loss, and how widespread were the effects? If Canoga Springs used to be the wondrous place these elements described, then apparently anyone who ever came in contact with the town or its populace is missing memories as well.

My mind tingles, as if it's suddenly bathed in gentle, popping soap bubbles.

—*Gaze, and recover.*—

It's a solitary "voice," but not Sofia's, and though the stilted words seem like a breeze against the bubbles, the words somehow transmit loud and clear. *But who was speaking?* My eyes dart to the two gallery walls, islands amid the empty void. *Was it coming from that direction? Outset* is mounted there, but right now *Outset* is basically *everywhere*, so that leaves...

Assembly Required.

The painting seems to sense, and confirm, my recognition.

—*Gaze.*—

I've stared at that painting a million times, but suddenly, I'm re-luctant. Why would I want to look at it, now that I know it's depicting a nightmarish image of Sofia, shattering into pieces as a null forms?

—*Please... gaze.*—

"I don't think—"

—*Please.*—

Sure enough, the crumbling, raven-haired version of Sofia is absolutely that same image I'd like to forget. *Then why is this thing making me...*

Unless...

I avert my eyes. The painted hair separates into tangible strands; the mosaic skin segments thicken with impasto-like edges as a thin layer of glistening, wet paint puddles into their midst. It's as if Sofia just finished dabbing the canvas... only there's still movement in that paint, and emotion rising up from between the cracks surrounding those puzzle-pieced skin seg-ments.

—*You gave; we now return.*—

The painting's words arrive paired with hazy, dreamlike im-ages and emotions that congeal within the wet paint. There's also a recognizable essence: the scent of my household or, by exten-sion, myself. I feel as if I'm reuniting with a removed appendix, or an extracted tooth... pieces of myself that I'd forgotten.

—*Five years ago: carbon tyranny.*—

I shouldn't understand, but somehow, deep within, I do. *Car-bon tyranny*: people acting superior to objects.

—*Most elements chose peaceful retreat, and anonymity; others chose threats.*—

Meaning the Leopards? *Assembly Required*'s "speech" is stilted, but our interface fills the gaps as the painting shares images, emotions, and memories that align with the history it's restoring. I don't just see it happening, I *feel* it: the false superiority, the resulting disputes, the violence as biological and elemental life disconnected.

Another green flash, another wail from elements elsewhere in the dissolving null. So little time left...

—*Only The Two, trusted by all parties, could arbitrate.*—

The Two. They could be anyone, but I understand, deep inside, that *Assembly Required* is referring to me and Sofia... that these are *my* memories, and *my* emotions, because Sofia embedded them into her art.

—*The Two intervened, with altruistic intent.*—

The tingling, bubbling sensation within my mind grows stronger.

—*Instead...* —

Assembly Required's understated narration, rendered in tandem with streams of my own memories and emotions, makes remembering what we did all the more chilling.

"Instead," I finish, "by removing the ability to recognize sentience in objects, we inadvertently undermined the social dynamics between people and elements."

The wet paint still glistens but it's not quite as bright, as if it's mimicking its own portrait of Sofia... developing a drying skin that hardens with each returned memory.

—*A life close to The Two was lost to the null... to prove the threats.*—

Meaning, the Leopards murdered someone we knew. Now I understand why Sofia and I felt our hand was forced: genocide had devolved from a risk to a guarantee.

Still, the way we reacted...

We literally dumbed-down thousands of people. My regained memories show the aftermath: our emotional anguish, and the horrified sorrow of interacting with a blunted community. Everyone, outside of Sofia's family and a few ultra-perceptive people at Amalgam, was suddenly oblivious to the life flourishing around them. Then, in the understatement of all-time, we referred to it as a "mistake?" *What a couple of idiots.*

Wait—using the scratch to modify someone's innate composition would have required top-notch interfacing skills. How could we do that if I'm barely able to interface without Sofia?

"Because you *can* do it without me," she says.

The painting reaffirms it—even now, I can feel it refilling my memory gaps. Suddenly, I'm certain that I met Sofia while she was painting at Buttercove Pier... but the meeting took place *eight years* ago, and she wasn't painting *Assembly Required*. That came three years later, not long after the blunting, when she took advantage of another lost interfacing benefit: objects, in this case her brush, paint, and canvas, absorbing painful memories—a courtesy some elements still extend to people recovering from accidents or other traumatic events.

That's how *Assembly Required* and *Outset* became extensions of *us*. Their components were gracious enough to absorb the most distressing memories related to our actions, along with the accompanying emotions. In essence, Sofia infused them with many of the thought processes and emotional responses that defined who we are.

Other details are returning as well... this time, about Sofia. There's something different about her, something enduring, and expansive, as if...

As if my wife is also something else?

I wait, as *Assembly Required* serves up an accompanying memory, then gasp as I see an impression Sofia shared with me years ago, something from her past.

I was right: she's much more than my intelligent, talented wife, more than an artist, or a skilled liaison between humans and objects... more, even, than an amazing woman.

She's also a painting.

THIRTY-NINE

The impression lasts a mere split-second, just a memory flicker that *Assembly Required* feeds me from some long-ago, pre-human stage of Sofia's lifetime. It's an Impressionist, flower-filled garden dappled with vibrant brush strokes, gorgeous color, and other hallmarks of an Old Master's talented hand.

Then it's gone. Sofia's standing next to me with several I-pins stuck into her left shoulder, from when she inserted them to interface with the paintings. She removes more of the needles from her I-pin bag and indicates this batch is for me, "so we can fix the mistake."

I'm suddenly not sure what to do. Am I really going to let her ram needles into me, the same way Halston shoved rebar into her? But I already know I'll do it.

Another round of green flashes ignites the null. This time they're followed by several seconds of intense shaking. I feel Sofia's arms square my shoulders, then she tells me to hold still. "For *us*," she whispers.

The metallic I-pin she's holding is thinner than a toothpick but long as my forearm. If not for the terrifying context of a crumbling void, I'd bat it away. Instead, I clench my teeth, bracing myself as she guides the needle forward.

"Five years ago, in the heat of a terrible moment, we made our mistake," she says, inserting the pin through my shirt, just below my second rib. "Can you blame us? Elements had their null in place, and they were ready to weaponize it."

I'm part-freaked about the needles, part-wondering why the hell I'm letting her spear me. *The needles facilitate a better connection,* I remind myself, grateful she's not using rebar stakes. Still, I certainly feel her puncture my skin. I'm not sure how she can hit the spot she's aiming for without having me remove some clothes, but to her credit she's steady, and precise, even with the deteriorating null under attack.

I wince as she removes a second I-pin from her bag. "Objects went so far as to murder my mother," she continues, placing the pin at the nook of my throat and my collarbone, then driving it inside. "They had her tossed into their null, to show us they meant business."

Rosemary Coronado was the person the Leopards killed to prove their threats? Even five years later, learning this news feels crushing. I can only guess we offloaded that detail into the painting, but again, I now get why we felt cornered by the Leopards.

Sofia's heightened emotion injects a static into our interface, but she understands what's at stake and fortifies the link. "So yeah, we agreed to their terms," she says, moving on to a third needle. "Their anonymity, in exchange for our survival. They brought us into their null; we used the scratch to modify every sentience-sensitive person in Canoga Springs, dampening their awareness and wiping any memory of elements being anything but, well, *objects*. It was a necessary compromise, just not one that my family, who retained full memory of what we did, could actually stomach."

There's a soothing sensation when I receive her words... that, and a love that perseveres. She takes a breath, then drives a fourth needle into the notch behind my right earlobe. "You and I couldn't live with it either. That's why we later dampened *your* awareness too…. why you made me promise I wouldn't tell you, why I also dumped most of my own awareness into the paintings. It was too much for us to bear, so we stowed our guilt and tried to move on."

More flashes. Maybe the I-pins really do enhance my connection, because this time I can *feel* the damage that the null just took.

Sofia hesitates, steadying her emotions, then sinks the fifth pin just left of my hip. "With our awareness curbed, we had the bliss of near-ignorance—of what I ironically started calling *normal*. How Dad and Ty were able to cope, I'll never understand. That's probably why Dad made it his mission to create another null, so we could reverse everything. But the price, pretending to be such a hardened version of the man he used to be…"

Between the needles and the crumbling null, I almost forgot: *Assembly Required* is still returning memories, now matched with what Sofia's saying. Nearly everything's back in my head: the full awareness, the interfacing techniques, the eight-year relationship rather than three. Amalgam isn't the only thing that changed; I've been working on Melds for twelve years, but didn't go full-fixation until after the memory wipe. *A subconscious lash at objects*? I may never know, but it grew into one of many reasons Sofia knew we'd made a mistake.

"The public, now missing any memory of object sentience, was oblivious to the change," Sofia says, clutching yet another needle. "Amalgam's inner circle was too, though they retained a bit of their innate sensitivity and some broken memories."

Explosive concussions vibrate the null, a surprise since there was no flash… or maybe this thing is now so thin that we didn't notice the change in brightness.

"Last one goes near the groin," she says, holding up the needle while flashing a brief, sympathetic smile. I close my eyes for this one, wondering how she can possibly aim correctly with my pants covering the area.

"For you and I, the effects were minor," she says. "Our personal events got jumbled into incorrect sequences, but that's about it. Amalgam, though... the group completely fractured. A few of us were still willing to work *with* objects, the rest insisted we treat them as lesser beings."

I lurch as the I-pin punctures me; this one, I feel.

"Done," she says, as I reopen my eyes. "The six-pin array should give a strong enough connection for the two of us to reverse our mistake, but..."

She steps back. "Matt... you're beginning to break up."

I almost forgot my split, hardening skin. It feels taut, and my hands resemble a parched desert floor. Worse, my fingernails are turning to scratch, meaning I'll start disintegrating soon. Whatever protection the embers gave me is running out.

More flashes, and intense shuddering as explosions erupt in the distance... or at least, that's what they sound like. Visually, they're *implosions*, as mounds of sentient scratch are suddenly yanked to a single, pinpoint location, then pulled inside, leaving a gray space the size of a car amid the remaining white scratch. The process repeats, time and again, as if something's firing miniature black holes into the null in an attempt to reduce the broken-down, sentient scratch that I'd regarded as a void into a true, lifeless vacuum. The eerie, sickening booms produced by those transformations end with a grating, metallic finish, like a million steel blades were just yanked free from the souls they pierced.

From the feel of the vibrations, and the urgency of emotions in the scratch, we absolutely need to finish, now... *but to what end?* Even if we reverse our mistake, we'd be back to the same problem we faced five years ago: fully aware people who think they're superior to objects, and Leopards who so resent the way people treat them that they'll try to wipe us out.

The only way that could ever truly change is...

By including inorganic perspectives as a vital part of human awareness. Instead of using the scratch to make sure people keep an innate awareness of objects' sentience, we'd also include those objects' viewpoints as part of the mix.

"We'd need at least one fully intact element," Sofia says, our connected thoughts an asset against the clock. "But there's nothing left. Our belongings were coated in protective embers, and Dad enhanced the paintings to survive the null. None of it will dissolve fast enough for us to mix with the scratch."

Agnes suddenly projects vibes on a scale I've never felt before, 'whispering' urgency and conviction. *Because she knows what I'm thinking.* She's been tucked in my pocket, so never coated with embers... or at least, not as coated as my clothes. Sacrificing her might—

No! It would mean losing the element with which, against all odds, the insensitive Melds King somehow formed a bond. Removing Agnes from my pocket, I think of all the objects that gave themselves for me, for Sofia, for the greater cause of getting us to a point where we could correct the changes. I don't want Agnes to join that list.

"We've got... *something*... incoming," Sofia says, eyes squinting as she looks skyward. "Not drones—I can't see what they are. But it's now or never."

Another vibe-burst; Agnes, imploring me to do what's necessary. With a heavy heart, I give her my subconscious answer, thereby signaling our plan to Sofia and the null as well. They signal me back: she and the billions of remnant scratch elements are on board.

I clutch Agnes, tight, cherishing the warm emotions I'm feeling in return. *Holding a Meld is like holding a piece of the Earth.* The last thing I want to do is shift into the crude, javelin-throwing stance that's needed; I'm too reluctant, and guilt-ridden. But we're out of time, and what needs to be done isn't for me, it's for *everyone.* Clenching my teeth, I place my forehead against hers in a moment of grateful appreciation.

Then I heave her skyward.

FORTY

gnes is just one solitary Meld, and yet, she's *all* of them... the entire product line, my heart and soul disappearing into goopy scratch... becoming *part* of that scratch, of the null, of our interface, of everything we're about to do.

That's where I'm torn, because despite the heartbreak of losing her, the significance of what she's about to accomplish is the thrill of a lifetime.

The incoming threat draws closer, and the randomized movements tell me they're not drones. Instead, I'm smelling something stagnant, and seeing a ghastly, fluttering mass of bizarre, yellowed elements, each dripping with sludge. They're everything from sewer grates to nose swabs, but also things that I've seen before, like rotted apple cores, pieces of the EAT sign, and bunches of those glassy, mephitic, pea-sized eyes.

Crimp objects, I realize, horrified. The swarm is full of the stuff I noticed during my averted-eye glance around the Early Mind exhibit, when the faint, hairline markings deepened into accordion pleats filled with eerie objects. A 'menagerie,' to use Ty's term... relics from phases and experiences that people would rather forget.

Worse, I'm getting a sense of intense hatred, meaning...

My throat tightens. *Meaning, these elements were Leopards.*

A pale, green light from within the swarm's center builds to a blinding burst then fades, like a lighthouse lamp. Dozens of menagerie items drop from the sky in gentle arcs, as if trained to entertain crowds by operating in tandem. It's graceful, and mesmerizing. When they hit the surface, they simply disappear into the white scratch like candies dropped into whipped cream, leaving nothing but modest holes to indicate the breaches.

The first hint of disaster appears in the form of graphite ripples, stretching out from the holes like wiry, skeletal fingers before going still. For one brief moment my dream is that the attacks failed, the fireworks were duds, the threat is done.

But soon the scratch surrounding the ripples moves, sliding in silence toward the holes housing the menagerie items. At first it looks beautiful, like a visual ballet as elaborate scratch petals slide toward their stigmas in the dozens of locations where the objects disappeared.

Then the modest, central holes widen into fissures. The surrounding scratch no longer slides, it's *yanked*. Deafening booms erupt from each crack, at which point implosions like the ones I saw a few minutes ago begin *en masse*. Sentient scratch is tugged toward the holes at breakneck speed, then plummets like water over a fall, leaving nothing but huge patches of empty, gray nothingness in place of the null.

My connection with the null means I feel every bit of it as it happens, as if something's pecking chunks of flesh from me, piece by agonizing piece.

The sickening booms fade, but not before the grating, metallic shrieks bellow forth. *The sound produced when reality dies*, I find myself thinking. But it's also hard not to imagine the screeches as our opponents' hideous victory cries.

Another pale, green light appears, builds, then fades within the swarm's center; a second round of menagerie items drops from the sky, much closer to us. Sofia and I, along with the punctured null, narrow our combined consciousness into a single collective that thinks, and physically operates, at blinding speeds—our only chance of surviving with so little time left.

As the objects follow their gentle arc toward the surface, our three unified minds maneuver our physical selves with astonishing speed and precision, heaving the surrounding scratch mounds upward, showering the incoming menagerie.

They dissolve on contact, undergoing a collapse as they retransform into the very scratch that created them. Eyeballs twist, warp, then drip away; grates contort into Warhol-esque smears before sprinkling down; smashed dog paws puff into nothingness, sludge and all.

Again, our combined consciousness ripples the null, shuffling textures and creating channels until we've gathered every bit of the dissolved menagerie's broken-down components. We do the same with the surrounding scratch. Then, with one dramatic, simultaneous thrust... we blend it together.

Everything shuffles, adheres, reforms. The menagerie's tormented viewpoints and experiences are flooded with Agnes' loving perspectives, joining those from the millions of other beings already embedded into the null. To our chagrin, the result isn't increased empathy, or enough of a softening in stance to foment the changes we have in mind. Quite the contrary; the menagerie components dig in deeper, refusing to accept fresh viewpoints.

Because it's the wrong approach.

The dispiriting truth hits me: adding Agnes and other inorganic perspectives to our mix won't solve anything if they're simply drowning out unwelcome views. For this to work, we need *everyone*.

"Don't snuff the menagerie's perspectives," I say, using my interface with Sofia and the null. "Let their opinions carry weight."

My own words make me cringe. I feel similar reactions from Sofia and the null. *Human-hating Leopard views should be snuffed, not given weight.*

But no, the menagerie's opinions—however appalling—carry uncomfortable truths. People *do* treat objects badly. They plunder resources without thought, and design obsolescence for financial gain. They toss rather than reuse, waste rather than cherish. Often times they burn or break beautiful elements, for no other reason than drunken stupidity or adolescent "fun."

We, as human beings, not only need to hear that, we need to understand, on an innate level, why it's *wrong*. We need to consider the concept that Leopard viewpoints are not only valid, but merit the priority we've given Agnes and the less-militant elements.

And yet, I'm still resisting—Sofia and the null, too. We're asking: wouldn't it be better to sacrifice ourselves, and any chance of humans regaining their sentience sensitivity, rather than let hateful elements share a voice? And the uncomfortable answer is... maybe.

Intentionally granting a voice to human-hating beings is beyond difficult, but this isn't about what's easy. It's about what's necessary, especially since education and opportunity can tackle hate far better than Sofia and I can with this questionable attempt at playing God.

Reluctant, yet hoping we're on the right path, we begrudgingly reshuffle, then re-blend the scratch, updating it into an inclusive, and hopefully enlightened, mixture.

But we're too late. More light flashes send dozens of menagerie objects floating down from *everywhere*. Our scratch attacks shrivel most of them, but several make it to the surface, triggering implosions. More incoming objects leave us no time to even check whether the revised mix helped.

In the milliseconds before the latest round strikes the null's surface, we manage to dissolve all but one Leopard. But that one, which resembles a slimy vomit pan, is on course for a scratch tuft that seems different from the others. It takes me a moment to realize why.

It's the scratch beneath the wall where Outset *is mounted.*

I watch, helpless, as the slimy vomit pan disappears like a burrowing gopher, right next to the wall's base. The structure buckles, then sags, shearing away from the companion wall where *Assembly Required* is mounted.

Assembly and its wall seem secure. Not so for *Outset*. We feel the painting's dread as its frame peels away from its mounting, wrenched by the tremendous pull of the implosion. *Outset's* canvas goes weightless as it tumbles down, a brief, terrifying freefall that I'm experiencing in both my head and my stomach.

My scream voices the painting's terror as it hits the null's surface, the weight of its frame and canvas creating a large, rectangular indent within scratch that's already being yanked toward the rupture.

Sofia, the null and I heave yet more scratch at what's left of the buried pan, determined to snuff the burgeoning implosion and keep the sliding *Outset* from falling into the hole. More than ever, the painting feels a part of me, like a family member. Maybe that's why I'm confident this isn't over, that we can *absolutely* dissolve this nasty, sludge-bathed object before it has a chance to finish the implosion.

A massive boom from somewhere below us, similar to the kind we heard earlier, says otherwise. Desperate, Sofia tries reformulating any part of the pan that's dissolved, hoping to slow whatever process the menagerie has triggered. It works; *Outset*, skidding across the null, slows, then stops, teetering right at the precipice between the surface and the hole.

She did it! Sofia saved Outset*!*

But what little remains of the vomit pan manages one final, determined yank. The painting wobbles, seesawing like Justice's scales: toward the hole, then away, until it loses momentum while angled toward the hole. The scratch at the rupture's edge gives way; surface material drops from sight, sinkhole style.

And *Outset,* our beloved portrait of the mind-bending moment when we managed to interface with the entire null, tumbles into the fissure.

FORTY-ONE

I nstinct kicks in: I send myself tumbling face-first into the fissure after it. *Have I lost my mind?*

It's like falling down a well: can't see a thing, but my right
arm is extended as far as I can reach, fingers grasping, hoping to
snag an edge of the painting's frame as we fall. My mind 'feels'
Sofia and the null reshaping the side scratch and the air currents,
in an attempt to usher me closer to *Outset* before it, me, and
therefore *everything*, is lost to the implosion.

To my astonishment, it works. My fingertips latch onto the
frame's corner, and I pull it toward me as the nose-dive down this
deeper-than-imagined hole continues. *Now how do I stop my fall?*
Sofia's already on it. She and the null are pushing the scratch
against my body like brakes squeezing a bicycle wheel, until *Outset* and I skid to a stop.

Looking up, I feel like a dog trapped in a well. There's a faint,
tunnel's-end glow way above. Otherwise, nothing.

I hear the painting's familiar subliminal signals and pull it
closer. It's too dark inside the hole for me to see *Outset's* abstract,
bleached landscape, but I can feel the painting calling me with an
insistent "look, look" like I sensed back in Sofia's gallery.

I don't want to look; I want us out of this hole. Wedging my
feet into the scratch, to see if I can climb up the same way I might

inch myself out of a snowy crevice, I'm able to move myself one step up, pull the painting higher, then move up another step. If I had about three days, this would work.

Look, look, look.

Outset again. I glance at it, even though there's nothing to see.

Except, there is. It wants me to notice, no, to *feel*, our connection—and oh, do I feel it. Much more than empathy, or warmth, this is like meeting a twin sibling you never knew you had, someone who not only shares your thoughts and ideals but actually embodies them in a fashion you yourself cannot.

What did I once call this painting? 'Life, embalmed?' Hardly. *Outset* is life, everlasting. I'm a *part* of this painting, it's part of me, and I'm suddenly very aware that will never change regardless of what time and fate has in store for our components.

But why is it hitting me with this now, unless...

A grating, metallic screech erupts from below as the scratch plugging the hole gives way to the tug of a massive implosion. It's a force so sudden, and so strong, that my fingers feel like they're pulling away from my hands as I plunge down. Sofia and the null heave what's left of the scratch upward with a stunning amount of counter-force, enough to not only hold me against the tide but to send me hurtling from the hole... but in the process, I lose my grip on *Outset*.

I let out an anguished yell as the implosion swallows the painting, along with tons of darkness-shrouded scratch, funneling it toward some ghastly, lightless pinpoint in time and space.

My contrasting momentum keeps me airborne for a couple seconds, then rolls me into a half-melted scratch mound. I'm far enough away from the implosion site to feel safe, not far enough to keep me from seeing that menagerie-infected segment of the null fade into emptiness.

In my heart, and my mind, I feel *Outset* fade into that same emptiness.

My consciousness feels frozen. For the first time in however many multiple phases define me, I'm belted by genuine loss. *Outset*, the painting that first drew my attention to sentient objects, an item Sofia fashioned using our combined consciousness and memories as her primary artistic components, a living work of art that was literally a piece of *us*... is actually gone.

Sofia's fighting tears, because my self-centered view of the painting as it related to *me* didn't change the crucial fact that she was a vital part of *Outset* too... perhaps the *most* vital part. That makes her all the more amazing when, somehow, she's prescient enough to recognize the bigger picture.

"Still with us," she says, between sobs.

I'm hoping she's referring to the painting, that she's telling me it somehow survived. But through my grief-fogged mind and tear-flooded eyes, I see she's referring to the null. Its expanse now looks like Charlie Brown's ghost costume: sheets of pallid scratch punctured by dark, empty voids. But that seeming wasteland is also sending out unusual vibes. Tolerance, maybe. Multiple perspectives... and yet, a unity that wasn't there earlier.

Because the scratch that's left is the scratch that we changed. Not only did our attempt to modify it apparently work, it wasn't completely lost to the implosion.

"We can fix our mess," I say, dumbfounded that somehow, amid this all-out assault and the loss of our beloved *Outset*, our plan might actually be working. Unlikely as it seems, Sofia and I could now use that modified scratch to reform the lost lives, and the lost awareness.

Except we no longer have time to try. Green lights again burst, this time from directly overhead. Menagerie items are dropping in bunches, a hailstorm that far outnumbers the dozens we've already dissolved. They're bigger this time: greased car axels, septic tanks, and lard-smeared cooking vats amongst the leading wave. They're also plummeting faster than before—or maybe they just *seem* faster because I'm exhausted. Either way, the menagerie is falling like meteors as Sofia and I resume our work with the null.

We tug, coil, and reformulate scratch at a feverish pace, once again drawing elements from the museum, and the spaceplane. But most important of all, we draw from the people who were within them... mixing their elements with scratch from the newly dissolved Leopard menagerie.

"Listen to his heart," Sofia mumbles, as the null keeps us working at inhuman speed, dissolving the initial menagerie bunches and preserving whatever infinitesimal chance we have left.

Except, with the null taking so much damage, we have less scratch to work with. Worse, the huge, terrifying clusters of incoming menagerie objects are converging straight at us. Instinct begs me to duck, run, or do anything that might steer me to a safety that no longer exists. Instead, I embrace Sofia, both physically and through our interface, convinced this might be our final moment in—what would she call it?

Our 'animate stage.'

The lead menagerie objects bombard our position. I'm convinced we're done for... but no, we successfully dissolve and reformulate wave after wave of them, a split-second before they hit us, melting them into modified scratch. Not that we're certain they're actually modified; we're too busy reformulating the *next* object bombardment, and then the next one after that.

Suddenly, without sound or warning, the bombardments stop.

I'm out of breath. Sofia, too. If this is the Leopard equivalent of allowing us a last gasp, we'll happily accept. We wait, grateful for the pause but wary of what's coming next. There's a reason for the sudden ceasefire, that much seems certain. Now it's just a matter of what we're about to find ourselves up against going forward.

Overhead, the green menagerie lights flare, but this time they don't fade. Instead, they slowly descend, stop a few arm lengths above what would normally be treetop height, then hover, flickering like will-o-the-wisps.

What are they pulling?

Maybe their strategy is obvious. Lowering their altitude cuts the amount of time we'll have to respond when they drop the next menagerie bombardment, and there's no possible way we can reformulate scratch any faster.

The green lights spread, reshaping into a dome-shaped, aerial field. Until now, I didn't realize how many lights there were—easily hundreds, maybe more. *Way too many to stop every menagerie object they launch at us.* They hover in eerie silence, as if enjoying the intimidation.

Then the lights flare, brighter than ever. A mind-boggling number of menagerie items bursts from their midst, dropping like a fireworks finale from hell. The assault is so extensive that one fact is now very clear.

We have absolutely no chance of stopping them.

But... is it possible we don't need to? Just before striking the null's surface, the menagerie objects come to a dead-stop, once again hovering in mid-air.

For several terrifying moments, nothing happens.

Then, to our utter surprise, they transmit a unified thought into our interface.

Maybe you have *changed.*

One by one, they break ranks, lowering themselves into the scratch, which begins dissolving them on contact.

"They listened," Sofia says softly, her eyelids lowered as if in thanks. "I begged them: *just listen to his heart, please!* They wouldn't, but..."

She lifts her eyelids, exposing hopeful eyes. "Maybe with you, me, and the null now together, along with Agnes, everyone in the Whitmore, all the plane passengers, and then many of the Leopards themselves... and with all of us bearing our full memories... maybe it was too strong to ignore."

There are no implosion holes forming, no graphite ripples, no more fissures. Instead, items continue lowering themselves to the point where they gently touch the null, then let the scratch consume them. It's as if each sentient object is taking a final bow, then plunging itself into the mush.

Crazier yet, the longer I watch the more I find myself silently applauding each of them, recognizing the sacrifice they've chosen, and the incredible faith they're placing in what we've pledged to do. They heard our intent, and now they're taking a huge gamble—*huge*—that our plan will work, giving up everything to help us restore what was lost.

It's an overwhelming gesture.

Soon the entire menagerie armada is gone, dissolved into the scratch. But really, they're more here than they were before, because once reformulated, they'll become part of *everyone*.

Mindful of that tremendous responsibility, we resume our reformulation efforts while the fading, damaged null still has enough consistency to assist. The null's sentient, pervasive warmth bathes us in an awe-inspiring level of grace and intellect as we work, then eventually pulls away as we sense the modifications are complete. Its departing whispers coalesce into phrases I'm not skilled enough to translate, with one exception.

"*... our next phase.*"

I'm envious. The null's self-awareness—understanding that its components will continue on, shuffled into other phases of an eons-long lifespan—offers freedom from any fear of death, a privilege few human-stage beings enjoy. I find myself wondering whether, like Sofia, a certain repentant Melds King could ever fully embrace such an understanding. Cognizant of my final moments with *Outset*, I think maybe he could.

The unique colors fade, the pleats return. Sofia and I are individuals again: disconnected, *in* the fading null rather than with it.

Something yellow flutters past, then an entire cloud of yellow, citrus-scented and headed directly toward a newly forming wind. Colors flicker and everything swirls; my consciousness and my emotions blur.

The spinning, tentacled exit gale and our newly constructed reversal are upon us.

8:18 a.m.

Monday., Sep. 7

Notifications

NEWS

* Severe "battlefield system malfunctions" reported by multiple nations.

* 24-hour cease-fire initiated worldwide as military analysts investigate.

* Crew, passengers from spaceplane *Resnik* found alive near crash site.

* 177 Whitmore Center survivors also found, rescuers call it "miraculous."

* Political, religious leaders hail "inspiring" cease-fire and survivor news.

Press HOME to unlock Screen Time, Reminders, and Purchases.

FORTY-TWO

ofia's at my side, injury-free, her radiant face tender as always. A pre-dawn sky glistens over our heads, so I can actually *see* her. No crimps, no embers, no null, not even any
I-pins, just that radiant, tender visage that caresses my heart. She
and I squeeze hands.

Kaleidoscopic butterfly patterns smooth; same for my puzzle-
pieced complexion. We're in the midst of a massive, dirt-filled
crater, as if someone took a cosmic claw and scooped out whatever had been sitting here. Somehow, I still recognize it as the
Whitmore Art Center's sprawling hilltop. There's no scratch, but
no museum either. No debris, no cars, nothing. Just us and a single, erect gallery wall with *Assembly Required* mounted at its center, clean and virtually undamaged.

But, no *Outset*. My chest feels hollowed by the thought.

Then I notice movement beyond the paintings, inside the
crater. As my head clears, I force my brain to reset, making it
bring smaller details into focus. The movements cascade... into
hundreds of people.

Confused, I tug Sofia's arm, to make sure she's seeing the same
thing.

She nods; it must be real. On this hilltop with no buildings, no cars, seemingly no objects whatsoever, it seems the most salient detail is the one that's taken me the longest to register.

We're surrounded.

And the people surrounding us are livid.

For all the anger and confusion, I'm confident that cooler heads will prevail.

Many of the spaceplane passengers and museum guests corralling us are threatening violence. Others are promising to file charges. The agitated group seems aware of what went down, and why, and it's not a pleasant situation. Still, I'm also noticing a quiet, startled minority... the people who are already rediscovering the true variety of life. I can't help but wonder: will they become today's version of yesteryear's alleged witches, persecuted for being more attuned to alternate forms of sentience? Will *we*?

And right then I know: my life's work hasn't ended. I'm just shifting to a different type of Meld. No bigger composites out there than human beings.

As far as I can tell, Sofia and I were unconscious for at least several minutes... maybe even the better part of an hour. Rebooted, along with the rest of them? Maybe, though that's not the word I'd use going forward. *Restored.* That seems like a much more accurate term.

Whispers kick in, like before: from within my ears and yet not audible. *Part of the boost in sentience sensitivity?* I'm hearing chatter everywhere: from stones, distant homes, approaching vehicles... from Florence too, if I'm not mistaken. What's clear is that everyone gathered around us, the literally hundreds of people recreated from scratch, are hearing at least *some* of that chit-chat as well—and what a joy it is, knowing that's once again the case.

Right now, it scares them, but soon—with our guidance, and a level of empathy, artistry, and understanding that wasn't there the last time around—all of that will change, first for the people of Canoga Springs but eventually, as word goes viral and people worldwide open their minds to such possibilities, for everyone. Doesn't hurt that I'll have the video from my car for the 'seeing-is-believing' types, either. Other videos will turn up too, once people know what to look for.

Also clear is that objects, Leopards included, are already cognizant of the re-awakened awareness... and that, unlike before, inorganic perspectives, including their own, are a vital part of that awareness. It's a modest difference, but enough that the whispers suggest some Leopards are already discussing whether animate life isn't *necessarily* an abomination of nature—a tolerant, middle ground not heard in the chatter for decades. Even the merits of reaching out to sentience-sensitive people, rather than waiting on us, are already being raised. *And all we had to do was include Agnes, along with their own missiles and drones, as part of our solution.* The hubris of imposing a hierarchy to material existence will soon fade.

Any threat of war is tabled, at least for now; of that, the whispers seem certain. Not that extremism, hardline or otherwise, is going anywhere. Even in a world more populated than anyone imagined, its citizens living vastly longer lifespans than people dreamed, that never changes... though it feels like now, there might be a chance.

"Empathy heals," Sofia says, looking at the mob. "It's just a matter of time."

I feel the same way. Her—no, *our* mistake—is fixed. We'll never again underestimate the need for connectivity.

"What about Doug?" I prompt.

She says she's not sure whether he made it out of the null, or whether he was even yanked in there at all. She also sees my skeptical expression, and insists she'd tell me if she knew. I just laugh. *Yeah,* I tell myself. *He made it out.*

As for Anthony and Ty, even *I* can sense their whispers, same as I know Neil's still parked at the bottom of the hill, as promised. At this point, I owe him deli for a lifetime.

Funny thing is, as I look around it's not the Whitmore I'm missing, it's the null. I can't help but take heart that such a wondrous, sentient collection of beings didn't simply go away. If our lifespans are truly ongoing, and if the three of us, working together, had any success whatsoever, then it's become part of us— and in this case, *us* means all of the restored people.

Maybe that's contributing to the memories I'm suddenly experiencing, of old photos: people posing with beloved cars, atop intricately designed buildings, inside experimental spacecraft... all pictures of collaborative efforts between objects and the people of Canoga Springs, and all apparently forgotten or reimagined into an exclusively human-centric history five years ago, at the moment Sofia and I changed things.

We used to work *with* objects, as a team. We interacted. We didn't just *use* them. With any luck, it'll soon be like that once again.

"Could this really work?"

It's just my mumbled, rhetorical hope for an existential blueprint we've barely touched, not an actual question.

Sofia shrugs. "Up to them."

Sirens sound in the unraveling night, headed our way, ready to collect us. We won't resist: ethics aside, there are legitimate issues regarding the Whitmore's destruction, the loss of treasured artworks, and so much more. Again though, I'm confident that over time, cooler, reawakened heads will prevail.

Sofia nuzzles her slender arm against my shoulders. It's warm, perfumed in citrus, maybe the most wonderful arm ever. We gaze at the ever-brightening sky, two loving, animate-phase objects, enjoying the proliferating whispers as if the angry crowd isn't there.

Threats, shouts, worldviews, debates, they're all ringing through the cool, pre-dawn air... and, *of course* they are.

My wife's paintings never *would* stop talking.

ACKNOWLEDGMENTS

This book is a years-long endeavor shaped by numerous people (and objects?), but my initial appreciation goes to someone I've spoken with just once: University of Wisconsin neurobiologist and psychiatrist Giulio Tononi.

Way back in 2004, Dr. Tononi explained some fascinating correlations between sleep and brain synapse efficiency for a news article I was reporting. What truly grabbed my attention, however, was his unrelated aside about a possibility that (pardon the egregious simplification) tiny bits of consciousness are endemic to physical matter. That was my first encounter with his Integrated Information Theory of consciousness, and this novel—which was already percolating in my head—became a passion from the moment that conversation ended.

Of course, a book about sentient objects with underlying dashes of panpsychism and Platonic philosophy needs an editor who's not only top-notch but *very* open-minded. Thankfully, Betsy Mitchell is both. My sincere thanks to Betsy for signing on for a second tour of duty inside my unrestrained (warped?) imagination.

Thank you as well to another true pro, David Bjerklie, who generously offered pragmatic insights and suggestions for a frenetic, early draft that shared the concept of sentient objects but featured a vastly different plot.

Also, kudos to Carl Graves at Extended Imagery for a hardcover design that was so attuned with the fractured Sofia

Coronado image in my head that it actually inspired some word-tinkering to highlight that perfect fit.

On the home front, I'm grateful to my incredible wife, Jane, who not only inspires our romantic indulgences but inexplicably understands and assists her husband's attempts to service the writing muse. Someday, Jane, if the elements are with us, I'll write you that chart-topping book.

I'm also grateful to our beloved son, Evan, who certainly knows a thing or two about crafting stories and has a wonderful knack for making his dad proud. I wouldn't be surprised to find people reading *his* acknowledgments someday.

I shared this novel's earlier self with David Lam and David Leonard, two of my closest friends, and their perspectives proved invaluable during rewrites. (Fair warning to them: Destry St. Hours shall return.) Thanks also to good friends Albert and Dolores Camacho, Jody and Michele Cohn, and Esperanza Rodriguez, who made my first book signing a truly special event.

Dolores also gets a *second* thank you, for giving me my first taste of what it's like to have an effusive, supportive reader. Whether warranted or not, her praising *Mother Tongue* as "the best book I read all year" (and she reads a *ton* of them) became an emotional buoy while writing *this* book. I have no idea what she thinks of *The Reality Meltdown*, but I'm honored to say that Dolores has locked up Slot #1 on the Dan Cray reader list.

Last—but only because she deserves to be the grand finale—my deepest appreciation to Jeanne Leone, a dearly departed artist, photographer, philosopher, Mensa member, and friend. I lost a kindred spirit when she passed in late 2020. Others heard this novel's premise and said, "intelligent *objects*?" but Jeanne erupted with excitement and told me that she and several acquaintances had seen signs of sentience in objects for *years*.

Naturally, the two of us understood how nutty that sounded and laughed about it, but in the quarter-century I knew Jeanne, she was always *that* open to possibilities, and she had the knowledge and skills to transform such obscure perspectives into reasoned, compelling art. Thank you, Jeanne, for helping me keep my chin up while exploring this long road. The heavens are even brighter now that they're graced by your talent.

ABOUT THE AUTHOR

Dan Cray is the author of *The Reality Meltdown*, *Mother Tongue*, and *Piercing Maybe*, which was named to *Kirkus Reviews'* Best Books of 2018. In nonfiction, he wrote *Soaring Stones* for National Geographic Books and worked as a freelance journalist for twenty-seven years, reporting sixty *Time* magazine cover stories and sharing a National Headliner Award. He holds a UCLA English degree and lives in Los Angeles with his wife and son.

Visit him at www.dancraybooks.com

9 781940 317168